CHASING CALIFORNIA

CHASING CALIFORNIA

An Edge of September Novel

Annie Jakes

*To Ava and Ross
no matter what*

CHAPTER 1

No one gives a damn about Hemingway.

Teachers act like every piece of information thrown at students in high school is going to be essential at some point, but the truth is: it's not. Never in Drew's life is he going to be sitting in a job interview or filing his taxes, trying desperately to remember what year *The Old Man and The Sea* was published. It just doesn't matter.

Except for right now.

The blank page stared back at him, mocking his lack of preparation. Mr. Hibbert paced around the room, glasses bouncing with each step. He weaved between the rows of students hunched over small metal desks, but they all knew he'd sit soon and completely forget they existed. Teachers were so predictable.

Drew clicked the cap off and on his pen until, finally, somewhere far beneath that fuzzy, brown sweater, that internal timer went off, and Mr. Hibbert returned to his desk, plopped into his rolling chair, and disappeared behind a book.

Drew slumped lower into his seat and kicked the chair in front of him. No response. He kicked again.

Ronny's shoulders tensed and his pencil stopped. Wait a few seconds. Drew's phone lit up from its hiding place in his lap.

Ronny: *Again?*

Drew's gut twisted and sweat coated his palms. He'd be screwed if Ronny wouldn't share his answers. Drew worked late last night and didn't have time to finish the book. Honestly, he'd read almost none of it. An order came in just as he'd planned to clock out for the night, and he couldn't turn it down. Huge tips. It had been worth the extra time but meant he'd fallen into bed well after one in the morning, book untouched.

He couldn't say any of this to Ronny, though, so he played it off—just the slacker kid, too cool for school and all that.

His fingers flew across his screen, arms stretched nearly under his desk.

Drew: *Sorry. Last time. Promise.*

Hopefully, one he'd keep.

It hadn't always been like this. He used to be a good student, or at least a decent one. But since his mom had lost her job last summer, Drew's income had taken priority over homework, and sometimes there just wasn't time for both. Hemingway would have gotten that.

30 seconds passed. 30 More. Shit. Ronny was going to draw the line now?

Drew's phone lit up again.

Image received.

His shoulders relaxed as he opened the file and found the test staring back at him. Complete answers in tidy handwriting filled the spaces that sat blank on his own test.

Thank you, Ronny.

***

"You're gonna get caught," Ronny muttered as they left Hibbert's room and turned down the hall toward their lockers. He could have been angry, but he obviously wasn't. Drew didn't cheat that often. A few times this year, max. He wouldn't do it at all if he could just find the time to read the loads of books their teacher assigned. He'd known last year when he'd signed up for AP Lit that it was a bad idea, but the high school counselor had insisted it was "the best opportunity." Apparently, simply showing up for class was grounds for expecting ridiculous amounts of reading and writing for all of senior year. Low standards for sure.

They shuffled down the long hallways lined with deep red lockers and wound their way through the crowds of students oblivious to the effect on traffic flow as they gathered in doorways and outside classrooms.

"I'm not gonna get caught," Drew said as they rounded the corner and reached their lockers. Nate was already there leaning against his own. He clutched his phone in both hands, eyes locked on the screen and completely oblivious to their arrival. "I always change the wording and purposely miss a few. I wouldn't screw you like that."

Ronny snorted, but all was forgotten as Cam and Brigid approached from the other direction. Cam smiled widely, but Brigid's face was hidden behind the book she held in front of her.

Ronny hooked his fingers through Cam's belt loops and pulled her against him. Cam's lips went straight to his. Drew turned his back to the nauseating couple and shoved his backpack into his locker. The thud of heavy books hitting metal broke Nate's concentration, and his phone disappeared into his pocket.

"Take it easy. It's not the locker's fault these two are disgusting." Nate rolled his eyes at the couple making out behind them and spun his own dial. A crooked grin undercut his annoyance. Cam and Ronny had been together for over a year. They'd all gotten used to the PDA.

"You save Drew's ass again?" Cam asked her boyfriend once she'd detached herself from his mouth. Drew narrowed his eyes at her lack of subtlety, but he knew her well enough not to take her teasing seriously. Cam giving him shit was her way. She didn't pull any punches. It was why he liked her so much.

"Always." Ronny winked at Drew, trying to get under his skin. Unsuccessful.

"My savior," Drew grinned back. Ronny flipped him off and pulled Cam tighter against him.

"Another tough test?" Brigid asked. She closed her book and shifted the straps on her backpack, freeing the smooth, blonde hair trapped beneath.

"*Old Man and the Sea.*" Ronny didn't need to say more

than that before Brigid was nodding her understanding.

"Not Hemingway's most interesting, but teachers love it. I've always preferred his short stories." She raised an eyebrow at Drew. "You didn't like it either?"

"Didn't read it."

"That would make the test tougher."

Cam popped her gum loudly and flashed another smile. "Not if you have a Ronny."

Nate slammed his own locker. "Joey's?"

The mention of food ended conversation immediately. Joey's Diner was their usual stop on Fridays when students had an extra half hour for lunch so teachers could have planning time. It was one of the few places in town that offered decent vegetarian options for Cam that the rest of them could stomach.

Drew dangled his keys from a finger in response and headed toward the main doors and out into the parking lot, his friends close behind.

***

They slid around their usual table in the corner of the diner. The old "Coca-Cola" light fixtures hung from the ceiling and cast a glow on the white tabletop. Ronny scooted the napkin holder and ketchup bottles to the end of the table, and there was something soothing about the red vinyl as it stuck to the back of Drew's arms.

Despite the I-don't-care face he was wearing, he was still shaking off the unease of Hibbert's test. Regardless of what his friends thought, he didn't like cheating. And he wouldn't

5

need to if he had the time required to plow through all the assigned reading.

He tucked it away. No reason to worry about that right now.

Food arrived only minutes after they sat—one of the benefits of being regulars. Steam rose from hot fries and the smell of burgers drifted from the heavy, square plates. Conversation slowed as they each scarfed down their food. Even with a standing order and the extra time, they'd have to hurry to make it back for last period.

"What's everybody doing next week? My parents are going to be at a peace rally in Seattle all week so I am going to spend spring break being crazy bored." Cam twirled her lemonade straw between her fingers, and her rings shimmered under the overhead lighting. Ronny sat with one arm splayed behind her, careful not to trap her nut-brown curls against the booth.

Nate wiped his hands on a napkin. "Working. My dad scheduled me almost every day once he found out I wouldn't have school. Getting me ready for graduated life, I guess." That was no surprise. Nate's dad was a piece of work. If he wasn't counting on Nate's diploma to get a plumbing license, Mitch probably would have made Nate drop out already. High school was a waste of time, keeping Nate from the real world and man's work. Bullshit.

"Extra practice," Drew answered without looking up. *Lie.* He'd love to spend the week tied to his guitar, amp cranked up high, but that wasn't any more realistic than Nate vacationing in Jamaica. He'd already signed up for shifts every day of the break. Hopefully if he brought in enough cash next week, he might be able to cut back a bit in the following weeks and spend even a little time prepping for that damn AP test.

Cam squirmed in her seat without responding.

"I'm hoping to catch up on some reading. There's been so much homework lately, I've gotten really behind on the fun stuff." Brigid smiled shyly but her eyes sparkled.

Brigid could read a book faster than Drew could get through the first chapter and remember everything she'd read. She should have been in AP Lit with him and Ronny, but she'd dropped for Honors English without any explanation the first week of the school year.

Their eyes met for a moment before Drew returned to the staring contest he was having with his Diet Pepsi.

"And I am studying," said Ronny. "My parents seem to think I need to know everything *before* I get to college." He shoved a fry in his mouth and rolled his eyes like he wasn't partially to blame for that. He was as excited to go to Berkeley as his parents were for him to go.

"Well . . . I had an idea." Cam glanced around the table, looking each of them in the eye before going on. She pressed her palms flat against the tabletop and leaned forward until she was nearly laying on her plate. "Let's all go on a road trip." She shot back against the booth letting her words take center stage. She looked at Ronny first. He never said no to her.

But Ronny looked as surprised as the rest of them, his tan skin and freckles pulling upward with his raised brows. Brigid sat frozen, burger halfway between the plate and her mouth. Only Nate seemed unaffected as he continued the steady stream of fries into the ketchup and then his mouth. Compartmentalizing was his M.O.

Even Drew's defenses slipped for a moment, and he felt his own eyes widen ever so slightly before he regained control. Cam was known to come up with some pretty wild ideas, but this was out there even for her. A road trip with no chaperones and in less than 24 hours? Impossible.

Ronny giving up a free week of studying and Brigid getting her parents to agree to a co-ed road trip were about equally as likely. Just about as likely as Nate's dad letting him out of work for the week. Drew could go, but it meant losing out on a week's worth of pay.

Ronny was the first to recover. A year and a half of dating Cam had quickened his reaction time. "That sounds really fun, babe. But I'm not sure everyone can make that happen on such short notice. Spring break starts tomorrow." He tucked Cam's hair behind her ear.

"I know it's short notice," Cam's brows pulled together, "but we could still do it. I'm thinking we head to California. It isn't that far, a day or two in the car, and we could go visit Berkeley. Your parents would let you go if they knew you were going to the campus. We could even get Liam to give us a tour." Ronny's eyes narrowed. A visit to his brother would be much greater incentive.

Cam was good.

Brigid reached across the table and squeezed Cam's hand. "It really does sound amazing Cam, but how would we pay for it? Even road trips cost money. And where would we stay?" Leave it to Brigid to be the logical one.

But Cam was ready for those questions. "I'll pay. My parents have plenty to cover a road trip for the five of us, and they would love it if I was to go travel and experience life. And we can stay at different places along the way. Hotels. Camping. I have an aunt that lives in California we could stay with for a night or two. Drew can drive."

Drew's head shot up. "Am I being volunteered? I don't remember saying I could go in the first place." As fun as a road trip might be, he didn't like the assumption he'd be on board.

Cam took a huge bite of her veggie wrap, chewed, and swallowed before responding. "I know, but you totally could if you wanted. And you are the only one with a car. No car, no road trip." Her voice held the confidence she always radiated, but her eyes betrayed her. Drew was far too familiar with that kind of hunger not to recognize it.

He continued eating without a response.

She was right about one thing. He'd have no problem getting his mom to let him go. She'd be thrilled to get rid of him for a week, if she noticed he was gone at all.

He also didn't mind taking his car. Actually, he'd prefer to drive. It would give him something to do with his hands.

But Drew couldn't tell his friends the real reason for his hesitation. They didn't know about that part of his life—the job, the money—and he wasn't going to bring them into that now.

Nate finally joined the conversation, mouth still full of fries. "I'm all about a road trip, but I'd have to get the okay from my dad, and you all know that isn't real likely. I'm sure Brigid might have the same problem with her parents." Brigid nodded slightly in agreement.

Cam closed her eyes and wrapped her arms around her middle. She somehow looked younger. More breakable.

When she opened her eyes, they were glossy and reflected the diner lights. "A senior trip is a right of passage. Our parents will understand that. At least ask." The slight wave in her usually steady voice was all it took. Objections stopped.

"It does sound really fun." Brigid's smile grew, and Drew could practically see her brain working through the ways to convince her parents to let her go.

"When were you hoping to leave?" Ronny rubbed Cam's back, and she visibly relaxed.

"First thing tomorrow morning. Early."

"I'll ask. But I may need some help convincing my parents," Brigid said.

"I'll stop by this evening." Cam winked at Brigid and returned to her lunch.

Drew's gut twisted for the second time that day. The conversation around him continued with ideas of places they could stay and thing to do along the way. Even Nate was getting into it. But Drew knew better than to hope. He couldn't go on a road trip, last chance or not, and Cam would be disappointed as hell because she had been right about one other thing. No car meant no road trip.

***

The house was empty when Drew got home. He dropped his backpack inside the door and sauntered to the front room windows. The latches were tight, but a few yanks got them sliding open. It was unusually warm for April, and the sun beaming through the glass would heat things up quickly. Drew was not going to pay for AC in spring. A breeze would be plenty.

Drew passed the kitchen, ignoring the cluttered counters and stale air that seeped out. The open windows would help with that too.

His room was at the end of the hall. It was the only hall in their two-bedroom, two-bath house, and it really wasn't much to see. Drew's friends, aside from Nate, had never even been inside. When they'd first started hanging out, they'd thought it was weird he never invited them over. They'd give him strange looks if it came up. Once, Cam had even asked if it was haunted. It had been long enough now no one questioned it anymore. Maybe they thought he was rude.

Fine by him.

Drew had decided years ago that it was better to let people believe the worst than know the truth. Then any time you exceeded expectations, you were a hero instead of the loser with the messed-up home life.

He closed his bedroom door behind him, tossed his bag into the corner, and slumped across his bed, an arm tucked behind his head. His worn, blue quilt pooled beneath him. He could use a nap. He was still exhausted from the week of overtime, and he didn't have to feel guilty about blowing off homework the Friday before spring break.

Drew glanced at the clock on his dresser. He still had an hour before he was expected to check in for work.

He had picked up the job last summer. Food delivery had become the new big thing last year, and delivery drivers could make decent tips if they were quick. He'd planned to quit when school started up in the fall, but his mom had still been unemployed, and they were behind on rent and other bills, so he'd kept it. He worked most evenings and nearly every weekend. He couldn't always pay the rent in full, but he'd found the last few months that as long as the landlord still had money coming in, eviction threats stayed away.

And that was the truth—the real reason Drew couldn't study for AP exams or take spontaneous road trips with his friends. Drew had responsibilities. He had a job to keep and rent to pay. His friends didn't have that kind of pressure. None of them were counting on a paycheck to eat this week or wondering if their parent was passed out in some loser's apartment.

Shit. When was the last time he'd heard from his mom? He'd checked in last weekend, but was pretty sure he hadn't seen her most of the week. Drew grabbed his phone and scrolled until he found her most recent call.

Last Sunday. Drew clenched his jaw but shot off a text.

Drew: *You alright?*

Shoving his phone into his pocket, Drew rolled off his bed and headed back to the kitchen. The stale smell was already dissipating. The sink was empty, as always, but pizza boxes and old receipts cluttered the counter. All from him. No empty liquor bottles or lipstick-stained glasses hinting that his mom had been here, and he hadn't cleaned in days.

His phone vibrated in his pocket.

Mom: *You don't have to check in on me.*

At least she wasn't dead.

Drew: *You coming home tonight?*

Mom: *Don't know. Take care of yourself.*

Her parenting summed up in four words. Drew could get her one of those ridiculous aprons with all the frills and pockets and those words sewn across the front in swirly letters for Mother's Day. She'd never use it.

Maybe one of those etched wine glasses instead.

Drew clenched the pen in his pocket. If his mom wasn't going to be around tonight, neither was he. He grabbed his keys, shoved his earbuds into his ears, and slammed the front door closed behind him.

CHAPTER 2

"You aren't even going to ask?" Drew watched from the beanbag chair in the corner as Nate connected Drew's iPod to the workshop. That was what Cam had named the area of Nate's room that housed his collection of electronics. The workshop was made up of two desks sitting side-by-side, spanning an entire wall, and a rolling chair Nate regularly moved between the two as he worked. At least two monitors were always set up on the desks' surface, but Drew had seen as many as six going at one time. Next to the desks was a storage container filled with devices. Nate left the lid on at all times so his dad would never stumble upon his collection, but Drew knew there were at least five tablets, three laptops, and no fewer than a dozen phones inside.

On the wall above the work station were lines of hooks holding every kind of cable and cord imaginable. Drew wasn't even sure what some of them did, but Nate used them all. The small, white cord tucked on the very end of the bottom row was the reason for Drew's visit.

He'd only been three steps out of his house when his iPod has crashed. It was an old, 3rd generation player. He'd found it in a drawer years ago and had never replaced it. His friends begged him to get rid of it and use his phone like every other person on the planet, but he wasn't quite ready to give up that piece of himself. Plus, he didn't ever add new music. He didn't need to. There was no new music that could compare to the classic rock that stocked this little gadget.

There were downsides to using such an old device though. Nate was the only one Drew knew who could reboot it, and the days were numbered before even Nate wouldn't be able to revive it.

"What's the point? I have plenty of other way to piss off Mitch, I don't need a new one." Nate clicked his mouse a few times before Apple music appeared on the nearest monitor.

"You think your dad would be pissed if you asked to go on a road trip?"

Nate shrugged one shoulder. "Wouldn't be thrilled. Definitely wouldn't say yes. You going?"

"Nope."

"Why not?" Nate knew more than anyone else about Drew's living situation, but even he didn't know everything. And it needed to stay that way.

"My mom needs me." A half-truth. She did need him. To pay rent. To support her drinking habits.

"She'd be fine for a week." Nate stuck his tongue out in concentration as he clicked buttons and entered some kind of coding into his keyboard. Drew had no idea what Nate was doing, but he had total faith his iPod would work perfectly by the time Nate was done with it. "And it would give you the chance to talk to Brigid."

Drew stifled a groan. How did they always circle around to Brigid? "And say what?"

"Oh, I don't know." Nate lowered his voice in a ridiculous attempt to sound more like Drew. "Brigid, I've been staring at you for months and I'm obsessed with you and you should date me and I love you. Wanna make out?"

"You suck."

Nate grinned at Drew over his shoulder. "Save the sweet talk for Brigid."

Drew reached for a shoe sitting a few feet from him and flung it at Nate's back. Nate arched at the hit but laughed anyway.

"Okay, so don't say it like that. But it's all true, and you know it."

"I don't want to scare her off. It hasn't been that long since her breakup."

"It's been months. What are you waiting for? She's not going to formally announce when she's ready for a new boyfriend. Girls don't work that way."

"And you're the expert?" Drew raised his eyebrows at Nate.

"I know some shit."

"Clearly."

Nate clicked a few more times on his laptop before pulling the cord from the iPod. He spun in his chair and tossed the device into Drew's lap. "Done. I'm just saying, a week alone with her would give you the chance to finally make a move."

"What did you do to it?" Drew chose not to respond to Nate's advice. He was done discussing Brigid.

"Just updated some stuff. You shouldn't notice a difference other than it shouldn't crash as often."

Drew nodded his thanks and tucked the iPod into his pocket. "Then, you aren't going?" If he could be sure he wasn't the only one staying behind, he'd feel better about it. Still guilty, just less so.

"I'd like to, but I don't see how it's possible. Mitch wouldn't let me go in a million years. You know I'm right."

Drew wished he had an argument, but there was none. Nate was right. His dad would never let him go. "Then the two of us can chill. We'll go to Second Dam or something."

"Hell, yeah. That beats the beach any day." The sarcasm dripping from Nate's words was practically visible.

Drew checked his phone and cursed under his breath. He was supposed to clock in for his shift ten minutes ago. He rose casually from his place in the beanbag chair.

"Thanks for this." He pointed to his pocket where his iPod was tucked away. "I have to get going."

"Busy again tonight?" Nate's question was innocent enough, but there was more behind it. They'd skirted around this topic for almost a year. Nate was curious about where Drew spent so much of his time, but he also knew Drew enough to know that if Drew wanted people to know something, he'd tell them.

Drew trusted Nate. He knew Nate could keep a secret

and would be more than willing to if Drew asked him, but it wasn't about trust. Drew didn't want Nate to know the truth either. Sure, Nate worked a job, but Nate's job was something his dad made him do. Income his dad thought was being saved up for a car or an apartment but really went toward buying the latest and greatest phones and tablets. Nate wasn't *supporting* his dad. He wasn't one bad month from getting evicted. He didn't skip meals to pay the power bill or hide cash from his dad to buy groceries.

Drew's was a life none of his friends would understand. They might try, but all it would lead to was pity. And that would be so much worse than their anger at his keeping secrets.

"Just stuff. I'll see you tomorrow." Drew was up the stairs and out of the house before Nate could respond.

***

Friday afternoons are shitty for delivery drivers. No one orders takeout at 4:00 on the weekends. Orders hadn't started pouring in until after seven, which meant Drew had had to work until ten to make enough to call it a night. At least he'd had the option to work late. That was the beauty of the job—it was clock in and out as you please. In Drew's case, that usually meant working extra hours.

Other than his delivery instructions, his phone had been surprisingly quiet. Not a text or call from anyone. He'd expected Cam and Ronny to be blowing up his phone all night, coming up with a thousand reasons he should be road tripping with them this week.

Not a word from his mom either. Didn't she wonder what he did with his time? Cam's parents let her do anything she wanted, but they at least checked in. Brigid's parents were crazy involved in her life. What if he was into drugs? His mom would never know.

Drew slowed his car into his driveway and cut the engine, leaving a window cracked in an attempt to air out the lingering scent of buffalo wings. Drew trudged his way through the dark to his front door until a silhouette shifted a few feet away. Drew held back a smile as he spotted a pair of long, tan legs draped across his porch steps. Cam's eyes reflected the dim streetlight across the road. She'd wrapped herself in a knitted, yellow blanket but remained in her cutoff jeans and flip-flops.

It was hard to not notice Cam. Physically. Her wild curls, tan skin, and wide smile added up to an incredibly pleasant visual. But it was more than just her looks. Some senior girls were still girls. Cam was a woman. She took command with just a smile and a wink. She radiated confidence and charm. And there was just something magnetic about her, like once you'd met her, you craved being around her.

If Cam wasn't eternally devoted to Ronny and if Drew wasn't hooked on her best friend, he might have fallen for her. But as it was, they were friends. Close friends, but friends only.

"A little late to be getting home, don't you think?" As Drew's eyes adjusted to the dark around him, he could better make out the eye-brow lift that accompanied her accusing tone. "Care to elaborate on where you've been?"

"Nope."

Drew sat on the step beside Cam and stretched out his own legs. They didn't reach more than an inch or so past hers. He wasn't particularly tall, and she was all leg.

Cam watched him closely, but Drew focused on the cracked cement driveway, unwilling to elaborate on his whereabouts that evening. Cam wasn't used to secrets. It was one of the first things he'd learned about her when they'd become friends the year before. She found no shame in being nosy and whether it was her charming personality or her ability to make friends with anyone, people tended to open up to Cam without much prodding. Drew was her Achilles heel, and it drove her crazy.

"Fine. You don't have to tell me who she is. Just be careful. Some girls like to take things slower than you seem to."

Heat rose up Drew's neck. "Are you here for a reason?"

Cam shifted to lean against the porch railing and face Drew. "I'm here to talk about the trip."

"I told you—"

"I know. You have to practice." Cam air quoted and rolled her giant eyes. It was sometimes hard to take her seriously. She had the facial features of a cartoon character. Big eyes, long lashes, a tiny, turned-up nose. He had to constantly remind himself that she also had claws. "But practice can wait, Drew. This can't."

"Is the trip even happening? Everybody's parents agreed?" Cam's and Ronny's maybe, but Brigid's parents would never agree to a co-ed trip and as on this afternoon,

Nate wasn't even going to ask his dad.

Drew pulled his pen from his pocket and clicked the lid on and off.

"Mostly. Brigid's took some convincing, and Nate is going to work on his dad tonight. I was at his house before this. But I need to know about you. You have the car."

"I see how it is."

"You know we want you to come. Don't be a dick." She slapped his arm. "If it was just about the car, I'd take my parents'. We want you there."

"Chill, Cam. I'm messing with you. Honestly, I'm not sure I can."

"Why not?"

Drew pushed out a breath.

Why not?

For starters, a mom who can't take care of herself and could be anywhere right now, likely with a new boyfriend who's as much of an ass as the last one was. Rent coming due in less than three weeks. AP exam that he's barely studied for all year.

But nothing came out.

Why not?

Any other senior could go. They could take a week just for them, to hang out with friends, forget about school, and do whatever the hell they want. Plenty will. The whole school was buzzing today with everyone's plans for the week: cruises, Disneyland, resorts. That ass, Mike Allen, wouldn't shut up about his parents' beach house in Bermuda. Or Bali. Or wherever. Drew had blocked him out.

Drew pushed the cap back on his pen and ran his hand down his face. He needed a break more than ever. Maybe this could be good. This could be a chance to reboot and finish out the school year strong. Just one week off the job and school. One week where he wouldn't have to check in with his mom to make sure she's alive or keep track of how many lights are on so the power bill doesn't blow up.

"I'll think about it." It was the most he could give.

Cam scooted close to Drew and rested her head on his shoulder. Her shivering shook him, but her skin didn't feel cold. He wrapped his arm around her back and held her close all the same.

The buzzing from the streetlamp was the only sound for a long while. After his crappy night, the dark was calming to Drew. A cool breeze ruffled Cam's hair, and Drew pulled her blanket tighter around her shoulders. When she didn't respond, Drew leaned forward as best he could to see if she was asleep. His stomach clenched at the tears trailing softly down Cam's cheeks and falling to the cement below.

This wasn't about the trip. Something was up with Cam.

This was the part he wasn't very good at. He didn't know the first thing about taking care of crying girls. "What's really going on, Cam?"

She swatted away her tears and sniffled. "This is important. Not just that I go, or Ronny. But all five of us. Things are going to change soon. We graduate in two months, and then that's it. Ronny will move to California. You'll go wherever your music takes you. Brigid will go to college, and

Nate will work for his dad full time. And I . . . well, I don't know where I'll be."

"I thought you were going to travel across Europe."

"I'm not sure about anything anymore." She cleared her throat and returned to her place on Drew's shoulder. "I need this, Drew. More than I can say. I need the five of us to go on one last adventure together. And this is the only chance we have. Please. Do this for me."

Drew hugged her against him. He wished he could say yes. He'd do anything for Cam, for any of his friends. But it was more complicated than that.

"Come on." He squeezed her once more before pulling her to her feet, arm still around her shoulders. "I'll drive you home."

Cam nodded silently but let him lead her to his car.

***

Despite never coming in contact with food, Drew always felt gross after a shift, like he was coated in French fry grease and barbeque sauce.

After getting Cam home, he'd returned to his empty house and shuffled into the shower. The hot water beat against his chest, and he let himself get lost in it until it ran cold.

He dried off, wrapped the damp towel tightly around his waist, and grabbed the pen he kept stashed in the bathroom drawer. He gripped it between his teeth, pulled the cap off, and, pressing the pen into his skin, began to trace smooth lines across his forearms.

The cool ink stung his skin, still too warm from his

shower. The scent of it filled his lungs as swirls and twists took shape, bands of black cascading down his hands and between his fingers. Inky escape, more calming than any mandated therapy sessions he'd ever been to and with far fewer questions about his dad.

Drew ditched the towel, slipped on sweatpants, and pulled a T-shirt over his head. Just as he was climbing into bed, his phone rang from where he'd left it on his desk.

Drew's breath hitched in his chest. There are very few reasons his mom would be calling him this late at night and even fewer that are good.

"Hello?" His voice sounded desperate, and he hated it.

"I'm coming home. I need cash."

Of course she did.

"I'll have some for you, mom. I'll leave it on the fridge."

"Such a good son. Be there soon."

Drew rifled through the jeans he'd left on the floor until he found his wallet. He removed a couple twenties and wandered to the kitchen. He slid the bills into the blue clip magnet stuck to the fridge.

This was the system.

He backed away from the money, and his shirt caught a stack of papers on the counter, knocking them to the floor. Drew scrambled to pick them up before his mom got home. Overdue bills and final notices all addressed to her. But really to him.

He dropped the papers and slunk to the floor.

He was drowning. Life was pulling him under, and he

simply couldn't stay afloat. He rested his head against the cabinet at his back and swallowed the lump in his throat.

One week. Then he'd come back and face all of it. It would be enough.

He was dialing before he could change his mind. Cam picked up on the first ring.

CHAPTER 3

Drew's alarm was about to go off anyway, but the call was still an unwelcome interruption to his sleep.

"Get up. It's nearly 6:30, and Cam asked me to verify you were awake. She doesn't want to leave late and assumed you'd be less than thrilled if she called you," Ronny stifled a yawn as he talked.

"I won't be late." Drew swung his legs over the side of his bed and rubbed his eyes with the palm of his hand, his other still holding his phone. "Tell your girlfriend to chill."

"Oh, I guarantee she is still asleep. She was tired after Brigid's last night and went to bed early. I woke up to a text that you'd be joining us. She must have woken up and sent it sometime in the night."

Drew's chest tightened. Cam was lying to Ronny about visiting him and Nate last night? That was new. If there was trouble in paradise, the last place Drew wanted to be was in the middle of it. Luckily, pretending everything was fine and ignoring problems were skills Drew had mastered.

"I'll be there."

Leaving his phone behind, Drew padded down the hall, slipped off his sweats, and stepped into the shower, letting the cold water finish the job Ronny had started.

He'd stayed up far too late, but it had been worth it. He'd given himself permission to use the empty house to hook up his guitar and play until his fingers were numb. When he finally did collapse in bed, he'd slept better than he had in weeks. Music could do that—push life and all its problems into a corner and let him just be. He could breathe in the sound like a gasp of fresh air.

A road trip. A smile spread across Drew's face, and he was grateful none of his friends were there to see the goofy grin he couldn't contain. Ten days he could spending relaxing and messing around with his friends instead of trying to keep shit from spiraling out of control.

His friends were insane, but they were low drama. It was exactly what Drew needed.

Brigid would be there. Drew's breath hitched and his fingers tingled. Possibly remnants of last night's jam session.

Probably not.

Drew dressed and headed for the door, his duffle bag in one hand and his backpack slung over his other shoulder. Only feet away from his escape, he found his mother passed out on the couch.

Even sleeping, her skin looked tired, but her face was relaxed. She was skinnier than he'd remembered, and her limp hair draped over the edge of the couch and hung halfway to the floor. Had it always been that long?

No one would have guessed they were related based on their looks. Physically, she was Drew's opposite in nearly every way. Her face was round with soft edges and petite features; his was sharp and angular. Her pale skin was a stark contrast to his year-round tan, and even her blonde hair was the cool ice to his shadowy, black spikes. Their only shared trait was their eyes: almond shaped and steel gray.

She hadn't come home yet when he had gone to sleep around one last night. Drew didn't want to wake her, but he hadn't told her about the trip yet, and he should probably let her know when he would be coming back. He knew what would happen if he left without a word.

He backtracked into the kitchen, pulled open the drawer by the fridge, and grabbed a pen. He spotted the receipt from the Chinese takeout he'd ordered a few nights ago sitting on the counter, flipped it over, and scribbled a note.

Going to Cali. Be back next week.

He stuck it to the fridge along with few more bills from his wallet. The ones he'd stuck there last night were already gone. With this and the leftovers in the fridge, she should have plenty to eat until he got back.

"Where you going?"

Drew took a slow breath before turning around to find his mom leaning against the wall just inside the kitchen, arms folded and eyes narrowed.

"I thought you were asleep. I was just leaving you a note to let you know I was going away for a few days with some friends. There's money for food on the fridge." Drew braced his arms against the counter, the barrier between them.

His mom snorted. "At least you had the decency to leave a note." She shook her head and stumbled out of the kitchen and toward her room.

In the years he'd lived alone with his mom, she'd become a master at cutting the deepest with the fewest words. Drew had learned quickly to bury any reaction. Seeing the damage she caused was fuel to her fire, and she'd just keep burning.

He shut the door quietly on his way to his car. It was a cool morning. Despite the warm afternoon the day before, Boise was still coming out of winter, and there'd be chilly days for another month. The breeze chilled Drew through his hoodie, but he pushed out a breath of relief when he saw it hadn't snowed last night. He really wasn't in the mood to dig his car out of a frozen mound of ice and snow.

Drew slipped into the driver's seat and turned the key. As the engine roared to life, something moved in his rear-view mirror.

He jumped and hit his head against the roof. "Shit!"

Nate's groggy eyes cleared quickly from his spot in the backseat as Drew spewed profanity. "Wait, what? Oh, sorry, dude. It's me."

Drew's breathing slowed as he processed what was happening and that he wasn't about to get murdered in his driveway.

"What are you doing?" Drew asked. Nate had a Skyline High blanket wrapped around him, and his backpack leaned against the car door like a pillow. He wore jeans, a pink

Hollister V-neck, and a zip hoodie that were definitely the same clothes he'd had on at school the day before. His blonde hair, a little longer than Drew's, stuck out in different directions. Drew couldn't remember the last time he'd seen Nate looking this rumpled. Nate's stylish clothes, trendy haircuts, and square jaw, along with the results of his daily gym time, caught the eye of most the girls at their high school.

"It's freezing. Did you sleep in here?" It must have been down in the thirties out here last night if the frost on the grass was any indication.

Nate shrugged. "I was just gonna hang out on your driveway, but then your car was unlocked, and it was kind of cold, so I figured I'd just crash here for a few hours until you woke up. My blanket kept me warm." He ran his fingers through his hair trying to control the chaos.

"But why are you here?" asked Drew.

Nate's eyes darted around the car before landing on his own hands as they rubbed together for warmth. "Well, I decided to come on the trip, and I didn't want you to leave without me. So, I made sure I was here early."

Drew turned forward and pushed the back of his head into his headrest. He breathed deeply before pushing on.

"Did you ask your dad?" He searched unsuccessfully for Nate's eyes in the rearview mirror. Drew and Nate had been friends for more than ten years. Nate had been there when Drew's dad left. Drew had been there when Nate's mom died and for those dark months afterward. They knew each other better than anyone else. Nate rubbed the back of his neck, likely sore from sleeping on the backseat of a Corolla.

"Nah, I didn't want to wake him up. It's good. He'll figure it out pretty quick." He finally met Drew's eyes, begging.

Nate's plans after graduation included working for his dad's plumbing business and about nothing else. He said he was cool with it, but that was a lie. Nate hadn't made a choice for himself since his mom died. His father made choices, and Nate went along with them. But Nate needed to make some choices before Mitch took over completely and Nate lost every last bit of himself that he had left.

Drew nodded once. This was Nate's choice to make.

As Drew backed out of his driveway, Nate pulled two energy drinks out of his backpack and handed the blue over the faded leather seat to Drew. "Thought you may need this this morning."

"After you tried to kill me?" Drew didn't glance at Nate as he took the can, opened it, and took a sip. "Why are we leaving so damn early anyway?"

Nate shrugged. "Cam said she didn't want to waste any time. Whatever that means."

It was only about a three-minute drive to Ronny's house, but the neighborhood was totally different. Drew and Nate lived in a neighborhood with chain link fences, fifty-year-old homes, and single parents. Ronny's was a brand new development with double doors, an HOA, and kids with trust funds. Ronny wasn't ever a jerk about it though. He knew his family had more money than theirs, but he acted like it genuinely didn't matter.

As soon as Drew pulled in, Ronny stepped out of his

house holding a suitcase. His brown hair was combed neatly to the side, and a grin spread across his face, interrupting the patterns of freckles. He had probably been up for hours by now. Ronny's parents used to make him get up an extra hour before school to study every morning, but that was before the letter had arrived a few days ago. Drew assumed the extra studying had stopped now that Ronny, like the other four Rosado brothers before him, had been accepted to Berkley. He realized now that Ronny had never actually confirmed that.

Nodding to them as he passed, Ronny loaded his stuff into the trunk, opened the back door, and landed next to Nate with a "Good morning, gentleman." Drew responded with a quick exhale through his nose. Nate's reply was less dignified.

No one mentioned Nate's unexpected attendance. Cam smiled as she climbed in and curled up in the middle seat between Ronny and Nate. She looked like she hadn't slept much the night before. She was wearing a white tank top and flannel pajama bottoms with hearts. Her hair was piled in a wild mess on the top of her head, and her eyes looked dark. She had nearly filled his trunk with two huge bags. When Nate pointed that out, she scoffed that they hadn't brought more.

"You never know what you will need on a trip like this, and you can't just wear the same clothes the whole time," Cam specifically eyed Drew for that last part.

"I brought clothes. I just didn't bring all of them."

"It is too early for your attitude, Drew Cox. Just drive." Drew nodded obediently and drove a few houses further down the street to the Foster's.

Drew reached for his door handle to help Brigid with

her bags, but before he could get out, Brigid's parents emerged from the house. Mr. and Mrs. Foster, each wrapped in monogrammed green robes, walked their daughter to the car and enveloped her in a hug before allowing her to get in. Mr. Foster's jaw tightened slightly as he offered a stiff nod toward Drew. It was clearly more of a threat than a hello, but it was the best Drew could have hoped for. It was amazing Brigid had gotten permission to go at all. A co-ed trip with an eighteen-year-old driver? Brigid and Cam must have pulled out everything they had for this one. Drew was grateful for whatever they'd done.

He returned the nod. An understanding and a promise.

Brigid's family was extremely traditional. Her parents had strict rules and expectations for their kids, and Brigid, as the oldest of six children, rarely experienced exceptions to these rules. It usually wasn't too bad though. Brigid got along with her parents, and they clearly loved her. It was a relationship Drew did not relate to.

Brigid buckled her seatbelt and pulled a notebook from her backpack. Papers covered in highlights and sticky notes lay neatly stacked inside, each peppered in her neat handwriting: addresses, times, and confirmation numbers. Drew chuckled to himself. Leave it to Brigid to put all this together in one night. Had she slept at all? Maybe Cam had been up all night helping her. That would explain Cam's clear lack of sleep.

Brigid didn't appear nearly as sleep-deprived. Her eyes sparkled and a brilliant smile lit up her heart-shaped face. Her smooth, porcelain skin nearly glowed. Light blue skinny jeans wrapped themselves around her hips, and her red sweater was just short enough to show a thin strip of skin at her waist. Drew forced his eyes back to the road and tightened his grip on the wheel, swallowing hard.

"Okay folks," Brigid said, "We have nine days to get as far away as we can and back again."

Damn, she was adorable. Drew fought back another grin. There's no way Nate wouldn't call him out for looking like some lovesick moron, and he wasn't ready to have that conversation yet.

"Today our destination is Logan. It's only about five hours from here, so we should get there by early afternoon if there's no traffic." Brigid pulled a fluffy, blue blanket out of her bag and up around her shoulders.

"That's fantastic. We'll have time to find something exciting to do tonight." Cam elbowed Ronny obnoxiously.

"I'm sorry. I have to know. How did you two get the Fosters to agree to this trip?" Ronny's eyes darted between the girls.

"You doubted us?" Cam's hand clutched her chest in overly dramatic disbelief, and her mouth hung wide in shock.

"Of course not, babe. I'm just constantly amazed at your endless talents." Ronny kissed the top of her head. They were beyond disgusting. Even so, a small fire in Drew's chest flared as he watched them in his mirror. He wanted that. Not with Cam—no, Drew and Cam would never be like that. He wouldn't know what to do with her, and he would drive her crazy. But to have someone that just wanted you for who you are, nothing more or less. It was kind of nice.

"We went with the "it's a high school rite of passage"

angle," Brigid said, making air quotes with her fingers.

"And that worked?"

Brigid chuckled lightly. "Not really. But then we swore up and down that Drew was a responsible driver, I wouldn't share a room with any boys, and I'd check in constantly."

"Even so, surprising." Ronny leaned back into his seat.

"I thought so too." Brigid's face was soft, and she was playing with a hair elastic on her wrist. Drew's fingers itched to weave through hers. Maybe driving wouldn't be enough to keep them busy.

"Music?" Nate asked.

Drew pulled his iPod from his hoodie pocket and plugged in the aux cord.

Seconds later, Whitesnake filled the car. Drew sat deeper into his seat and locked in the cruise control.

CHAPTER 4

Despite being nearly inseparable for years, the five of them had never spent any extended time together in a car, and it became clear almost immediately what Drew should expect from his passengers in the following days.

Nate was asleep before Drew passed the exit for the next town over. Drew glanced at him in his rearview mirror every so often. How long had Nate spent in his car last night? He must be straight up exhausted to be sleeping through the spirited license plate game taking place between Cam, Ronny, and Brigid. It was like a smoke detector that needed batteries—dead silent for a minute or two and then suddenly a "H!" shouted from all three, each trying to be the first or the loudest.

By the time they'd reached W, Ronny's stomach was grumbling so loud that Drew could hear it over the music. His own stomach wasn't far behind. In the rush of the morning, he'd skipped breakfast. Nate obviously hadn't eaten, and Drew would put money that Cam and Brigid hadn't either.

"Will it throw off your plans if we stop for food real quick?" Drew asked just loud enough that only Brigid could hear him.

"Not at all. I'm actually really hungry." She twisted her body beneath her seatbelt to face the backseat. "How do you all feel about getting something to eat?"

"Yes!" Cam blurted. "I am starving."

"Why didn't you say anything?" Ronny's brow creased in concern.

"I wasn't hungry until right now." She elbowed Nate, and he opened one eye.

"There's no way we're there already."

"Nope. Food."

Nate stretched awkwardly. He really was too tall to be crammed in the backseat, but Drew wasn't going to say a word. Nate would never even consider asking Brigid to give up shotgun, and Drew certainly didn't mind having her by his side.

Drew took the next exit and found a Carls Jr not far from the offramp. They each tumbled out of the car, stretched, and followed Cam through the large red doors at the entrance of the restaurant.

It smelled like a Carl's Jr, even during breakfast—grease, burgers, fries. All of it.

Cam wrapped her blanket tighter around her shoulders, marched to the register, and ordered way more food than they'd ever eat. She removed her parents' credit card from its place in her sock, swiped it through the machine, and led them all to a table in the back corner to wait for their breakfast.

"Where are we?" Nate held a fresh cup of coffee with both hands and took a long drink.

Brigid flashed her phone to show everyone the map. "Heyburn, Idaho. Just outside Twin Falls."

A kid who looked about 14 approached the table with a tray piled high with breakfast sandwiches, French toast sticks, and hashbrowns that looked an awful lot like tater-tots. Brigid sorted through the food and handed Drew his breakfast burrito.

Drew peeled off the paper wrapping and took a bite. It was much hotter than he'd anticipated. His tongue was on fire. No, burnt to ashes. He grasped at the nearest cup, took a drink, and nearly spit it out.

Dr. Pepper. This was not his drink.

His eyes drifted from the cup up to Brigid's face. She'd sucked in her lips, biting them both to keep from smiling, but her eyes danced.

"Not a fan?"

Drew forced himself to swallow. The burrito had managed to kill off most of his tastebuds, but there was no mistaking that syrupy sweetness.

"Sorry. I didn't realize it wasn't mine." Drew set Brigid's drink back in front of her. She picked it up and took a sip, still watching him. Then she set her cup down, reached for his, and took another sip.

Drew definitely was not thinking about her mouth on his straw.

"I still don't taste a difference."

"That's because there's not one." Cam dipped her French toast stick in a container of syrup she was sharing with Ronny. "Diet and regular taste almost exactly the same."

"Not for some drinks. Some taste completely different. Like coke and diet coke." Nate said as he unwrapped his own burrito.

"That doesn't count. Coke is disgusting."

Ronny wiped his mouth with a napkin and nodded. "It is disgusting. Nonetheless, it is the number one selling soda in the country. Makes no sense."

"How do you know stuff like that?" Nate asked.

Ronny shrugged. "I read a lot."

"So does Brigid, but she isn't the human equivalent of Wikipedia."

"It's not about the taste," Drew cut in. Nate seemed especially irked at Ronny this morning, and Drew had no interest in continuing down that road. "It's the sugar. Non-diet soda is too syrupy."

Brigid took another sip of both drinks. "I guess I kind of get it. I can tell there is something different. That must be it."

"If you drank only diet for a few weeks and then tried regular, you'd definitely notice. You'd never go back."

Brigid raised her eyebrows. "Is that a challenge?"

Drew let a hint of a smile through. "It's a promise."

Brigid held his stare for a moment before she stood from her place at the table, walked to the soda machine, and dumped out her Dr Pepper. Drew watched closely as she refilled her cup with fresh ice and pushed down purposefully on the Diet Dr Pepper button. She kept her eyes locked with his the whole time.

Drew's stomach flip-flopped. Was she flirting with him? He could never tell with Brigid. Most girls who wanted his attention that way were much more forward about it, dropping obvious hints about their parents being gone for the night, touching his arm, or grabbing his hand.

Brigid wasn't like those girls. There were moments, like this one, when Drew was so sure there was something there. An electricity between them that she must feel too. It could be completely in his head, but based on the raging silence coming from the other three members of their circle, he'd bet his guitar he wasn't the only one noticing the undercurrent.

Drew's phone buzzed on the table, rattling the tray beside it and ripping him from his thoughts. An unknown number lit up the screen, and he nearly shoved the phone into his pocket. No one had this number but the people sitting around this table.

Except his mom. She could have borrowed someone's phone or called from a landline. If she'd gotten into some kind of trouble, he needed to know before he got any further from home.

"Be right back." Drew left his burrito on its paper wrapper and made for the doors. He wasn't sure what he'd have to say to his mom and didn't need anyone overhearing it.

"You're answering that now?" Ronny lifted an eyebrow and motioned to the discarded burrito.

"It's probably a girl." Cam wiggled her eyebrows.

"Chick from last night, I'd guess."

Drew ignored Cam and stepped outside, refusing to look at Brigid.

"Hello?"

"Hey buddy! Haven't talked to you in a while." Drew's heart stumbled. Of all the people he thought might be on the other end of the call, his dad had not been one of them.

Drew could count on one hand the number of times he'd spoken to his dad in the last six years. He'd call out of nowhere, claim to want a relationship, and disappear again.

New phone number. New life.

"What do you want?" Drew kicked a rock on the sidewalk and it flew across the mostly empty asphalt parking lot.

"Actually, I've got a job for you. I work with some pretty big names in the industry, and it just so happens that I've got a band in need of a lead guitarist. I've seen your stuff online. It's good, champ. Come on out and play with them. They've got a gig in three weeks."

Drew nearly dropped his phone. It was too much, too fast. His dad was calling. With a job offer. Lead guitarist for a band. Away from here.

He leaned against the hood of his red Corolla, letting it hold him up.

Playing music was all he'd ever wanted. When he was young, he'd watched his dad play the guitar, studying the way his fingers moved over the frets. Drew had gotten his first guitar for Christmas when he was eight. He'd cried. Then he'd played it until his fingers bled.

As his friends planned for college, jobs, and travel after graduation, he'd been hesitant to voice his own dreams for the future. He'd mentioned playing music, but he'd never shared just how big that dream was. Playing rock music to crowds of thousands. Living off the music. Never worrying about money—he'd have more than enough.

His dream wasn't like his friends' though. He couldn't just study music for a few years and then assume he'd have a decent career like Ronny could with law school. There was no job application for a rockstar. You had to know someone in the industry who could help you get in front of the right people. Drew only knew one guy that fit that description.

And if he'd learned anything in the last six years, it was that this bastard didn't do anything to help his son.

Cold spread through his entire body as reality clawed its way back in. Even if he was willing to trust his dad, he couldn't leave. His mom needed him. She hated him, but she needed him. She'd never be able to afford food or the rent without the money he brought in.

Drew studied his friends through the window. Nate dumped most of a bag of hashbrown bites directly into his mouth, and Brigid was laughing at something Ronny was saying. She covered her face and her hair fell forward, shining in the morning sun.

"No, thanks," Drew said, "I've got some stuff that needs me here right now."

"I won't accept that answer, Drew. This is a once-in-a-lifetime opportunity. Think about it. I'll be in touch."

The call ended. He was gone.

***

Drew took in the sights as they drove down main street. Logan gave off a small-town vibe, not in a backwoods way but more of a Hallmark-Christmas-movies-take-place-here way. People walked up and down the sidewalks, stopping into small shops and boutiques. The Book Table. The Rage Salon. Something called Locker 42 that appeared to sell memorabilia for the local university.

He hadn't visited Logan, but he would have to live under a rock to live near Boise and not have heard of Utah State University. The two schools were heated rivals. He didn't much care, but it was clear that this town was all about their school. Nearly everyone was wearing a school t-shirt, hat, or hoodie. That Locker 42 place must be doing just fine.

Drew slowed the car and pulled into a small diner on the corner, The Center Street Grill. He was starving. His appetite had disappeared after the call from his dad, and his breakfast burrito had gone untouched until Nate asked to finish it off.

"Do you know this place?" Brigid asked him.

"No. But they have lunch," Drew responded. He turned to Cam, "And this is a college town. I guarantee a diner like this is full of locals you can interrogate for ideas on how you'd like to spend your evening."

He was right.

The place was packed with people between the ages of eighteen and twenty-five.

Cam had brought clothes to change into, and after a

surprisingly short time in the restroom, reappeared looking like someone who had not just spent five hours in a car. Brigid grabbed her hand as they ordered and stepped aside for the others. Nate, Ronny, and Drew each ordered burgers and then followed the girls across the restaurant to find a place to sit.

"Day one and so far all we've done is eat." Cam pouted and crossed her arms.

"No complaints here," Nate chuckled, "but if you are upset about it, find us something to do. You were the one who came up with this trip."

They tore into their burgers, and Cam scanned the restaurant around her, eyes thinning as she scrutinized the college students at each table, looking for just the right target.

She found her mark only a minute later, grabbed Brigid's hand, and dragged her to a table just across the aisle where two guys were sitting. They set their own burgers down when they saw the girls.

Drew tensed as he watched the two college guys sweep their eyes over Cam and Brigid. He understood Cam's choice. These two would tell the girls anything for a shot with them. Brigid was breathtaking, and Cam was that crazy kind of hot that made guys say and do stupid things without thinking twice. Drew thought about joining them, but he could hear from where he was and following them seemed a little too "don't touch my property."

"How can we help you ladies?" one of the college guys asked. He was skinny and had a smile that showed way too many teeth. His friend, a redhead with tons of freckles shoved a French fry in his mouth without looking away from Cam.

"Well, it just so happens we are visiting from out of state and are looking for some exciting things to do today. We wondered if some college guys like you might have some advice," Cam batted her eyelashes at the boys. Drew relaxed. As much as he felt the need to protect them, he sometimes forgot how fierce Cam was. She'd have no trouble handling these two boys if they got handsy. And Brigid was stronger than she let on. She was more reserved than Cam, but she was smart. They could take care of themselves.

"Oh, I definitely know what you should do tonight," the kid responded, showing all those bright, white teeth and meeting Cam's eyes without reservation.

Drew stole a glance at Ronny and Nate sitting in the booth beside him. Ronny's jaw was tight as he watched an older guy drool all over his girlfriend. Understandable.

Nate was grinning from ear to ear.

The redhead spoke up at this point, discreetly elbowing his friend. "This time of year, most people just stay inside. Or go home for spring break. There isn't a lot to do around here during the winter."

"But it's April," Brigid said. The snow had long since melted in Boise. Drew hadn't seen any around here as they'd driven through town either.

"Yes, well, in Logan, winter can go through May," the redhead replied. "It gets cold."

Cam would not be so easily deterred. "There has to be something. Some random thing that students do to keep things exciting, even in the winter." Her bottom lip pouted just a tad.

The guys exchanged glances. "Some do the Ultimate Aggie Challenge, but I doubt you girls would be into it."

"What is it?" Brigid asked. Her voice lacked the swagger Cam's held, but it was loud and clear. Drew wasn't fooled. She was hating every moment of this.

"There's this bronze bull statue on 10th north and 8th east. It's kind of a local college thing that students will ride the bull."

"Why wouldn't we want to do it?" Cam asked.

Teeth-guy turned toward her. "We ride it completely naked."

Nate snorted loudly and choked on his Mountain Dew, finally drawing the attention of Cam's admirers. Ronny slapped his back as Nate coughed and sputtered.

But if Cam was surprised or shocked, she hid it well. She placed her hands on her hips. "Sounds perfect. Thank you for the recommendation."

"You two want company?" He kept his eyes locked on Cam, but his redheaded friend eyed Drew from across the aisle.

"No, I think we'll have plenty." Cam motioned to their table before returning to her seat and plowing into her salad like nothing had happened. Brigid scrambled into the booth right behind her.

Nate chuckled under his breath, "You're awful. You know that right?"

"I don't know what you mean," Cam replied, not looking up from her salad. Her words dripped with indifference. She shuffled the food around her plate with her fork until she found the strawberry she'd apparently been hunting for, speared it, and popped the entire thing into her mouth.

"You shouldn't mess with guys like that. It's not okay to lead them on." Ronny's face was relaxed but he his eyes continued to dart back to teeth guy who'd returned to his own burger.

"It's also not okay to assume that every girl who talks to you, bats her lashes, and smiles a pretty smile wants to have your tongue shoved down her throat." Cam's eyes pierced through Ronny, and her lips tightened to a thin line. She held perfectly still, daring Ronny to disagree with her.

Drew, Nate, and Brigid all slunk just a little deeper into their seats.

Cam and Ronny were a great couple. They were disgustingly in love with each other and their personalities worked well together. Cam was extremely opinionated and never backed down from a fight, whereas Ronny was generally pretty chill and willing to go along with Cam's absurdities. But every now and then they crossed paths and things could get ugly.

Ronny rested his forearms on the table and placed both hands over Cam's. He leaned closer and softened his voice.

"Then I believe you taught him a very valuable lesson today." A small smile appeared and his warm eyes were all for her.

Drew looked away. He'd not grown up in a family that showed a lot of affection, and it could sometimes be hard to watch. PDA was whatever, but seeing the way they looked at each other was like coming out of a dark room and looking straight at the sun.

"I believe I did." And as quickly as it had come, the tension was gone.

"We aren't actually going to do that naked statue challenge are we?" Brigid asked.

Everyone glanced around the table until all eyes landed on Cam. She raised her brows in feigned confusion but lowered them again as a wicked grin spread across her face.

CHAPTER 5

They left the hotel just after midnight. It had taken more planning than they'd expected to adequately prepare for their adventure. They'd needed to dress strategically. Drew opted for flannel pajama bottoms and a hoodie. Nothing underneath. Ronny and Nate had gone with the same strategy. The less you had on, they less you had to take off.

Brigid had also grabbed a few towels from the swimming pool. She said she wanted an easy cover and that it wasn't stealing if they took them back. It was borrowing.

The hotel was quiet. Empty halls connected them to the lobby where lights had been dimmed for the night, and only one employee stood at the reception desk. Hopefully the rest of the town had also shut down for the night.

They were already shivering when they reached Drew's car.

"29 degrees currently. And snow forecasted for tomorrow," Nate announced from the backseat. "If it starts snowing, I'm out."

"We'll be out of town before the storm hits. It's just cold." Brigid had resumed her place as co-pilot, a stack of blue hotel pool towels on her lap.

"Where did that guy say the statue was?" Drew turned the wheel and pulled out of the parking lot.

"10th and 8th." Brigid handed him her phone. "Here's the navigation."

Drew set her phone on his leg and focused on the dim streets. He'd been right in hoping that the town would be quiet this late at night. The bustling sidewalks from that afternoon were now empty and only two other cars were on the road.

They weaved through neighborhoods until they reached an enormous football stadium. Drew slowed to a stop near the lot entrance.

"Park up a side street. We don't want to draw any unnecessary attention," Ronny whispered even though they were still in the car. "Berkeley is coming up, and I can't have anything affecting that. No cops."

Drew turned up a side street and parked along the curb. A tree blocked most of the glow coming from a nearby streetlight, and all the houses were dark. They crept down the street and back to the corner where the bronze statue stood.

The bull was a lot bigger than he had expected, but then again, it had to be rather large if grown men had been known to ride it. It was about four feet tall and six feet long and rested on a cement block that was an additional three feet tall.

The bronze looked aged and worn all over, but nowhere more so than the bull's bean bags. Those had been rubbed to a shine. Shocker.

They approached the beast. Cam inhaled deeply and whispered, "Let's do it."

"Who's going first?" Nate rubbed his arms with both hands.

"Why don't we let the ladies go first so we can give them a little privacy and keep a look out for other people?" Ronny suggested.

The girls nodded and the boys turned and each walked a few yards away, backs to the statue.

Drew wrapped his arms tighter around his chest. This was definitely near the top of the list of stupidest things they'd ever done. He could see his breath fogging in front of him, and he still had getting naked to look forward to.

A gasp and hushed "Oh my God!" sounded from behind him followed by a thud. Drew chuckled to himself. Sounded like Cam was down. He continued to listen and heard Brigid gasp and puff as she climbed the statue in the cold. Another loud thud told him Brigid had also jumped from the statue.

"You can turn around!" Cam called from behind him. He turned and walked back to where the girls were standing, fully clothed but shivering worse than ever beneath hotel pool towels.

"So, how was it?" Ronny smirked. Brigid shot him a dirty look.

Cam responded, "Thrilling! But cold." Her teeth chattered between each word.

"We'll be in the car," Brigid added, grabbing Cam by

the wrist and dragging her away.

"Okay, gentleman," Ronny eyed Nate and Drew mischievously. "Who's up?"

"Cam's been a terrible influence on you." Nate rolled his eyes, stripped his clothes off, and awkwardly climbed up the statue.

Drew glanced up and down the street watching for cars or cops. Nothing.

Nate landed on the ground beside Drew a moment later and quickly threw on his sweats.

"Holy shit, that's cold." He nodded at Ronny. "Your turn."

Ronny was back on the ground in less than a minute, shivering but fully clothed.

Drew swallowed hard, pulled his hoodie over his head, and dropped his pajamas. Every muscle in his body tensed. His chest shook, trying to warm itself. As cold as it had been dressed, it was nothing compared to the chill of being naked in 29-degree weather.

Which seemed like a tropical beach compared to the bronze of the statue against his skin.

The cold metal burned his palms as he wrapped his hand around the horn and hauled himself up and onto the back of the bull. The stinging cold penetrated through his body, and every inch of him was frozen.

How long did he have to stay up here? Nate and Ronny had each landed only a few seconds after they left the ground.

Drew leapt from the back of the bull, landing hard on the ground beside his deserted clothes. He'd never dressed faster in his life. It barely took the edge off.

The three of them dashed back to the car at a full sprint, whether to leave before they got caught or as a rush for the heater, Drew wasn't sure. But either way, the heat inside the car was a welcome relief.

Drew drove off at full speed before anyone said a word. They arrived at the hotel parking before long, but no one moved from their spots in the car. The only sound the whole way back was the sound of teeth chattering wildly.

But as cold as he was and as ridiculous as he felt, Drew was also exhilarated. He hadn't felt this alive in months. A smile broke free, still partially frozen. He had forgotten what it felt like to throw all caution out the window and do something simply to say he had. Or to focus on nothing besides doing something stupid.

A chuckle arose from someone in the backseat. Drew looked to see all four passengers grinning from ear to ear as they shivered. Ronny's smile turned to a laugh followed closely by Cam's. Within a few moments all five of them had lost control and the entire car shook with laughter.

"I cannot believe we just did that," Brigid giggled.

"I will never thaw." Ronny's arms were wrapped around Cam, attempting to warm her. "This is your fault."

Cam just laughed harder and kissed him.

***

Hot showers and a few hours of sleep went a long way to reheating everyone. They had agreed the night before to meet in the breakfast room at eight o'clock before scurrying into

53

their respective rooms.

Drew hadn't eaten anything yet, but his focus remained on his energy drink. Eight wasn't particularly early when you were used to getting up before seven for classes, but it had been another late night last night.

Brigid sat across from him, looking more at ease in a clean pair of jeans with holes in the knees and a green Aeropostale t-shirt. Her eyes were calm and the ever-present creases in her brow had smoothed. She sipped coffee, alternating with bites of an almond poppyseed muffin.

Nate slouched into the seat next to Drew and sipped from his own cup of coffee. He and Drew had joined Brigid for breakfast since Cam and Ronny were taking forever. Drew had a few guesses why.

But when they walked in a moment later, it was clear Drew had been wrong. Ronny was all smiles and freckles, but Cam looked beat, unlike her normal, energetic self. Drew didn't remember mornings ever being a struggle for her before, but clearly it was not her time of day.

"What's for breakfast?" Ronny asked. Cam took the seat next to Brigid, and Ronny grabbed a chair from the neighboring table and pulled it over to join them.

"Whatever you'd like as long as it's a bagel, muffin, or toast," Brigid said. Nate stood and walked to the underwhelming breakfast options, Drew right behind him.

"Grab me a muffin, will you?" Ronny called after them.

"You want something, Cam?" Nate shouted back.

"I think I'll stick with water this morning." Cam tipped forward and pressed her forehead against the table. She looked paler than normal too. Her tan skin was dull, but it was probably the terrible lighting in the hotel.

Drew and Nate each toasted a bagel, schmeared them heavily with strawberry cream cheese, and returned to the table. Nate carried a plate with an assortment of muffins and placed it on the table in front of Ronny who immediately tore into a banana walnut.

Drew sank into his seat and finished off his drink in one long pull. Nate circled the long way around the table, placed a hand gently on Cam's back and crouched down next to her.

"You okay this morning?" Nate whispered, head tilted forward and brows drawn together.

She twisted her head on the table so she was turned to him and smiled weakly. "I'm fine. Just worn out from last night."

"There's nothing I can get you?"

Ronny cleared his throat loudly. Nate flinched and removed his hand from Cam's back.

"I'm really fine, Nate. Thanks for asking." Cam scowled at Ronny. Nate nodded and returned to his own place at the table.

They ate in an awkward tension for a moment before Brigid stood from her place and pushed in her chair. "I'm going to go check that I'm all packed. You want to come, Cam?"

Cam nodded and followed Brigid toward the door.

"I'll come, too," Ronny added. He brushed the remaining muffin crumbs from his fingers and followed the girls through the dining room door toward the elevators, shooting one last look at Nate on his way.

Nate slumped deeper into his seat.

"Wonderful." He pushed his bagel around on his plate, swiped a finger of cream cheese off the top, and shoved it into his mouth.

"What the hell was that?" Drew asked. Ronny was a jealous guy, but it wasn't usually directed at Nate or Drew. They'd all been friends for long enough that Ronny trusted them. Or, at least, Drew thought he did.

"Things have been a little tense between Ronny and me the last little bit." Nate replied. "He doesn't like when I get too close with Cam."

"That's bullshit. You two are friends and have been since before she even knew Ronny. What changed?"

Nate sucked down another finger-full of cream cheese before answering. "A while ago Cam mentioned to him that I'd slept on her couch before. That lead to her telling him all about how I used to sleep over at her house when her parents were out of town. Apparently, Ronny doesn't approve. He hasn't gotten mad or anything, but he's definitely been more aware of me when I've been around her the last few weeks."

"How have I not noticed this?" Drew took a bite of his bagel. He glanced behind Nate at the vending machines lining the wall. He could use another energy drink.

"You aren't around all that much. You're always busy with whatever you have going on."

Drew ignored the thinly veiled question in Nate's words. "So now Ronny thinks you two had sex?"

Nate shrugged. "I don't know. But he's making sure I know Cam's his girlfriend and off-limits."

"You could tell him the truth."

Nate ignored him. He pushed his plate away and sat up straighter. "What about Brigid?"

"Does Ronny think you slept with her too?"

Nate kicked him under the table. "Smart ass. You two were flirting like crazy all day yesterday. When are you going to make a move?"

Drew didn't have an answer for that. He'd wanted to ask her out forever. She'd been single for a few months now, and it was probably okay for him to make a move at this point. But he was nervous. Flirting wasn't the same thing as wanting a relationship.

He pulled his pen out of his pocket and began drawing smooth lines across his right arm.

"If I ask her out and she says no or things go south, it's gonna mess everything up. Our friendship will go to shit."

"Don't be an idiot. She's going to say yes."

Drew rolled his eyes. If only he could be sure.

CHAPTER 6

"Brij, you sure this is the place?" Drew had followed Google's directions, but they stopped in an empty lot that was apparently parking for nothing. No hotels, or any kind of buildings, were anywhere around. They were completely isolated in what seemed like a canyon, but instead of the snow-capped hills of Boise, reddish rock and dirt surrounded them. Trees sprinkled the area, and the gurgling of running water was somewhere close. Rolling out of the car, he saw a small path in the dirt with a sign that read *St. George Yurts.*

Brigid nodded and bit the side of her lip. "Don't be mad. I thought it might be fun to try something a little different than a hotel since we'll pretty much be in those the whole trip. So, I booked us a night in a yurt."

"A yurt? What the hell is a yurt?" Nate asked.

"It's like a tent. A large, circular tent," answered Ronny.

"We're camping?" asked Drew. He hadn't been camping since he was a little kid. His dad had never taken him as that was nowhere near Elliott's range of interests. Drew had gone with Nate's family a few times, though. He didn't mind it, but he had a hard time picturing Cam staying anywhere without a functioning bathroom.

"We are glamping. It is *like* camping, but we have modern amenities. We just get the cool nature aspects of camping." Brigid's shoulders sunk, and she looked at the ground. "I'm sorry. I thought you all might like it. I should have asked."

Cam grabbed her hand. "No, you should not have. This will be an adventure, all of us bunkered down together under the stars. I love this," Cam slipped her arm through Brigid's. Drew was grateful she'd stepped in. He was having a hard time keeping his own arms from wrapping around her.

"So how do we get to our yurt?" Ronny asked, good mood unaffected.

"We have to check in over there," Brigid pointed to a small building hiding behind some trees that Drew had missed before, "and then I think we hike. This is Zion's National Park. I think you pretty much hike everywhere here."

Drew had to admit the hike was impressive, and not particularly strenuous, which was a relief. The rock that made up the mountains here was a deep orange red, and it gave the entire area an adventurous feel. The smells of nature swirled around them, and Drew pulled off his hoodie to take in the warm sun.

Upon reaching the yurt, Drew was pleasantly surprised. Brigid had been right—this was not camping. The yurt was much larger than he'd expected. Inside, there were three sets of bunk beds. Each had been made with clean sheets and what looked like handmade quilts of nature-themed colors. Everything here was based on nature: natural wood table and chairs, a wood burning stove. Even the yurt itself was made from some kind of animal hide and framed with exposed wood beams. Only the refrigerator looked manufactured.

Outside the yurt was a firepit and a wraparound porch. Cam immediately set out to explore and the others followed close behind. Drew took a quick breath as he rounded the yurt to see what lay beyond. The yurt had been built toward the edge of the mountain and overlooked the entire canyon.

The hills were endless. They cascaded over each other covered in new green trees and grass and set against that red rock background. The sun was beginning to sink into the horizon shooting light across the world.

This was what he needed. A place with a view as endless as the possibilities he could pretend were his. No tests staring him down or bills piling up.

Goosebumps covered Drew's arms, and he vaguely felt his friends on either side, speechless as well. They stood there for some time before Brigid spoke up.

"We probably better get our things settled before it gets dark. We can bring some chairs back out after if we want."

The others claimed their beds as soon as they entered the yurt, Ronny in a bottom bunk with Nate above him. The girls in a similar arrangement in the next bunk over. Drew dropped his bags on the final bed.

Brigid and Cam disappeared with fresh clothes to hunt down the bathroom. Ronny dug through his bag and pulled out a protein bar, and Nate lay sprawled across his mattress playing on his phone.

"You guys getting any signal?" Nate made a face at his phone. Ronny and Drew both checked their phones and shook their heads. Apparently, the scenery came with a price.

Drew sunk into one of the kitchen chairs, uncapped the pen from his pocket, and touched up the ink on his right arm.

When he'd first started drawing on his arms nearly ten years ago, it had been easy to see he was right-handed. His left arm would be smooth and precise while his right would look like a kindergartener found a Sharpie. He'd gotten better though. Now he felt the same working with either hand.

He knew a lot of people wondered about his arms, why they were always covered in ink. He'd heard people's theories: he's camouflaging his tattoos. He likes that they are intimidating. He does them to attract girls. And while there was a touch of truth in every theory, not even his friends new the truth.

He didn't really care if people knew why he did the things he did, but he'd never mentioned it because it was nobody's damn business.

High school was full of people who wanted to know everything about everyone to distract themselves from the fact that they know nothing about who the hell they are.

Drew had no interest in becoming the latest gossip in the halls of Skyview High.

"When does the sun go down?" Cam asked as the girls strolled back into the yurt.

Nate waved his phone at them. "Not sure, no signal. But probably not until around eight. That's about when it went down yesterday."

"Let's go on a hike or something. There has to be a path close by," Cam said.

"Sounds like a good time. I'm in," Ronny said. Nate followed them out of the yurt, leaving Drew alone with Brigid.

"You going?" Drew asked.

"Sure." Brigid's eyes were dark. All they'd really done today was drive, but she'd had to plan everything and probably spent the whole day worrying. Her anxiety often sat right at the surface on days like this, but she'd never admit it.

"We can come back early if we get tired," Drew held the door of the yurt open for her. Her eyes brightened slightly, and she led him out into the fading sun.

Cam was right, just on the other side of the fire pits was a walking path that headed directly into the trees.

As they wound through the trees, Drew was relieved to find it was much more of a leisurely walk than a strenuous hike. But the scenery was incredible. Trees loomed high above, swaying slightly either from a breeze too high for Drew to feel himself or from animals living in their branches. Rocks and twigs crunched beneath their sneakers, but after a few minutes, the rushing of water he'd heard earlier began to drown it out. The path sloped down, and a river came into view. Water moved slowly over mossy rocks, and bushes lined the edge. But no bridge.

"Well, this is dumb. Why would someone have a path that just ends like this?" Cam asked. She stood on her toes, looking down the river each direction.

"The path is probably meant to bring you to the river and no farther. I think this is the end." Nate picked up a rock, rubbed the dirt off with his hands, and flung it into the moving water.

"Should we head back?" Brigid's eyes shifted anxiously over the surrounding.

Cam mounted her hands on her hips, still searching for a way across the river.

Drew realized what she was about to do a second too late.

Three large rocks poked out above the water, high enough to be dry at the peaks. With zero hesitation, Cam leaped to the first. Ronny and Nate both called after her and threw out their arms as thought they could catch her from the shore if she missed. But she landed smoothly, teetering slightly as she stood from her stooped position, arms out in an attempt to balance herself.

"Cam, are you crazy? Get out of the river." Ronny's face was pulled tight, brows creased. He edged toward the river bank, Nate beside him.

Drew glanced to Brigid standing safely beside him, a few feet from the others. Her eyes were wide with terror, but she stood frozen, watching her adrenaline-junkie best friend chase the rush.

The river seemed to move quicker now. What was a smooth rush of water before was now a threat, fast enough that if Cam fell, she'd have a hell of a time swimming against the rapids.

Drew's stomach swirled as Cam leaped to the second rock. She landed it again, and it wasn't a full second before Nate was behind her on the first. He said something the rest of them couldn't hear.

Ronny still stood on the shore. His eyebrows were pushed together and a deep frown pulled his face downward. "Babe, be careful."

"I got it." Cam waved his worry off and jumped to the final rock. Nate followed her, landing on the second.

But Cam had over-jumped.

Her feet made contact with the rock but her momentum propelled her forward toward the water. Nate's feet sprung from the second to the third rock without stopping. He landed the jump, grabbing Cam's waist before she hit the water. He pulled her against him, keeping them both balanced on the small surface.

Drew's heart raced as he watched two of his closest friends standing still in the center of a rushing river. Nate held Cam tightly, and she tucked herself into him. Her shoulders rose and fell drastically.

Drew tried to slow his own breathing. Cam had always been a little reckless, chasing adventure and acting without thinking. But this was extreme. She'd never put her life at stake like this before. Drew thought back to their conversation on his porch. Cam suggesting the trip at lunch on Friday. She'd been acting different that day too. Ever since, really. Had that only been two days ago?

A throat cleared loudly. Ronny still stood on the shore watching his girlfriend in Nate's embrace. Even from behind,

Drew could see his clenched jaw.

Nate loosened his arms, and Cam leaned away as best should could without falling off. She made the final leap to the opposite shore without trouble. Nate landed next to her a moment later.

Ronny followed them across the river, taking each jump a bit more precisely than Nate and Cam had. On the other side, he wrapped an arm around Cam's waist. Drew didn't miss the dismissive look he sent toward Nate as he passed him.

Nate was clearly under Ronny's skin. Hopefully Cam would smooth that over before it got any further.

Drew tore his gaze from the drama across the river to find Brigid standing so close their arms were nearly touching. Her eyes were still wide, but her color was returning. She still looked like she needed a moment though.

"You want to go back?"

She nodded silently, but her shoulders eased.

Drew lifted his arm to wrap it around her but stopped himself. They'd never been physical like that. Cam was physical with everyone and had shredded that barrier long ago, but Brigid had always been more reserved. Now was not the time to push that.

"We're going to head back and make a fire," Drew called across the river.

Nate shot him a look that promised death if Drew left him alone with Ronny and Cam, but Drew pretended not to see it. Maybe some time alone would give the three of them a chance to have it out.

Brigid's lips lifted to a small smile. "You know how to build a fire?" She was trying not to laugh.

"I'll figure it out."

CHAPTER 7

Outside the yurt were two large fire pits, each surrounded by benches that had been made by cutting a large tree trunk in half. Drew sat on the smaller of the two and began building a fire. There was a large stack of firewood and kindling a few yards away, and within about fifteen minutes, Drew had a decent fire started. It wasn't that hard despite how people make it look. He sat next to Brigid on the bench, their backs to the yurt.

"You didn't have to do this, you know," Brigid said, "You could have gone with the others."

Drew gave her a small shrug. "I didn't really want to go. Nature is fine and all, but I don't feel the need to bask in it. I'm a little surprised they did." His friends weren't exactly "outdoorsy".

"Well, thanks anyway. It is nice to have someone else here." Brigid looked around them at the fading light. "It is already getting dark. I don't think they realized how much earlier it gets dark in the middle of a canyon."

"Probably not. But they'll be fine. Ronny is smart, and they'll stay on the path."

Then sat in silence for a time, watching the sky darken and listening to the fire crackle. Drew twisted the pen from his pocket.

"You ready to graduate?" Brigid poked the fire with a stick she'd found by the logs.

"I'm ready to not have to deal with classes anymore." He'd miss other things though, like seeing his friends every morning and the excuse to not be at home.

"Me too. But then I guess I'll just have college classes. So maybe not."

"Did you decide what you are studying?" Brigid had received her acceptance letters from half a dozen universities, but had been stressing about it ever since, unsure of what she wanted to do. Drew couldn't decide which was worse: not knowing what you want out of life or knowing exactly what you want but knowing you could never have it.

"Not yet." Brigid laid the stick carefully on the ground. "I keep thinking I could study English since I like reading so much, but I don't want to write or teach, so I don't what I'd do with my degree."

"You don't have to decide yet."

"Good thing, because I have no idea."

The silence between them was comfortable but got heavier as the minutes passed. Nate's words resonated in his memory. *She's not going to announce when she's ready. You have to ask.*

Drew had been waiting for a chance to talk to Brigid

alone, and if he didn't take it, he wasn't sure when he'd get another one. He had to step up.

"Is everything alright?" Brigid asked him. How long had he been zoning out?

Drew pushed out a breath and shoved his pen back into his pocket. "Actually, I wanted a chance to talk to you."

"Oh?" Her eyebrows lifted, and she turned toward him more fully.

Drew forced himself to face her, letting those ice blue eyes sear straight through him. He wasn't going to half-ass this. He'd wanted her for too long. Months. But she'd been with Mike, and Drew wasn't about breaking up relationships. So he'd waited. Even after they broke up, he waited, giving her time to move on or whatever she needed. But he couldn't just keep waiting.

"Yeah, I wanted to tell you . . . or ask you . . ." He sounded like a moron. Drew shook his head, trying to get his thoughts straight. "Do you want to go out sometime? After we get back?"

Brigid turned back toward the flames. She swallowed but said nothing. If she hadn't turned so abruptly, Drew would have wondered if she'd even heard him.

The silence beat through him, and he regretted everything.

After much too long a pause, Brigid whispered, "I don't think that would be a good idea."

It was a punch to the gut. He shouldn't have been surprised. Her response had not given him reason to think she was interested, and truthfully, he didn't deserve her.

But the shock was still there. Not even a maybe or one date. Just no.

They'd been flirting for weeks. He was sure of it. Even Nate had seen it.

Drew didn't move or say anything for long minutes. Flames licked the sky and heat seeped into his chilled skin.

Eventually, Brigid mumbled, "I'm sorry."

"You don't have to be sorry Brij." Great, now she pitied him. He braced his arms against his thighs and let his head hang. "I shouldn't have asked. Just forget it."

"No, it was nice of you. Really. I just don't think it would be what either of us want." She bit the corner of her bottom lip. God help him.

"Because you don't want it?" The sun disappeared behind the hills, and the fire cast long shadows across the yurt behind them.

"Not necessarily. But look at our histories. I am more of a relationship person, and you are more of a date around kind of guy."

He flinched. "A date around kind of guy? Or a sleep around kind of guy?" Is that really what she thought of him?

"That's not what I meant, Drew." Brigid's breaths were coming quickly, and her hands clutched at her stomach.

"Oh, I think I know exactly what you meant," Drew spat and stood from his spot on the log. Heat that had nothing to do with the fire burned up his neck.

"No, I just . . . My last relationship ended so badly, and I can't let myself get hurt again."

He froze. "I'm not him, Brij, and the fact that you think

I am tells me everything I need to know." Drew crashed into the yurt without looking back.

She thought he was like her dirt-bag, asshole ex. The idea that he'd ever treat her, or any girl, that way made his blood boil. He didn't know exactly how things ended between them, but Cam had assured him that Mike Allen had hurt Brigid in unforgivable ways. Just the thought made Drew feel sick.

Drew had been with more girls over the last year than he cared to admit. He'd stay with each for a few weeks, sometimes only days, before he'd break it off and move on. Most had stayed in the "PG" range. But he didn't use them, didn't hurt them like that.

He also couldn't commit to them, not when he felt the way he did about Brigid. It wouldn't have been fair to them. So, he'd end it. He was attracted to them, but he couldn't drag them into a relationship when he was in love with someone else.

Blood pounded in his ears. He'd done this. He'd led her to think he was a player. A guy who used girls in the worst way and then dumped them for the next in line.

He needed space to process and cool off, but there was nowhere to go. And Brigid's breathing was escalating. He needed to help her get under control before she had a anxiety attack and passed out in front of the fire. If he sent her spiraling like that, he'd never forgive himself. Drew grabbed her blanket off her bed and headed back outside.

Crashing sounds approached as Drew stepped out of the yurt, and Ronny and Cam burst from the path at a full run.

Both were looking a bit ruffled, and both were out of breath.

They were alone.

"Where's Nate?" Drew demanded.

Brigid looked around frantically, still breathing too quickly.

"We were hoping he'd be here. He hasn't come back? We've been looking everywhere for him. He must have gotten lost," Cam panted.

"Shit." Drew motioned to Ronny. "We'll go. Stay with Brigid." Cam nodded and made her way to the fire.

Drew wrapped the blanket around Brigid's shoulders and bolted into the path where Cam and Ronny had just emerged.

***

Ronny was falling behind, but Drew didn't slow. They'd been searching for fifteen minutes, and it was only getting darker.

He had to find Nate. There was no way his head was in a good place if he'd actually run away from home yesterday. Drew should have checked in with him earlier. Nate's emotions could be a risky balance.

Three years ago, after his mom died, Nate had gotten pretty depressed. He had grieved for her, but then he hadn't come out of it. He sank lower and lower until he was buried in pain and uncertainty.

Nate had stopped attending school. He stopped programming and messing around with his electronics. All he did was lay around all day. Mitch had been completely unaware of what had been happening, lost in his own grief and emptiness after the loss of his wife. Drew was the only one who knew. He checked in on Nate every day, helped him find a reason to keep fighting.

Nate had improved a lot over the last year. He'd gotten help from professionals and found a balance in his life, but Drew also knew Nate had to fight every day to keep from spiraling. He worried that, one of these days, Nate would plummet again, and next time, he might not make it back out.

Drew cut back in a different direction, Ronny still on his heels. A few yards further into the woods, he caught a glimpse of light in the dark. He shuffled forward to see Nate sitting against a tree, staring at his phone on the ground in front of him. Drew put his hand against the trunk, allowing it to hold him up as he caught his breath. Ronny arrived a moment later, also winded.

"Oh, thank God you are alright. We have been looking everywhere for you," Ronny gasped.

Drew scanned Nate.

"Sorry, guys. Really. I just needed a minute. I'll come back soon," Nate said, still staring into the open woods in front of him.

Drew signaled for Ronny to head back to the girls. He nodded and took off running as quickly as they'd come. Drew watched him as far as he could see in the darkness before he lowered himself slowly to the ground next to Nate.

"I really am sorry, man. I know it was stupid," Nate said without looking at Drew. They sat in silence for a minute before he went on. "When we got high enough, I caught signal for just long enough for a text to come through. It was from my dad. He wants me home."

Drew nodded slowly. Mitch would be pissed that his son had left without permission.

"I didn't ask him before I left. I just left. Then I sent a text this afternoon. Couldn't even call him." Nate stood, picking up a rock and flung it as hard as he could into the emptiness that lay before him.

"And when I get home, he's going to have all these things to say to me. Things about how I'm a letdown. How a real man doesn't neglect his responsibilities. But he won't actually say any of it. He'll look at me the way he always does, like I'm not the son he wanted, and then we'll go back to life as it was. Me doing whatever he says and him having no clue who I really am. He doesn't! He doesn't know anything about his own son, because I'm too much of a coward to tell him." Nate dropped back to the ground next to Drew and wiped the moisture from his cheeks. "I'm just like him."

Drew kept silent. This wasn't something Drew could fix with words anyway.

The two sat in the dark for a few more minutes as Nate got himself back under control. He let out a long breath before going on. "Ronny's pissed at me again."

"He'll get over it."

Nate shrugged. "Maybe. I wasn't trying to get that close, but it was a really small rock for two people to fit on without both of us taking a swim."

"You're not ready to tell him?" Drew asked.

Nate shook his head slowly. "Not really. I told Cam she could tell him if she wanted, but she never has."

The night rippled around the trees and settled deep into Drew. He'd always liked the dark, but out in the middle of nowhere, with no houses or streetlights, there was nothing to hide the skies. Millions of stars filled the space above them, unending in their intensity. Tiny rays of light fighting their way through the darkness where they belong.

"Did you tell Brigid how you feel?" Nate asked.

"I asked her out."

"Finally. You two make out in the yurt?" Nate nudged Drew slightly, but when Drew clenched his jaw, Nate backed off. "She said no? Is she crazy? You are totally hot, and you'd be an awesome boyfriend."

Drew let a small chuckle escape. "Shut up. She said she can't go out with me because I sleep around, and she doesn't. She is a relationship person, and I am a player."

"She said that?"

Drew nodded slowly. Nate's brow creased. The two sat in silence for a few minutes. Tension smothered any further discussion.

"I guess we should go back before they start to worry about us again." Nate stood, brushed the dirt from his jeans, and walked the direction of the yurt. Drew pushed off the ground but hung back.

"You okay, Nate?"

Only Drew called him that. He was Nathan to everyone else, but Nate was the guy Drew knew. The guy he'd been before his mom died. That hadn't ever changed to Drew.

"I'll get there."

"And tomorrow?"

Nate gave a small smile that didn't reach his eyes. "Yeah, tomorrow."

Drew clapped him on the back, and they strode into the darkness.

***

Tension enveloped the car the next morning as everyone stared quietly out their windows. Ronny appeared to be over what had happened at the river and was doing his best to keep the peace, but Cam was still pissed at Nate for taking off. Drew and Brigid hadn't so much as looked at each other since their conversation by the fire the night before.

Drew was livid with himself. How had he let Brigid come to think that he would ever be like Mike? He squeezed the steering wheel until his fingers hurt.

Brigid and Mike had just gotten together when Drew met Brigid halfway through junior year. Drew still cursed his luck that he hadn't met her just a few months earlier. If Mike hadn't been in the picture, Drew would've asked her out the day they met.

But she was in a relationship, and Drew respected that. He'd watched in silence when Mike picked her up an hour late for junior prom or when she'd miss a Friday lunch to go out with him and his friends and then get ditched once she was there. As long as she was happy, who was Drew to interfere?

Things ended between them just before Christmas. Drew hadn't been there that night, but Cam had. Brigid showed up on her porch at nearly midnight, anxiety attack underway. Cam was the best at getting Brigid back in control outside of her own parents, but Brigid didn't want her parents knowing what had happened that night.

Drew spun the wheel at their exit and snuck a glance at Brigid. Her eyes were swollen and red.

After they'd gotten back to the camp last night, Cam had sent the boys straight to the yurt saying she needed some time with Brigid. Drew had obeyed, stopping only long enough to get confirmation from Cam that Brigid's anxiety attack was under control.

He never should have asked her out. He knew it was going to blow up in his face. Why would she ever say yes to him? And not only did it possibly ruin their friendship, he'd nearly sent her into a anxiety attack in the process. He was such a dick. Maybe he was more like Mike than he realized.

CHAPTER 8

Vegas was somehow exactly and nothing like the movies. The whole place was lit up and people were everywhere. Oversized casinos and hotels lined the strip, but it lacked the extravagance the movies always seemed to portray. Maybe it was because the sun was up and people weren't out to party yet.

Drew turned off the main road and onto a little street with a sign that read "Cosmopolitan Parking." The parking structure lead directly into the hotel lobby. Drew threw his backpack over one shoulder and carried his duffle in the other hand. Ronny somehow managed to haul his bag and both of Cam's in one trip. Cam carried her blanket.

The lobby was incredible. Shiny tiles covered the floor, reflecting the lights from high above. The entire back wall was a line of reception desks, each with a Cosmopolitan employee clicking away on a computer. Between Drew and those desks were two rows of enormous square pillars, each around five feet across. Glass panels covered all four sides of the pillars from floor to ceiling. The glass emanated different colored lights and designs. Drew couldn't tell if the art was projected from inside the pillar or if the panels themselves were screens, but the overall impression was stunning.

Despite the impressive art that made up the Cosmopolitan's lobby, the smell of cigarette smoke and booze nearly knocked Drew over. It smelled like his mom after a bad night—times about a hundred.

Cam and Brigid checked in at the receptionist desks and returned with a handful of keys, handing one to each of them. They weaved their way through the pillars until they found an entire wall of elevators.

"You guys go ahead. I'll be up," Nate said. "Cam, could I talk to you for a sec?"

Cam nodded and shooed Drew, Brigid, and Ronny toward the elevators. There were a thousand of them, so they immediately found an empty one, pulled their luggage in, and hit the "6" button.

No one else entered their elevator on the way up. The doors opened, and they walked down the hall to their rooms, bags in tow. Brigid stopped at 608 and swiped her key.

"See you guys in about an hour?"

"Sounds like a plan," Ronny answered.

Drew nodded in agreement as she disappeared behind her door and it shut with a click.

Ronny whistled. "Shit went down with you two last night, didn't it?"

Drew ignored him and moved on to 609. He swiped his key and held the door open for Ronny to step in.

"Oh, Brigid didn't tell you?" Ronny rubbed the back of his neck. "We've got three rooms here. You and Nate will be in this one, and Cam and I are taking 610."

"That works," Drew said and slipped into his room. It was nice—nicer than anywhere he'd stayed in a long time. Most of the space was filled by two queen beds with puffy, white comforters and blue leather headboards. Modern aesthetic oozed from the bathroom with sharp edges and two sinks. There were geometric shapes and glass panels everywhere, and everything was shiny. The view was pretty incredible though. Floor to ceiling windows overlooked the entire strip.

Ads screamed at him from every direction. Bright colors advertising the addition of a new dance show at a nearby hotel and the best place to hire tonight's female company. Thousands of people littered the streets, most of which seemed either drunk or on their way to become so. Didn't these people realize it was broad daylight?

He'd been to Vegas once before, but he'd only been about six and didn't remember much. Elliott had taken him for a weekend while his mom traveled for work. Drew had spent most of the weekend alone in the room watching cartoons while his father schmoozed musicians and gambled away any of Drew's college funds that might have existed.

A beep and a click announced Nate's entrance. He dropped his bag on the foot of the opposite bed from where Drew had left his own.

"Talked to Cam," he said.

"You tell her what happened?" Drew asked without

leaving the window.

"Basically. I told her I had gotten a not real happy text from my dad and needed to cool off. Then I begged her forgiveness and promised her my soul. She's good now. You going to shower or do you care if I get in?"

Drew nodded his head toward the shower in answer. Nate grabbed a few things from his bag, walked to the bathroom, and closed the door.

As he waited for the shower, Drew's thoughts again drifted to the call he'd received the day before. Elliott had a gig for him. If he was contacting him out of the blue, it must have been a big deal.

Drew had heard from his dad only three times since he left, and all within the last two years. His mom had no idea, and Drew would never tell her. She'd probably kick him out on the spot if she knew. She'd never forgiven Elliott for leaving all those years ago. Neither had Drew, but it was different. His mom was angry. Drew simply didn't care anymore.

He swiped his phone to life. A few junk emails. No texts. No calls.

He frowned at the blank screen, throat tight. He hadn't heard from his mom since he'd left, not that that was surprising. He went days without hearing from his mom even when they were living in the same house. He'd ignored the burn in his gut as his friends had answered calls from home in the yurt this morning. Well, everyone except Nate who still hadn't responded to Mitch's texts. But at least Mitch had sent something.

Nate stepped from the bathroom, wet hair dripping

down his neck and into the collar of a fresh T-shirt.

"All yours." He shook his head, spraying water like a dog. "Unless you need some help in there." He sent a crooked grin at Drew.

Drew flipped him off and closed the bathroom door behind him. Nate's laugh echoed from the other side.

***

People lined the strip on both sides, and cars filled the street, nearly forming a parking lot. Billboards lit the sky even in the light of day. Blues and reds bounced off the sides of glass hotels, each larger than anything you'd find in Idaho and housing enormous casinos. Cam asked if anyone wanted to try their luck before they went off to see the strip, but gambling wasn't really why they were there.

The people around them were nearly as interesting as the hotels and shops. They lined up to take photos with aspiring actors in knockoff Disney costumes. Some played instruments in the hopes they could earn tips from passersby. Drew threw a five in the hat of an especially talented violinist playing AC/DC.

In front of the NewYorkNewYork, they stumbled across some girls dressed in what looked like skimpy swimming suits that turned out to be nothing but body paint. Cam grabbed Ronny's hand and hurried him past. Drew stared at the sky, or the ground, or anywhere else. He felt like a perv even walking past them. Weren't they cold?

The most interesting person they met along the way was a street artist named Kai, an artist that worked in spray

82

paints. Drew was skeptical as they pushed their way through the crowd to watch him work. Graffiti was intriguing, but he'd never really found it all that impressive.

But this was not graffiti—or anything close.

Kai worked fast. It was difficult to follow the cans of paint flying in and out of his hands, both stained with smears of rainbow. He used a small square of plastic to create clean lines and shadows. Drew stood mesmerized as, slowly, the night sky over a wide ocean began to take form on the canvas.

It was stunning. Stars streaked across a sky of blues, blacks, and purples and reflected off the rolling waters of a living ocean. Every inch of it sang of freedom and expectation.

Drew tore his eyes from the painting and watched Kai as he put the final touches on his masterpiece. Despite being bent over a piece of canvas, his shoulders were pulled back, pushing his chest forward, chin held high. Pride flared in his eyes.

A familiar flame burned deep inside Drew. Kai had found his calling in life. He knew what he wanted and went after it. If only life were that simple.

Maybe someday it could be. His mom might put herself together, or he could work his way to a job where he could support both of them and still have time to play music. It could happen. And if not, maybe Drew could find himself a spot on the strip somewhere between Kai and the painted women. At least he'd be playing music.

Drew pulled a couple twenties from his pocket and bought the canvas.

***

"It's the only thing I absolutely have to do while we're here," Ronny pulled Cam into the Stratosphere, the rest of them falling in line behind her.

"Why? There are rollercoasters everywhere. You can go to Six Flags all the time once you live in California."

"Yes, but this is a coaster on *top* of a skyscraper. We have to do it." Ronny led them through the lobby and over to the elevator that would take them to the coasters.

Drew wasn't a major rollercoaster buff, like Ronny apparently was, but he didn't mind them. He was fine to go for a thrill ride if it was what the others wanted. Cam, however, was looking pretty pale.

"I think I'm going to sit this one out. I'm a little tired, and could use a few minutes to chill." Cam kissed Ronny and took a spot on a nearby bench before he could stop her.

Drew kept his face blank, but his mind was swimming. Twenty-four hours ago, Cam was jumping rocks across a raging river, but now she needs a rest?

"We can't leave her alone on some bench in Vegas." Ronny blew out a mouthful of air. Brigid grabbed his arm as he took a step toward the bench.

"I can stay with her. I wouldn't mind a break either, and I'm not a huge fan of heights." Brigid found her way to Cam's bench and took a seat. Cam rested her head in Brigid's lap and closed her eyes.

Ronny blinked. "You both know," he continued, voice even lower now, "we can't leave them alone either." His eyes shot between Nate and Drew, looking for one more volunteer.

"I'll stay," Drew said. "I wouldn't mind a minute to

talk to Brigid, and you two can go get yourselves off on a coaster."

Ronny clapped him on the shoulder, and he and Nate entered the elevator.

Cam was already asleep in Brigid's lap when Drew got to the bench. Her eyes were dark. Was she not getting enough sleep? That was very unlike Cam. Brigid was the worrier. Cam lived life on full blast. She met the world head on and always came out on top.

"Is she okay?" Drew asked Brigid with a nod toward the sleeping pile of brown hair on Brigid's lap.

"I think so." Brigid stared at Cam like she could read what was happening in Cam's head like one of her books. "Probably just tired. We've been going pretty hard today."

Drew nodded silently. They only had two days in Vegas before they needed to move on to California, so they'd seen as much as possible today.

He took a spot on the bench next to Brigid. What was the proper distance to sit next to a friend who'd recently rejected you? Six inches? Ten?

The Stratosphere was one of the cheaper hotels on the strip, sitting a little further north and not quite in the heart of the action. They'd had to drive to get here.

A young couple strolled past wearing "He's my Husband/She's my Wife" T-shirts with arrows pointing to the other person. A minute later came a young family, kid crying while the mom pulled a bag of cheerios from her oversized backpack.

Drew and Brigid sat in a thick silence. This was his

fault. They were friends. She liked him as a friend. That should have been enough. He had to stop hoping for more out of life than what he was being offered.

Brigid twisted the elastic at her wrist, looking anywhere but at him.

"Brigid?" His voice came out squeaky. Awesome. "I'm sorry about last night. It was stupid of me to mess with what we have. I didn't mean to upset you."

Brigid finally met his eyes. Damn, she was beautiful. Having her full attention was like standing on stage with a spotlight shining directly on you. Other people can see you, but all you can see is light.

"*You're* sorry?" Her brows pulled together, and she blinked quickly a few times, long lashes brushing her cheeks each time. "I was going to apologize to you! You were so nice, and I was awful. I didn't mean anything the way it came out, and then I got all… well… me. I'm so sorry." Brigid placed a hand lightly on his arm, her pale fingers dramatically contrasting his inky skin. She bit the corner of her bottom lip.

That lip was going to be the death of him. His skin heated under her fingers.

Words. He could form words.

"You don't need to be sorry, Brij. Can we just move on, act like it didn't happen?"

"Yes. Please. I want that." A smile lit her face. Drew pulled his arm away from where her fingers still held him, unable to endure the burn of her touch any longer.

"You two are stupid," Cam mumbled, eyes still closed.

"How long have you been awake?" Brigid asked.

"Long enough." Cam sat up slowly and glanced around like she wasn't sure where they were. "Are Nate and Ronny back yet?"

As though beckoned by her question, Nate and Ronny exited the elevator.

"Babe, you missed out. That was so exhilarating!" Ronny scooped Cam into his arms and kissed her firmly, holding her against him.

Nate's eyes found Drew's, and he didn't have to say a word for Drew to read his thoughts. *Get a damn room.*

CHAPTER 9

The group split up for a quick stop before they continued making their way down the strip. The bathrooms in the Stratosphere were fancy. Chandeliers sparkled above them and cast shadows across the golden floor tiles. Vanilla-scented hand soap permeated the air and only the paper towel dispensers reminded Drew that they were in a public bathroom.

He checked his phone as Ronny washed his hands. Still nothing. He'd texted his mom a few hours ago to check in, but hadn't heard back yet. He told himself that was probably a good sign. If she'd gotten in trouble or run out of food money, he'd definitely have heard from her.

The girls' bathrooms were down the hall from theirs, so they took up a spot against a wall as they waited for them to finish. Cam and Brigid emerged soon after but were cut off just outside the doors. Two men stepped directly into their paths, blocking their way to the other end of the hall where Drew leaned against the wall, Ronny and Nate on either side.

"Excuse us." Cam pulled Brigid to step around the men, but they were again cut off.

"What's your rush, sweetheart?" The larger of the two men took a step toward her. From behind, Drew could tell he was lean but muscular—stronger than he appeared.

The second guy was turned toward Brigid, who was looking more than just a little uncomfortable under his gaze.

What was it with creeps? Did all girls have this problem?

Drew pushed off the wall, and the three of them approached the men from the side, stopping about ten feet away. Close enough to be seen, but not to take control.

"We're on our way to meet our boyfriends." Cam motioned toward Ronny, Nate, and Drew. They may have only been eighteen, but all three appeared older. Ronny had to be at least 6'2" and was uncharacteristically broad-shouldered for a high school student. Nate worked out every day and definitely had the build to prove it. Drew wasn't as built or tall, but he knew how to make himself intimidating. The ink on his arms flashed as he crossed them. He could hold his own.

"These boys?" The man nodded toward where Drew stood, and a slimy smile spread across his face. "Beautiful women like you deserve to be handled by real men." He winked.

Drew's entire body tensed. This had gone way too far already, and he had no problem handing these guys' asses to them. He took a step forward, but Ronny put a hand on his arm, holding him back.

"We're leaving. And if you say one more word to

either of us," Cam met the man's eyes and leaned forward slightly, "I'll let them kill you." She motioned once more to where they stood, fury evident in each clenched jaw, balled fist, and fiery stare.

Cam took Brigid's hand once more and pushed through the men. Ronny wrapped an arm around Cam's shoulders, and Nate slipped his hand through Brigid's. The five of them walked out of the casino and didn't once look back.

***

The Cosmopolitan had two pool areas. As the outdoor pool was overrun by families with young children playing Marco Polo, they opted for the indoor pool where they'd have a bit more room to themselves. A large swimming pool filled most of the area. It was nearly empty aside from a few swimmers methodically doing laps. Three hot tubs surrounded the shallow end of the pool. The air was thick with humidity, and chlorine invaded every breath.

Cam had informed them on the way in that she needed some time with Brigid and to keep to themselves for a few minutes. So as the girls headed to the deep side of the pool and dangled their feet over the edge, Ronny nudged Nate and Drew toward an empty hot tub.

They sat in silence, enjoying the warmth of the water after a long day of wandering around the strip. Drew's feet ached from the miles they'd covered as they explored all Las Vegas had to offer. Cam wanted to do everything. If she never made it back to Vegas again, she could still claim to have not missed a thing—besides the rollercoaster.

Drew watched Cam and Brigid across the water. Brigid twisted the hair tie on her wrist, brows pulled together, as Cam spoke. She nodded slowly, listening intently to whatever Cam was saying and biting that damn lip.

Even after a long day on the strip, she was a knockout. He couldn't keep from noticing how Brigid's red bikini top stretched up her shoulders and tied around her slim neck. Silver rings at her hips held the fabric together and left little to his imagination. Drew's fingers itched to slide through those loops and pull her against him.

"Your tongue is hanging out." Nate hit him in the arm.

Drew flipped him off.

Ronny chuckled but then became serious. "Everything okay? You've been a little off since this afternoon."

"They might be able to take care of themselves, but that doesn't make me hate those assholes any less. We should have done something." Drew was practically growling. He needed to get a grip. He never got this unhinged. This trip was doing weird things to everyone.

"You and I both know Cam would have been pissed if we had stepped in. And Brigid. They can handle themselves," Ronny countered.

Nate chimed in, "Dude, you are gonna creep her out if you stare at her all the time. Why don't you do something about it? You could get any girl you want."

Drew's gaze found Brigid again. She was saying something to Cam now, concern and care still written all over her face. That caring was as attractive to Drew as any physical attribute, of which Brigid had many. She was so much more than that, though.

"She isn't any girl. And you of all people know that relationships aren't that simple." Drew turned to Ronny. "And not all of us can have the perfect one." Ronny and Nate both held his stare for a moment before conceding defeat.

"That doesn't mean you just give up." Ronny dipped further into the hot tub.

"She thinks I use girls for sex."

"So, prove her wrong. Show her the real you."

"She knows the real me. We've been friends for a long time."

"Ronny has a point," Nate slowly kicked his feet in and out of the water. "She knows your personality, but how well does she know you as a person? What does she know about your life?"

None of his friends knew almost anything about his life. Nate knew more than any of the others, and even he didn't know much. Drew kept his life contained, a bag of trash you tie up tight to keep it from getting anything around it dirty. He was doing them a favor by not dragging them into his world of night shifts, cheap booze, and overdue rent.

"You can't expect her to let you into her life if you won't let her into yours." Nate clapped him on the shoulder and slid completely under the water.

They were right about one thing if nothing else. Drew couldn't just keep staring at Brigid all the time, pining after her like a lovesick puppy. He had to do something—either change her mind or move on.

Drew had replayed their conversation in his head at

least a hundred times since the night before. Brigid hadn't said she didn't like him or wasn't interested. She'd said she didn't think them dating was a good idea. So maybe she was interested. He just needed to show her she could trust him, that he was nothing like that bastard she'd dated before.

He could do that. He could let someone into his messed-up world, at least a little bit, if that someone was Brigid Foster.

"Is this seat taken?" Brigid appeared over his shoulder and took the space next to him, dipping her legs into the warm water. Cam walked around the wet concrete and sat on the edge opposite them, near Ronny.

"All yours," Drew smiled back.

"This feels so good. That pool water was too cold." Cam filled her cupped hands with warm water and trickled it over her shoulders. "Guess what I did."

"Did you pee in the pool?" Nate splashed water lightly at Cam, sprinkling her hair.

"Gross! No!" Cam kicked water back his way, barely missing Drew in the crossfire. "I got us tickets to a show tomorrow. It isn't a real Vegas experience without a show."

"What show are we going to, babe?" Ronny asked. He slid next to Cam's legs and ran his hands along them under the water.

"Chippendales."

"What?" Nate lost his footing and slipped under the water. He reemerged with wide eyes darting between each of them.

Brigid was stiff next to Drew.

"Kidding." Cam rolled her eyes. "It's a magician."

"Really, babe? A magic show?" Ronny paused in his leg massage to glance up at her.

"He's supposed to be really good," Cam shrugged. "And if it sucks, it'll make for a funny story later."

Drew wasn't big on magic. It was all a little too fake for him. Magicians were for reality tv shows and children's birthday parties. But if he had to choose between watching some guy do card tricks for an hour or watching male dancers take their clothes off, he'd happily attend the magic show.

***

Day two in Vegas got off to a late start. Ronny and Cam had rented a bunch of pay-per-view movies the night before, and they'd all stayed up watching raunchy comedies, eating overpriced microwave popcorn, and making enough noise to get a call from the front desk. Drew, Nate, and Brigid had finally staggered back to their rooms around three in the morning. Drew didn't care to know how much later Cam and Ronny stayed up.

They hunted down coffee and energy drinks around noon and began the day's exploring.

Cam looked better than she had the last few mornings. Sleeping in had clearly done her a lot of good.

They would be leaving for California first thing the next morning, so it was their last day on the strip. Brigid had made a list on her phone the night before of all the things Cam still *had* to do before they left the city.

They watch the Bellagio fountains, visited the M&M

94

Store, and waited 45 minutes for hot chocolate from some place called Serendipity. It was "just like in that movie!" according to Cam.

It was a strange sensation to have someone else paying for all Drew's expenses. Every meal, drink, or entrance fee had Cam pulling out her parents' credit card. He knew they wouldn't mind—the Wests were extremely generous and extremely wealthy—but it was unfamiliar all the same.

Cam's parents had gotten married really young, right out of high school. They'd been pregnant with Cam when they'd graduated. Her dad had gotten a job working for some call center company to pay the bills, but they were both major social and environmental activists. Fast forward about five years, Cam's dad had founded some eco-friendly company that was a big deal. He sold it not long after for enough that they were pretty much set for life. Now they saved the world full time.

Somewhere between the Coca-Cola Factory and Madame Tussauds, Drew's phone went off in his pocket.

He hadn't heard from his mom since he'd left. All his texts had stayed on "read," and all his calls had gone unanswered. Apparently three was the magic number of days before she'd worry about her son being out of the state without a chaperone.

Drew slowed his pace and let his friends distance themselves before swiping his screen to life. One new message.

Mom: *I'm out of cash. You didn't leave enough.*

Drew's chest sunk. He cleared his throat, pushing

away the tightness that sat unwelcome there.

Drew: *I left a hundred dollars. That should have lasted the whole week.*

She responded immediately.

Mom: *It didn't. Where's the rest?*

Drew: *There should be a few more twenties in the drawer by the sink.*

No response. She must have gotten what she needed.

Drew's stomach twisted. That money was supposed to be for next week's gas. Guess gas money would be coming out of their food budget now.

Nate appeared and bumped Drew's shoulder with his own. "Everything okay?"

Drew nodded and slid his phone back into his pocket.

"Your mom?" Nate asked.

Drew nodded again.

Nate shrugged. "Don't worry about her. This week's for us. She'll still be there when you get home." He clapped Drew on the back.

She would. Drew knew that. She'd still be there because she needed him. But just once it would be nice if that wasn't true. Just once it would be nice if she was there because she wanted him.

"Here we are!" Cam called from a few yards ahead, "Our tickets are for the early show. You have to be 21 to get tickets to the night show." She veered toward Caesar's Palace and pointed to a lighted billboard across the street from where they stood.

Eye liner and a crooked smile gave the magician a dark,

mysterious aura. He was dressed head to toe in black. The sleeves of his dress shirt were rolled most of the way up his forearms, and in his hands was a deck of cards. The queen of hearts stuck halfway out of his shirt pocket. Giant gold letters across the top read "Matias Wolf now performing at Caesar's Palace!"

Nate wiggled his eyebrows at Drew before grabbing his arm and pulling him along beside him.

CHAPTER 10

It was a smaller venue than he'd expected. Instead of an arena, they entered a small ballroom room lined with black curtains. Colored lights kept the room dim without making it too dark to see. Small round tables were scattered across the floor, each with a black tablecloth that draped to the floor and three to five chairs around it.

They found a table with enough chairs for all of them and took their seats. At the front of the room was a stage. More black fabric hung from the ceiling at the back of the platform, and a lone microphone stand stood abandoned at the side.

A waitress appeared at their table to take drink orders. Drew ordered a diet soda, and when his heart flipped a moment later, it definitely did not have anything to do with Brigid ordering the same. That would be pathetic.

Tables were full by the time their drinks arrived. The lights dimmed further and any conversations halted in the darkness. A spotlight appeared at center stage, but there was still no sign of a performer.

Seconds passed and hushed whispers arose from the audience.

A deep, raspy voice sounded from the shadows to Drew's left.

"First rule of magic: everything is a distraction." The man from the billboard stepped from the shadows and into the dimly lit room. He swept past their table and made his way smoothly to the stage and into the spotlight.

He was younger than he'd looked in the ad, probably only twenty something. His face was catlike with thin eyes and lips. He wore the same black clothing, but his hands were empty, no cards yet.

"You see, when I was just a boy, my father taught me about magic. He said to me, 'Matias, there will many people in your life that will claim to know magic. They are all liars.'" He scanned the audience, before locking eyes with Drew. "There is no such thing as magic."

Matias smiled that crooked, wicked smile. Every eye in the room was locked on him. Even Drew held his breath, waiting for whatever this guy had planned. Crazy or not, he knew how to command a room.

"I decided I would create it. I would manipulate the rules most magicians live by to give the illusion of magic, and by doing so, bring each of you into the magic itself. You see, I need each of you to make the magic work. First, I need you each to take a card." He snapped his fingers loudly. "Will each of you please check your pockets?"

Drew reached into his front pockets. Phone, keys. He shifted to check his back pockets. In one he found his wallet, as usual, but in the other, he discovered a smooth, crisp playing card. The five of spades.

He glanced around the table. Ronny and Nate each retrieved a card from their own pants' pockets. Five of diamonds and five of clubs.

Brigid discovered the five of hearts in her backpack.

Cam's card was in her jacket. Six of hearts.

Gasps from around the room signaled similar experiences from everyone. Each person in the room was holding a single playing card.

"Fifty two. There are fifty two people in the room." Ronny scanned the room again, verifying his count. "A complete deck."

Applause broke out around them as others made the same discovery.

"Tuck those away where you found them. We might need them later," Matias directed from the stage. He extracted a boxed deck from his shirt pocket, opened it, and slid the cards out into his hand.

Drew barely registered the waiter setting a fresh diet mountain dew in front of him. As much as he didn't enjoy magic, Matias was hard to look away from.

"Second rule of magic: a magician never reveals his secrets." Matias splayed the deck of cards for the audience to see. He stepped effortlessly from the stage. Drew had a feeling this guy didn't do anything that wasn't smooth and calculated.

He walked through the tables weaving in and out so all could see the cards that made up the deck in his hands. An entire deck of aces.

"Now, that just won't do. Any trick I do with this deck will be an illusion. A fake. However, we might need to save just one card. You never know when you might need it." He winked at a woman at the table next to theirs. She giggled and flipped her hair.

Matias drifted around to back side of their table, flipped the cards upside down, and fanned them toward Cam. "Choose one please. Look at what it is, but don't tell me."

Unlike the giggler, Cam locked eyes with Matias and, without hesitation, plucked a card from the deck. She glanced at it briefly and tilted it toward the ground.

"Would you mind just sticking that in my pocket for safe keeping?" Matias grinned again. Ronny sat up a little straighter.

Cam confidently lifted the card and popped it into Matias's shirt pocket.

"Thank you, miss." He strode through the room and returned his voice to performance level. "We won't need the rest of these." He tossed the remaining cards in the air just as he reached the stage. They spiraled around him in all directions. Another distraction.

But Drew kept his eyes on Matias this time.

"I'll just have to use your deck instead." He waved his hands, motioning for them to retrieve their cards.

Drew reached into his pocket for his card, but came up empty.

The card was gone.

Brigid rifled through her backpack, and Cam removed her jacket completely to check again. All their cards had disappeared.

A woman across the room held up a card. "I still have mine."

Matias wrinkled his brow. "That's strange. Our deck needs 52 cards. No more. No less." He paused. "Unless we have a duplicate."

A gasp, barely audible, escaped Cam's lips. "The Ace of Clubs," she whispered under her breath.

"What is your card?" Matias asked the woman.

"Ace of Clubs," she called out.

"Oh my god." Cam's eyes bulged.

Matias reached into his pocket where Cam had placed a card mere moments ago and retrieved none other than the Ace of Clubs.

The audience lost it.

***

"Come on. You have to admit that was cool." Cam elbowed Ronny as they made their way out of Caesar's Palace.

"I can't figure out how he did it. Any of it." Brigid's brows pulled together and scrunched up her forehead.

Matias had been pretty impressive. Drew had to admit he'd enjoyed the show more than he'd expected. Trick after trick, Matias had wowed the audience. No one could guess what he'd do next, let alone know how he'd done it. Halfway through the show, Drew had stopped trying to figure it out and just let himself be entertained.

Nate looked up from his phone for the first time since the show ended. "Looks like that Matias guy is a big deal in the

102

magic world. He's one of the youngest magicians to ever get a headline spot on the strip. He's especially popular with the ladies."

Shocker.

The sun dipped slowly behind the casinos as they entered the final destination of the day, The Venetian.

They pushed through the doors, and Drew was surprised to find himself still outside. Or not really. The hotel was designed to feel like an outdoor attraction. Lights and clouds sprinkled the ceiling. Sidewalks led them down a winding tunnel and into an open square. Even the air smelled fresher than it had outside.

Italy—or at least the way Italy looked in movies—complete with a river winding through the middle of the walkway in place of where a street would be in other cities. Boats filled with tourists floated their way down the center of the river steered by a driver who stood at the front and pushed through the water with some kind of giant oar.

"Gondolas." Brigid nodded at the boats. "These are the Venetian Gondolas. The Gondoliers drive the boats down the river. It even winds outside for a little ways." Her cheeks were pink and her eyes sparkled. Had she been waiting for these all day?

This could easily turn into a very romantic situation. As badly as Drew wanted to use that to his advantage to impress Brigid, he knew that wasn't the way to win her trust. He pushed the instinct down deep.

The line moved quickly, and they were loading before long. As they approached the boat, Drew realized they only held four passengers. His friends also hesitated briefly.

"Ronny and I will go in one," Cam smiled, but it was strained. Brigid nodded to her once, and Drew didn't miss the way she squeezed Cam's hand before allowing her to climb in behind Ronny.

Their boat floated away and another took its place only moments later. Drew stepped across the loading dock to climb in. A steel railing had been installed, separating the dock from the water. Drew grasped the cool metal in one hand and placed one foot carefully into the vessel. It was more stable in the water than he'd expected.

He'd once been kayaking at a birthday party and nearly tipped the whole thing over trying to get in. These were much sturdier, probably held in place by all kinds of wires and tracks beneath the surface.

His other foot landed in the gondola, and Drew turned to help Brigid climb aboard. She took his hand without hesitation, but dropped it the moment she had her footing.

Nate clambered in behind Brigid, and their gondolier pushed off. They floated only about fifteen feet behind where Cam and Ronny's own boat made its way down the river.

There was plenty of high-end shopping in the Venetian. They passed a Hugo Boss, Gucci, and Louis Vuitton within 50 feet of each other. The unique atmosphere, outside while inside, was captivating. Drew nearly forgot they were in Vegas and not making their way through Venice.

"I need to tell you both something," Brigid whispered from across the boat. She sat alone across from him and Nate, but the seats were close enough that her knees nearly skimmed his.

Drew locked his attention on her, and instantly knew something was wrong. Her forehead was wrinkled, and she rubbed her arms as though she was cold, even though it was probably at least 80 degrees. He nodded for her to continue. Nate leaned forward, listening intently. Drew couldn't be more grateful for a best friend who treated Brigid the way Nate did.

"Cam and I talked last night, and she needs me to tell you both something. She's talking to Ronny right now, but it's something you both need to know." She swallowed hard. "Cam's pregnant."

Drew blinked. Pregnant. The word swirled through his brain without taking root.

"Cam's having a baby?" Nate stumbled over his words like they were too big for his mouth.

Brigid nodded quickly.

Cam was pregnant. Ronny and Cam were pregnant. How could this happen? That was a stupid question. Drew knew exactly how it happened. But hadn't they been careful? Used protection?

The flutter of adrenaline that filled his stomach quickly turned to a weight. His skin went cold.

There would be a baby.

A little kid.

"What's she going to do?" Drew blurted, more aggressively that he'd meant to be. "Is she keeping it?"

Brigid blinked quickly as she rebounded from his abrupt response. "I… I don't know. I think so, but she didn't really say."

"And she's telling Ronny right now?" Nate asked. Brigid nodded again. The three of them turned to in their seats to better see the gondola ahead.

Something was definitely going down up there. Ronny sat bent over with his head in his hands. Cam covered her mouth with both hands. Drew couldn't see her eyes very well, but her shoulders were shaking like she was crying.

Ronny sat up abruptly and faced Cam head on. Even sitting side-by-side, he'd managed to put at least a foot between them, as though every inch mattered. Anger contorted his features as he spoke. Cam's eyes went wide and her mouth dropped open.

Drew could barely process what was happening as Cam stood from her place beside Ronny and jumped out of the boat.

The river wasn't particularly deep, only reaching the middle of Cam's back, but it splashed as she hit the surface and soaked her from head to toe. The last few inches of her hair floated along the surface as she trudged through the water toward the edge of the walkways. Water ran from her jeans and hair as she pulled herself over the edge and disappeared into the bewildered crowd of onlookers.

Both gondoliers, Ronny's and their own, stopped their rowing. They looked around expectantly for what to do next. They'd probably never had someone jump out before.

Ronny remained seated in the boat, jaw tight, eyes on the hole in the crowd where Cam had disappeared.

"Excuse me, sir," Brigid motioned urgently to the

gondolier, "Can you please pull over right here?"

Drew was sure the answer would be "no", but the gondolier probably wasn't thinking straight either. He steered them to the side of the river and Brigid stood to exit.

Brigid reached for the edge of the dock, but Nate wrapped a hand gently around her fingers. "Let me go after her. I'll make sure she gets back to the hotel safe, and you two can figure out what happened with Ronny."

Brigid hesitated for only a second before nodding. Nate climbed out of the boat and faded into the crowd where Cam had only a minute before.

Brigid slowly sunk back into her seat.

"He'll take care of her." Drew wasn't sure what else to say. His mind was still spinning.

They shoved off the edge, and continued making their way down the river, keeping Ronny in view. He sat slumped in his seat. Head in his hands and completely alone.

Drew barely registered the rest of the ride. Questions swarmed his thoughts, each more complicated than the last, but one question burned its way to the forefront, more crucial and revealing than any other.

What about the kid?

Their ride came to an end before Drew was ready. The gondolier docked, and Drew didn't miss the look he threw them as they left the boat and hunted for Ronny.

He'd landed on a nearby bench. His face still held the vacant expression he'd worn since Cam had jumped from the boat.

"What happened?" Brigid demanded, a touch of fire in

her voice.

Ronny shook his head repeatedly. "Cam's pregnant." The words came out weak and breathless.

"Why did she jump out of your gondola?" Brigid held his stare.

"I. . .," Ronny ran his hand down his face, "I didn't react very well."

"Explain."

"I asked her if it was mine."

Shit.

Drew couldn't blame Ronny for being shocked. Drew was in shock, and it wasn't even his kid. But to essentially accuse Cam of cheating? That was cold. No wonder she'd jumped.

Brigid stared Ronny down. A muscle moved in her jaw, and her fists clenched tightly at her side.

"We need to get back to the hotel."

Ronny hesitated and then nodded.

***

The Cosmopolitan elevators opened on the 6th floor, and Drew, Brigid, and Ronny made their way silently down the hall. The whole walk back from the Venetian had been tense. Brigid was clearly livid with Ronny, but she'd never let him have it for something that was Cam's to deal with.

They arrived at their rooms, and Ronny cleared his throat.

"I can't . . . Cam and I share a room, and I'm not sure she wants me to . . ." Ronny trailed off without making eye

108

contact. He shoved his hands deep into his pockets.

He was right. Cam needed space, and Ronny couldn't invade that.

"You can come in with Nate and me." Drew pulled his key from his wallet, swiped, and pushed the door open. He held the door for them and then followed Ronny and Brigid to where they had both frozen just inside his room.

Drew stepped between them and stopped in his tracks.

On Drew's bed sat Nate and Cam, his arm wrapped around her shoulders. Cam wore nothing but a bra on top, and Nate was completely shirtless.

This didn't add up.

But it looked really bad.

"Ronny, what are you doing here?" Cam asked. She shot up from the bed and out of Nate's arms.

Ronny only stared at them, his face shifting from shock to anger.

"This isn't what it looks like, Ronny. Nathan was just helping me calm down." Cam stumbled over her words. Even in Drew's ears they sounded guilty.

But Ronny wasn't listening anyway. "And you had the nerve to be mad at me?" he shouted. "Looks like I was totally justified in wondering if it was mine. I came to Drew's room so you wouldn't have to see me, to give you the space you needed, and I find you two having your own little therapy session. You could have at least had the decency to hang a sock on the door so Drew wouldn't interrupt."

"It wasn't like that," Nate said, finally standing from his place on the bed. His sculpted chest accentuated the rise and fall of each breath. It wasn't helping his case for sure.

"Nothing happened, Ronny. We were just talking." Cam reached for Ronny's hand, but Ronny pulled away.

"Hey, don't let me stop you. I'm out of here. You and I-" he motioned between him and Cam- "are done."

Ronny stormed out the door without looking back.

"Shit," Nate whispered under his breath, and he chased Ronny out the door, still shirtless.

Cam fell back onto the edge of the bed, mouth hanging slightly open and eyes unfocused. Brigid sat next to her, taking Nate's place from earlier.

Something wasn't adding up. There was no way things actually happened the way it looked. Drew needed to fix this, to help Cam and Nate and Ronny, but he first had to know. No matter how impossible it was, he had to be sure that nothing had happened between Cam and Nate.

"Explain." Drew demanded, unable to look at Cam.

It took a few moments for her to respond, like she heard him but couldn't process the question. "We came straight back here. I didn't want to go in my room in case Ronny came back. Nate said I could wait in here until Brigid came back with her key."

"And the clothes?" He folded his arms across his chest.

"My shirt was soaked. Nate hugged me on the elevator, and my hair soaked his as well." Her voice sounded wrong, empty. "We were cold."

The door beeped, and Nate reentered the room. A fountain of blood poured from his nose.

"He hit you?" Brigid asked.

"It isn't a big deal. It's not broken, and I've had worse," Nate snatched a white hand towel from the counter and held it to his face. "I am so sorry, Cam. This is all my fault. I shouldn't have brought you here. We should have found the others. Or gone somewhere public. Or basically anything else."

Nate slunk into the chair in the corner of the room, towel still pressed to his face. He pushed his fingers through his hair with his free hand.

"Where's Ronny?" Drew asked.

"He was just outside the elevators when I caught up to him. He headed down, but I got the feeling he didn't want me to follow him." Nate motioned to his nose. Blood soaked through the towel creating splotches of red in the white.

"You and Brigid stay here with Cam. Keep her out of her room. I'll find Ronny and take him back there."

Drew glanced once more at Cam and Brigid. Brigid continued rubbing Cam's arms, trying to thaw her from a freeze only she could feel. Cam's eyes remained unfocused, staring at a spot on the wall ahead. Her entire face was blank, completely void of all emotion.

He'd help with this later. For now, he needed to find Ronny and keep him from doing anything stupid.

CHAPTER 11

Finding Ronny was easier than he'd expected. Drew stepped out of the elevator on the main floor and nearly walked right into Ronny standing frozen in front of the elevator doors.

Drew clapped him on the shoulder, squeezing slightly. He didn't really have anything to say.

They stared out at the bustling casino before them. A large carpeted area spanned most of the room, portioned into different types of gambling. Tables lined the far side of the space: poker, roulette, craps. Past that was the slot machines. They had slots everywhere from a penny to a few bucks. Cam had played a penny slot earlier. She'd said they had to gamble at least a penny's worth while in Vegas. It was bad luck not to.

Ronny glanced sideways at him. "She send you?"

Drew shook his head slowly. "No. I came for you."

"I don't need a babysitter."

"Then what do you need?"

Pause. "To get rip-roaring drunk."

Drew had only seen Ronny drink once or twice ever

and only one beer and only during the summer. But who was he to tell Ronny what to do?

He opened his wallet and pulled a fake ID from the folds. Ronny's eyebrows rose in question.

"I got it a few months back in case I ever needed to get into a bar or club." He'd hoped it would be to play. The only time he'd used it so far was one night when his mom had been passed out drunk and her boyfriend at the time had ditched her at some bar. Drew had found her unconscious under a table.

"Then let's get the hell out of here."

***

An hour later they were back in Ronny's room. Ronny slumped on his bed, propped up by pillows, and nursed his third beer. Or maybe fourth. Drew had driven him to the closest convenience store but had put his foot down on buying anything stronger than beer. The last thing they needed was Ronny getting alcohol poisoning.

Drew sat on the floor and sipped from an energy drink.

"What am I going to do, man? I'm gonna be a dad." Ronny's words were foggy. He rubbed his eyes and squeezed the bridge of his nose.

Drew didn't respond. He didn't know the first thing about being a dad. He didn't even have one.

"I can't believe this. She's pregnant. I dumped my pregnant, cheating girlfriend." Ronny ran his hand down his face. "This is so screwed up."

Drew nodded.

"I can't take care of a kid. I didn't ask for that kind of

responsibility. I don't want that."

Drew leaned against the mattress at his back. He knew all too well what it meant to grow up as a child that wasn't wanted. He was that kid. No one came to your second-grade parent-teacher conference. No one offered to take you to the movies just to spend time with you. Your dad didn't stick around, and your mom was never an actual parent, just a roommate who kept you alive until you were old enough to return the favor.

Was that going to be Cam and Ronny someday? Drew couldn't believe that. He wouldn't let himself believe two of his best friends could ever be as big of losers as his own parents were.

Ronny's empty bottle slid from his fingers and clattered to the floor. "How do I even know it's mine? Who knows how long she's been screwing Nate."

Drew winced. "You really think they've been hooking up?"

"You saw them in there just now. And they've always been too close. I knew they were keeping something from me, but I thought it was a past relationship. Not a current one." He sat forward and squinted at Drew. "Did you know they used to have sleepovers?"

Cam and Nate were close, closer than Cam and Drew ever were. Nate had also known her for longer than Drew had. That was actually how they all met. Nate and Drew grew up friends, and as Nate got closer the Cam, Drew naturally joined them. Brigid moved in down the street from Cam junior year, and the two were instant best friends. Right about the same time, Cam met Ronny in a chemistry class, and they got together, adding Ronny to the group as well.

When Drew had first met Cam, Nate had told him all about how he used to go over to Cam's when her parents were out of town, which was a lot. The Wests would fly all over the country for peace rallies and freedom marches, and Cam would stay behind for school. So, Nate would go over, and he and Cam would make cookies or watch movies. He'd sleep on her couch so she didn't have to be alone in her house at night.

But that was it.

Nate and Cam had never been together romantically. Or physically. Drew would stake his life on it.

A snore came from across the room. Ronny was out cold, his head bent awkwardly over the pillow.

That was for the best. He could sleep it off. Drew tossed the empty ice bucket on the bed next to Ronny, stole the key card from his wallet, and closed the door behind him.

***

In the next room over, Drew found Cam and Nate each passed out in a queen bed, both wearing clean, dry clothes. Brigid slumped in a neighboring chair, wide awake. Her cheek rested on the back of the seat, but her eyes were locked on Cam.

"She barely said a word all night. Fell asleep about half an hour ago. Nate wasn't long after," Brigid whispered.

Cam shifted under the blanket. She slept soundly, but her face betrayed her emotion. Worry lines creased her brow and her lips tugged down ever so slightly. She'd been in love with Ronny since they'd gotten together. Losing him would

115

wreck her, not to mention the added complication of a pregnancy.

Everything snapped into place as Drew watched Cam sleep. She'd wanted a last-minute road trip because it was her "last chance." She'd looked terrible the last few mornings and had eaten almost nothing this whole trip. Skipping the roller coaster should have been a huge red flag for an adventure-chaser like Cam. He'd been blind to all of it.

So had the others, except maybe Brigid, but Nate and Ronny had both been as shocked as Drew today.

Drew eyed Nate. His nose had stopped bleeding, but it looked swollen. Despite what Nate said earlier, Drew wasn't so sure Ronny hadn't broken it.

Brigid yawned softly from her place across the room.

"You should get some sleep," Drew whispered, careful not to wake the others. Brigid's eyes were dark, and she tilted in the chair like she might slip right out of it if she relaxed her muscles at all.

"I don't think I can sleep yet. Too much to process."

"Then let's go somewhere. We'll let everyone else sleep."

"Where can we go? They're in here, and Ronny's in his room, and my room is . . . I mean, I'm not supposed to. . ." Brigid blushed.

She'd promised not to have boys in her room.

"The roof. Fresh air and plenty of people."

***

The Cosmopolitan was known for its rooftop oasis turned

nightclub. There was an enormous pool, cabanas, private jacuzzies, and a thousand people who were all too loud. But Drew was grateful not to be anywhere too private with Brigid right now. She led him to a small table near the edge of the roof. It was one of those tall tables that was meant to be stood around, so there were no chairs. They ordered sodas and watched the people on the strip below.

"It's still so busy, even late into the night." Brigid's eyes danced across the crowded walkways.

"Are you okay?" Drew asked.

"I am," Brigid answered, "Just worried about Cam. I don't think that went the way she had hoped it would."

"Didn't seem like it." Drew took a sip from his Diet Coke before asking, "How long have you known?"

"About Cam?"

He nodded.

"She told me at the pool last night. She wanted to see if I thought she should tell Ronny or not."

"And you told her she should?"

Brigid spun the hair elastic around her wrist. "I told her she needed to decide for herself but that I thought he had a right to know."

"He does."

"Cam agreed. She just didn't want him to give up his future out of feelings of obligation toward her or the baby."

"That does sound like Ronny." He made the smart choices and always thought things through. If Ronny felt something was his responsibility, then that was what he did regardless of whether it was really the right decision. Drew took another sip.

"You still thinking of moving away after graduation? Finding somewhere to play?" she asked.

Drew nearly choked at the unexpected shift in conversation.

He didn't know how to answer that. He wanted to. He'd wanted to find a band and make music his whole life. Boise was not a great place for a professional musician. There were no bars or clubs to play. Nowhere to get your name out. He would have to leave to chase that dream.

But he still couldn't abandon his mom. She wouldn't make it a month without his paycheck to support her.

He wasn't sure he was ready to leave Brigid either. He'd miss Cam, Ronny, and Nate, but he'd stay for Brigid.

"Maybe. I'd like to, but it's more complicated than that," Drew said.

Brigid nodded. "Seems like everything is." Drew studied her face as she took another sip of her soda. Worry lines still creased her brow, and she bit her lip nervously. But her pale blue eyes sparkled in the light reflecting off the pool.

"How long have you played? When did you start?" she asked.

Drew blew out a breath of air as he thought back to his childhood. "Nearly ten years ago, I think. I mostly just taught myself."

"I've always wanted to play. I mean, I've never taken lessons, but I always thought it would be neat to know how," Brigid said. A timid smile spread across her cheeks, finally smoothing the lines that had been etched into her forehead all night.

"I could teach you." The words were out before Drew could stop them. He didn't want her to think this was another attempt to ask her out. Her chuckle put his worries to rest. "I mean, if you really wanted to learn."

"I would love that. I'd pay you for the lessons."

"Absolutely not."

"Oh, come on." She nudged his arm playfully. "I can't expect you to do that for nothing. It doesn't have to be money. There has to be something you want."

Oh, Brigid. You have no idea.

But there really was something she could help him with.

Drew felt around his pocket for the pen he knew would be there. He clicked the cap on and off. "Tutor me. I have the AP Lit test in three weeks. I'll never be ready in time without help, and you're the best at it."

"I do like books." She spun her straw between her fingers, a habit she must have picked up from Cam. "It's a deal."

They sat in a comfortable silence, watching the people around them. People in Vegas were practically another tourist attraction. A group at the neighboring table were playing some kind of drinking game, and a couple near the pool was making out in a pool chair. The pool itself was nearly empty aside from a bachelor party that was clearly too drunk to be anywhere near water.

"Can I ask you a question?" Drew generally didn't pry, but it was a night of revelations. "Why aren't you in AP Lit?

You obviously could have been."

Brigid took a slow breath before answering. "I was signed up. I even went to the first week of classes."

"I remember."

"But Mike talked me out of it. He said it was better to take the normal English class with him and get an easy A than to chance damaging my GPA in a tougher class. Honestly, I think he knew that he'd get to copy all my homework if we were in the same class."

"That sucks."

She nodded. "It did. But really, I think I would have dropped it anyway. I love reading. It's an escape from the anxieties that like to take over my mind. I wanted to be in a class that was all about losing myself in those other worlds, but I was also scared. What if I didn't have what it takes?" Brigid lowered her chin. Drew wanted so badly to reach out to her.

"Have you ever wanted something so bad it scared you?" Brigid shook her head. "That sounds stupid."

"It doesn't." Drew's chest tightened. "There are a lot of things I want, and I'm terrified."

Drew held her stare, the air tight between them.

"Well, either way, it was probably the wrong decision. I've been jealous of you and Ronny all year." Brigid shrugged, and the tension fell away. "We'll start next week. Where's the best place to meet? My house? School?"

"You can come to my house."

Brigid blinked a few times. "You want me to go to your house?"

"Sure. I already have all the amps and guitars set up.

You'll need a guitar to practice with, but I have one I don't ever use. You can borrow it," Drew offered, "but it might be kind of tough at first. You'll need to build up some calluses on your hands. That's why mine are so rough."

Brigid gently grasped his hand from across the table and ran hers along the inside, feeling the proof of his words. Her finger traced along the outside of his palm and up his thumb. "They aren't as rough as you think," she said. She flipped his hand over to feel the tips of his fingers along her own.

Drew's breath caught in his chest. Her hands were cold from holding her drink, but her fingers burned a path along his skin. He wanted them to keep going—up his arms, around his neck, into his hair.

She had frozen as well. Her hands still held his, the tips of her fingers barely grazing his own. She lifted her head from where she'd been staring at their hands and met his gaze. Even on the crowded roof, silence hung heavy between them.

Drew swallowed hard.

Brigid's phone lit up and buzzed loudly on the table where it had rested since they'd arrived. Drew flinched as the world crashed down around them. He yanked his hand back and shoved both in his pockets as she checked the message.

"Nathan." She waved the phone at him. "Wondered where I went."

They left a few bills on the table and made their way back to the elevators in silence. Drew replayed the last few minutes as they wound through the hotel. Brigid had agreed to meet with him for guitar lessons. She'd initiated physical contact. She must have felt even a fraction of what he had as she'd held his hand. There was no way that had been entirely one-sided.

They arrived at their rooms, and Brigid disappeared behind her door with a quick "goodnight" and a click. Drew inhaled deeply, his heart still racing, before slipping into Ronny's room.

CHAPTER 12

Drew met Brigid and Nate in the hall in the morning while Ronny slept.

"How's Ronny?" Nate asked.

"He's hungover, but he'll be fine after he hydrates." Drew had stayed in Ronny's room the rest of the night. Ronny woke up early in the morning, threw up, and went back to sleep.

"Cam is struggling," Brigid reported, "I think she'll be alright, but it is going to take time. The breakup has really crushed her. And on top of everything else?"

"So… do we go home?" Nate asked. He looked almost as bad as Ronny. Dark circles shadowed his eyes, and his nose was bruised and swollen.

"I think we better." Brigid's fingers flew across her phone. "We can get home by this afternoon if we leave soon. I think it might be worth it."

Drew nodded.

Back in the room, Ronny was still passed out. Drew

gathered the few items he'd left around the room—a hoodie, toothbrush, socks—and shoved them in his bag. Ronny's bag was already meticulously packed. Ronny only removed things as they were needed and returned everything the second he was done with it.

Ronny's girlfriend, or ex-girlfriend now, was his opposite. Cam's stuff was everywhere. How these two had lasted more than a day as a couple would forever be one of life's great mysteries. But they had. Drew could hardly remember life without them together. They had been the one relationship that had made Drew think maybe people could truly find lasting happiness together, until last night. Maybe they could still fix things.

Unlikely. Ronny may have been the dumper, but he'd also been a total asshole. Once the shock wore off, Cam would be pissed, if she wasn't already. They had to get her home before that kicked in or the drive would be unbearable.

Drew glanced around the couple's hotel room again. How had Cam managed to leave clothes on every single surface? Drew wasn't going to touch any of it. Brigid would have to come pack for her.

Drew circled around the bed to the nightstand in the corner and unplugged his phone. As he did, it lit up with a call.

Elliott.

Drew stared at the phone for a minute before answering. He really didn't want to deal with his father this morning. Bracing himself, he swiped the green button. "Yeah?"

"Morning, buddy! You give any thought to my offer?

Show is only a few weeks away," his father crooned. His was the voice of a man who was used to getting his way, smooth and confident. He'd been in the music business since before Drew was born. He had introduced Drew to rock music, given him his first guitar. It was the one thing Elliott had done right for his son.

Drew brushed his thumb across the iPod in his pocket.

"Nothing has changed. I'm still needed at home."

"You're needed here! You're gonna love this band, Drew. It's just what you've been waiting for."

"No, thanks."

"You'll change your mind. Call me when you do."

***

The ride home was long and boring. The car was mostly silent except for a few attempts at conversation from Brigid. Nate, Cam, and Ronny each slept on and off. Brigid stayed awake but had given up shotgun to sit between Cam and Ronny in the backseat.

It had become clear when they'd checked out this morning that putting Cam, Ronny, and Nate in the backseat together would be disastrous. Cam hadn't said a word the whole morning, and every time Nate so much as looked at him or Cam, Ronny's fists clenched at his side. Drew was certain that Nate was headed for another nosebleed if they didn't stay at least an arm's length away from each other.

Drew took the shorter, less scenic route through Nevada to save time and didn't stop other than to fuel up on gas or food. It paid off when they exited into their

125

neighborhood before sunset that evening.

Drew stopped at Cam's house first, and both girls pulled their bags from the trunk. Cam slunk up her porch steps without a word, dragging her bags behind her and disappearing through the front door. Brigid hesitated next to Drew's open window.

"Call me?" She raised a single eyebrow in question.

Drew nodded, and she followed Cam into the house.

Brigid would spend the rest of the break at Cam's. Cam was in no place to be alone, and who knew how long her parents would be in Seattle.

He pulled into Ronny's driveway next, and both Drew and Ronny got out, leaving Nate alone in the car. Drew walked around the hood and met Ronny just as he passed Nate's door.

"You alright?" Drew asked.

Ronny shrugged casually and adjusted his suitcase in his hand. He'd rebounded from his hangover pretty well on once he'd stopped hurling.

"You going to talk to Nate?" Drew tried again.

"Nathan Lankford can go to hell." Ronny's voice was even, but his jaw was clenched.

"You still think he slept with Cam? And that Cam would cheat on you?" Drew crossed his arms.

Silence. Ronny finally mumbled, "I have to go." Drew let him pass, biting his tongue on any further argument. Ronny trudged to his door and slammed it closed behind him.

Drew climbed back into the car but didn't back out of the driveway. He just sat there, staring at the steering wheel.

"He didn't mean that." He knew Nate had heard all of

it.

Nate nodded unconvincingly. They both knew. Ronny did mean it. If Ronny had had issues with Nate and Cam's relationship for a long time, then yesterday had been the breaking point. Ronny had meant every damn word.

Drew went straight home from there. Nate only lived a few houses down and could walk the rest of the way. Nate slunk down Drew's driveway but stopped at the sound of Drew's voice.

"And tomorrow?" Drew asked. He had to check, to make sure.

Nate took a long time to respond. Finally, he nodded without turning around, and then continued home to face his father.

Drew trudged into his own house to find his mom draped across the couch in the living room.

"Look who's home," she'd drawled. Red wine sloshed in her glass.

"I told you I'd be back in a few days," Drew said. He dropped his bag at the edge of the hall. He'd unpack later.

His mom stood from the couch and walked into the kitchen. Drew obeyed the unspoken order to follow her. He leaned against the edge of the kitchen table as his mom grabbed the bottle of wine from the counter and refilled her glass to nearly full. She held out the bottle, offering him a swig. Drew shook his head slowly.

"So, was California all you thought it'd be? You going to take off and make something of yourself?" Disgust bled through her words, but so did fear—fear he'd follow in his father's footsteps.

Drew wondered what she'd say if she knew about the calls from his dad. She'd be angry. And hurt. She hated Elliott for what he'd done, and Drew was a daily reminder of that man. She barely put up with him as it was. Knowing he was in contact with the husband that had abandoned her would push her over the edge.

Flame burned in his chest, and he nearly did it, nearly wielded the words he knew would hurt her the way she constantly hurt him. The one truth he knew would sting.

He swallowed them instead. Their relationship was strained enough with her pushing him away. They'd only get worse if he pushed back. So, he buried the words deep inside with the rest of the truth, hurt, and pain that he'd been burying for years.

Drew shook his head.

"You're back earlier than I expected." It was both a judgement and a question.

"We had some problems in Vegas and decided to cut our trip short." Understatement of the century.

She set her glass on the counter and pointed a long, red fingernail at him. "Did you get in trouble? Because if you need a lawyer, you are on your own—"

"I'm not in trouble. We just came home early," Drew interrupted.

She eyed him suspiciously and took a long drink of her wine before going on. "Well, good. I'd hate to see you make the same choices as that bastard father of yours. Although it wouldn't surprise me. You are just like him with that damn guitar. One of these days you probably will."

Drew clenched his jaw and let the blow land. His mother hated his guitar, but music was the one thing she hadn't been able to take from him yet. The one thing he'd be willing to fight for.

A knock at the door broke through the tension soaking the room. Drew padded to the entryway. He took a deep breath to clear his head and decompress. He thought of his friend a few houses down. Nate's dad may not understand why he left, and he'd be hella pissed, but at least Nate had been missed.

Drew twisted the knob. Behind the door stood a man much taller than him. The visitor wore work pants and a tight t-shirt. He had short hair, buzzed nearly to his scalp. Tattoos covered his arms, similar to Drew's own, but while Drew's were dark from fresh ink that morning, this man's were the faded color of real ink that had been done years before. He looked Drew over once before Drew's mom pushed the door open wider, inserting herself into the line of sight.

"Benny! I'm so glad you are here. It's been such a terrible day." His mom's voice was much higher than normal and dripping with syrupy sweetness that turned Drew's stomach. She stuck out her bottom lip, pouting like a teenager.

"Tell me all about it, baby." Benny pushed his way through the doorway and led Drew's mom to the couch, pulling her down on his lap.

Drew took this as his cue to leave. Keys still in his pocket, he walked out the front door and pulled it closed behind him. He'd go anywhere that meant he wouldn't be here.

***

"Are you going to ask her out again?" Nate chucked a rock into the running water beneath him.

"Yes, because I'm looking for more opportunities to get rejected." Drew shot him a look. "I'm just going to help her learn the basics on the guitar, and then we're going to study for a while."

Nate shrugged and looked out over Second Dam. They'd discovered this place last summer on accident when Cam had borrowed her parent's convertible to take them all on a joy ride up the canyon. She'd missed the turnoff for First Dam, a popular hangout for locals to fish, swim, or picnic, and had ventured further up the mountain in search for a place to flip around. About five minutes up the road, they'd come across another dam, smaller than the first, and tucked back into the mountain a ways. You had to park and walk down a path to get to it, but it was worth the walk.

Unlike First Dam, Second Dam (Cam had named it, of course) was quiet and secluded. Water rushed over the edge of the manmade barricade, slowing but not completely stopping. A bridge crossed over the river and led to a small lookout point on the other side.

Second Dam had become their personal oasis—a place to hide from parents, avoid homework, or waste a summer evening. It was technically a public area, but they'd never once seen anyone else there.

"Study for a while." Nate put air quotes around it.

"Isn't that code for 'make out in your car'?" He leaned against the bridge rail and threw another rock into the running water.

"You're running out of rocks." Drew watched him carefully from the bench in the outcropping. He hadn't been able to get Nate out of his head since they'd gotten home yesterday, so he'd picked him up as soon as Nate was done with work and headed here. Drew filled him in on his deal with Brigid. Knowing his mom would be long gone by seven, he'd invited Brigid over for her first guitar lesson. Nate wasn't buying that their plans that evening were genuinely innocent.

He also had yet to say a word about his dad.

"You want to talk about it?" Drew didn't like to push Nate, but sometimes somebody had to.

Nate sunk to the ground, dangling his legs over the edge of the bridge.

"There's really not much to talk about. It played out exactly how I thought it would. I walked in. He stared at me. I stared back. We both moved on with our lives."

Mitch wasn't a bad guy. He didn't like Drew all that much, but all in all, he tried to take care of his son, which was more than Drew's own father could claim. But providing for your kid wasn't the same as knowing him, and Mitch did not know the first thing about Nate.

"What about Cam? Have you heard from her?" Drew pushed again.

"No, but I bet she stays away for a little while after what happened."

"It wasn't your fault."

Nate shrugged. "If it wasn't for me, they'd still be

together."

"You don't know that."

"I know that Ronny didn't like how close I was to Cam. I know that he thinks we are having sex. And I know that Cam is now single and pregnant." Nate closed his eyes and squeezed the bridge of his nose. "I can't believe she's pregnant."

Drew made a mental note to check on Cam. He hadn't heard from her either. He was sure Brigid was with her, but he still needed to see if there was something he could do.

"Come on." Nate nudged Drew. "We need to get you back for your date."

Drew flipped him off and headed for the car.

CHAPTER 13

The doorbell rang at exactly seven o'clock.

Drew found Brigid standing uncomfortably on the step. She glanced around like she might be in the wrong place, even with him standing right in front of her.

Her hair was pulled up into a ponytail, and she wore a tank top and black leggings that hugged everything.

Girls highly underestimate the power of leggings.

He invited her in, and she edged through the door, like she was exploring a cave and the floor might give way at any moment.

"I've never been in your house before." Her eyes darted around the room to the worn couch. The faded curtains. Drew had cleaned the empty bottles off the counter before she arrived.

"Not many people have."

Drew led Brigid through the house to his room. He'd thought about moving his guitars out into the living room for their lesson, but the house was empty. It didn't really matter where they were. No one was going to walk in on them. He left his door open all the same.

"How's Cam?" Drew unwound the cord and flipped on his amp.

"I'm not really sure. She's been sleeping pretty much nonstop since we got back, but I'm not sure if she's depressed about the breakup or if the pregnancy is making her tired." Brigid sat on the edge of his bed. His blue comforter brought out her eyes. Drew shook off the thought.

She scanned the posters covering his wall. Most were posters he'd gotten from concerts. Old 80s and 90s rock bands his dad had introduced him to before he'd left.

"Have you seen all these bands live?" Brigid asked.

"Some. KISS did a tour a couple years ago, and I've seen Foo Fighters a couple times. Some stopped touring before I was old enough to buy a ticket."

"So where did those posters come from?"

Drew removed his spare guitar from its case and sat next to Brigid on the bed before answering.

"They were my dad's."

"He was into music?"

"It's why he left." Drew hesitated. He didn't talk about his family, especially not his dad. This was uncharted territory. But the wariness that usually wrapped itself around him at the mention of Elliott didn't come. "He left to pursue his music career."

"He's a musician?"

"Manager. He plays too, but he went to Los Angeles to manage." Brigid waited quietly for him to continue.

"I was twelve. I'd come home early from school. I was supposed to be taking a math test, but I'd blown off studying the night before to go to a Foo Fighters concert, so I cut class. No one was supposed to be there."

He'd coasted into the driveway on his bike and found Elliott's Mustang idling in the open garage. Drew still didn't understand it, but he'd known right then that his father was leaving. Not on another trip or to meet with a band. Leaving for good.

Elliott had emerged from the house moments later to find his only son frozen in shock, standing in their garage, backpack forgotten on the ground next to him. Six years later, Drew could still feel the burning of unshed tears. He hadn't let them fall, not for this man. Elliott just stood there, like this was just another day.

"I asked him why," Drew continued, "At the time I thought it mattered. He hadn't even had the decency to look guilty." Elliott's eyes had thinned, and he'd crossed his muscular arms across his chest. That was how Drew always remembered his father, face all angles and sharp lines.

He'd said, 'This isn't what I want—you, your mom. I've got to live my own life,' and that was it. Drew never saw Elliott again.

Brigid rested her head gently on Drew's shoulder. Not flirty but supportive. Drew's shoulders relaxed and tears threatened to fall.

He'd kept this piece of him buried, tucked away where no one could see it and he didn't have to face it.

Elliott had broken more than a promise that day. He'd

shattered a kid who wanted nothing more than to grow up to be his dad. Even now, despite how much he hated him, Drew still idolized Elliott. He would always be the man who taught him to love rock music and play the guitar. It was why he still used a ten-year-old iPod. It was the best Elliott had to offer.

"We should get to work." Drew cleared his throat and blinked away any evidence of moisture before Brigid could see it. He was trying. Truly. But he wasn't ready for complete transparency. He may never be.

Brigid nodded. Drew switched to his desk chair and rolled it toward Brigid so they sat knee to knee. He placed the guitar in her lap and showed her where to place her fingers. Every touch made his hands tingle, but he forced himself to concentrate on the placement on the guitar.

"These are the frets," he motioned to the guitar. "You'll need to learn the finger placements for each chord.

Brigid was a fast learner. After an hour, her fingers were shaking, but she could play most of the major chords.

"You're a natural." Drew packed the guitar gently into its case.

Brigid blushed. "Now it's your turn. Where's your books?"

Drew ruffled through his backpack until he found *The Old Man and the Sea,* still hiding, unread, within the pockets. He flung it on the comforter next to Brigid, and nodded to the novels stacked nearly two feet high on the floor on the other side of the bed.

"Have you read any of them?" she asked, no judgement in her voice.

Drew nodded.

Brigid rolled her eyes. "Which ones?"

"All of them."

Her eyebrows shot up. "You've read all of those?"

"Well, The first half of all of them. I never finish in time for the tests. I liked them though. Except *The Old Man and The Sea.* I barely started that one, but it really sucks so far."

She didn't laugh. Her brows pulled together, deep in thought. She stood and walked to the stack of novels, leafing through the titles. She stopped when she reached *The Count of Monte Cristo.*

"That's the only one I finished." Drew said from behind her. She stood slowly, eyes still locked on the book in her hands.

"I love this book." She finally turned to face him. "I didn't know you read like this."

"Read like what? The first half of old books?"

"A mountain of old books. This isn't light reading, Drew. Even just the first half of this stack is thousands of pages. You don't need my help passing if you read like this."

"Except it's still only half. Knowing half the questions on the AP exam is still failing." Drew slunk back into his chair, pulled out a pen and started tracing lines across his left forearm.

This was why he needed her help. He understood the stories, but he couldn't take on the sheer volume she could. Even if he read every spare minute for the next three weeks, he'd never make it through everything.

Brigid's eyes followed his pen. "Sometimes it's not

about how much you know. It's what you do with it."

Drew glanced up at her.

"Literature isn't about memorizing facts or learning equations," she explained, "It's using fictional worlds and made-up characters to learn about real life." She returned to her spot on the edge of Drew's bed, still holding his copy of *The Count of Monte Cristo*. "There are at least ten shorter books in that pile, but you finished the one that's over 500 pages. Why?"

Drew thought back to last fall when he'd plowed through the novel in a matter of days. He hadn't been able to put it down.

"Edmond had nothing—no family, no girl, no money. I wanted to see how he'd change all that when he had no options."

Brigid's fingers tightened around the faded pages in her hands, and a smile curved at the edge of her lips. "I read it differently. I thought he had every option, and I wanted to know which one he'd choose."

***

Saturday mornings were Drew's favorite. His mom was never home Saturday mornings or if she was, she'd passed out so hard an earthquake wouldn't wake her. He had no reason to clock in for work as no one in their right mind orders delivery before eleven on the weekend. And he didn't have homework due anytime in the next thirty-six hours.

It was time just for him.

Sometimes he spent Saturdays at the dam with his

friends. Last summer, it had become so standard they would show up without even discussing it first. He'd pull up as the sun rose and they'd all just be there—Cam usually in pajamas and half asleep, but she was there.

He didn't expect his friends would be there today. Everyone had been pretty quiet this week. Aside from his visit to the dam with Nate and his guitar lesson with Brigid, he hadn't seen any of them. He texted each of them a few times, but after the disaster that was Las Vegas, it seemed like everyone needed a little space.

Without his friends drawing him away, he was left with his other favorite option. Drew tuned his guitar carefully, tightening the strings until they rang true to pitch. He needed new ones, but these would work for today.

He plugged the cord into his guitar and connected it to the amp in the corner of his bedroom. His pedal board lay before him, powered on.

A knock sounded at the door.

"Come in!" Drew called through the door. Nate had probably needed some air and time away from Mitch.

Drew nearly dropped his guitar when his mom walked through his door.

She looked . . .

Nice.

Her blonde hair was smoothed and held back in a pony tail just above her neck. She wore one of those suit dress combos that was made of a black suit jacket on top and a skirt on the bottom. She stood as tall as Drew in heels. Drew couldn't remember ever seeing his mom in heels, except maybe those slutty ones for Halloween.

Her face had the most significant change. Her eyes were clear and bright. Her makeup was softer somehow, more natural looking than usual.

She was smiling.

"I need a ride. Benny took my car to get the transmission flushed." She held her hands clasped in front of her.

"Where to?" Drew asked. He couldn't look away from the woman in front of him. She looked ten years younger.

She glanced at the watch on her arm, another anomaly, and blinked quickly. "Can I explain on the way? I need to get going."

Drew flipped the power off on his amp, set his guitar gently on his bed, and followed his mom out the door and into his car. She climbed in silently but rubbed at her hands. She hadn't stopped moving since she'd knocked on his door.

"Where am I going?" Drew asked as he turned the key and reversed out of their driveway.

Mom pointed down the street. "Downtown."

Drew weaved through the neighborhood until he reached the freeway. He merged into traffic before he spoke again. "What's downtown?"

He couldn't even try to guess where they were going. His mom didn't generally ask for rides, but when she had it had been to pick her up from somewhere sketchy or take her to pick up something even sketchier. She'd stumped him this morning. She wasn't dressed for those kinds of activities, and nothing sketchy went down at nine in the morning on a

Saturday in Idaho.

"I have a job interview."

Cold shot through Drew's entire body, and he laughed out loud. "You're getting a job?" he sputtered.

"You don't have to act so shocked. I have had jobs in the past. I've just been taking a little time for myself recently. I always planned to go back to work."

"What's the job?" Drew signaled and moved into the fast lane.

"It's an office assistant in a medical billing firm. It's a lot like what I used to do." She smoothed out the wrinkles in her skirt.

"On a Saturday?"

"It was the only day they had any time. They are shorthanded."

"That's great, mom." Drew smiled sideways at his mother, still fidgeting nervously in the seat next to him.

She entered an address into her phone's navigation and set it in the center cupholder so Drew could see the directions.

"I'm ready to make some changes, Drew." She returned his smile. "This is just the beginning."

The phone navigation brought them to a large, glass building with plenty of parking and large signs above each entrance. Drew shifted into park outside the office building with ten minutes to spare. He'd driven a little faster than necessary, but if his mom was going for in for an interview, he was not going to drop her off even a minute late.

"Good luck," Drew called after her as she climbed from the car and closed the door behind her.

He watched her walk toward the building until she disappeared into a glass revolving door.

His fingers tingled, and he had trouble catching his breath. She was ready to make changes. She was trying to get a job. This was good. This was really good.

If this job panned out, Drew might be able to quit his, or at least cut back on hours. He could focus on school and his music. He wouldn't have to support his mom and pay rent. No more threatening letters from their landlord. No more late-night calls for drinking money.

A grin spread across his face until his cheeks hurt.

His reached for his iPod buried deep in his pocket, connected it to the car stereo, and hit play.

His mom emerged from the revolving doors more than half an hour later. Drew tried to remember what he'd learned about job interviews in school.

Nothing. Literally nothing.

He had no idea how long interviews were supposed to go. He'd gotten his job by having a car and no felonies. No interview necessary.

He watched as his mom made her way back to his car. She had a small smile on her face and a bounce to her step.

She climbed in, and Drew shifted into drive. He waited for her to say something, just in case. No one wanted to be asked about a bad job interview, or so he guessed.

"You aren't going to ask me how it went?" His mom scowled.

"How did it go, mom?"

"It went so good!" She clapped her hands together and

bounced in her seat. "The gal I spoke with loved me—I could tell. You know how you can just tell sometimes? She asked me about my experience and my skills, and then we just chatted. Turns out we both have kids that go to the same high school. Do you know a Kaitlyn?"

"Kaitlyn Howser? Yeah, I've met her," Drew answered. Cam always said she was one of the few girls she'd call a real bitch.

"It was her mom! Isn't that funny? Anyway, we talked, and I think the job is definitely mine. She said she won't be making calls for a few weeks because she's got more interviews and then a conference she has to go to. So she said I shouldn't worry if I don't hear from her right away. But I'm not worried."

It was possibly the most he'd heard his mom say in years. Her cheeks were flushed, and her eyes lit up as she watched the cars pass by.

"I'm really glad, mom. This is exciting."

"It is exciting. This is a new beginning. A chance to start over."

His chance.

CHAPTER 14

Even with how things went down in Vegas, Drew was still paying for it. Taking a few days off had seemed like a good idea at the time, but rent was coming due, and he was nowhere near ready to pay it. Aside from his guitar lesson with Brigid, he'd worked every afternoon since they'd returned and for as late as possible each night.

He'd clocked in first thing after he and his mom had gotten home from her interview. She hadn't thanked him for taking her, but she hadn't criticized anything about him or his life the whole drive home, and that was really more than he could have hoped for.

Hours later, Drew was parked in the back corner of a parking lot, waiting for another dinner order to come through. His car smelled like buffalo wings. He'd have to leave his windows open all night to get rid of the smell. His iPod sat in the passenger seat, the cord wrapped around the shifter and plugged into the stereo.

Brigid had loaned him some audiobooks to help him

catch up on his reading, Nate had worked his magic with the iPod, and now *Grapes of Wrath* filled his car. Drew relaxed into his seat and closed his eyes. His phone buzzed, and he waited until the end of the chapter before checking the order.

Brigid: *Can we talk?*

Drew jolted upright, fingers fumbling as he rushed to respond to her text.

Drew: *Where? When?*

He stared at his phone, not daring to blink in case he missed her response.

Brigid: *Tonight? When are you free?*

Drew: *I'm free. Where should I meet you?*

Brigid: *Can you pick me up? Maybe go for a drive?*

Drew: *Be there in 10.*

Drew clocked out of his shift on his phone and turned out of the parking lot. His fingers tingled, and Drew squeezed the wheel to control his nerves.

Brigid wanted to talk. Drew's mind whirled. When people asked to talk it was either really good or really bad.

Brigid had been with Cam all week. Maybe something happened. Was Cam sick? Or hurt? Drew had heard stories of women who got hospitalized when they were pregnant. Maybe it was one of those situations.

Brigid hadn't sounded upset, but what did he know? It was a text. She could have been sobbing on the other end, and he'd never know.

He pushed the gas a little harder and shook his head out. He was being ridiculous. Most likely she just wanted to talk guitar stuff. No doubt, she'd already mastered everything he'd taught her a few days ago.

Drew forced himself to come to a complete stop at each stop sign and red light on the way. Everything was fine.

Ten minutes later, Brigid was in his car. She smelled incredible, like coconut or pineapple—something tropical and insanely delicious.

"Where to?" Drew shifted to drive and forced himself to focus on the road.

"Drinks?" Brigid buckled her seatbelt and leaned deeper into the seat. Drew ached to pepper her with questions but held himself back. If it had been an emergency, she would have said something already. Even so, it was all he could do not to pullover and start demanding answers.

She didn't look upset. More . . . contemplative? No sign of tears. So maybe she wanted to talk about something good.

Drew shoved the thought away. If life had taught him anything, it was that you may not have to assume the worst, but you definitely should never assume the best.

But he'd be damned if he didn't make the most of this time alone with Brigid.

Drew drove to the soda shop down the street. Soda shops were a staple in their town—drive through joints where you could order custom sodas and other fancy, non-alcoholic drinks.

"Dr. Pepper?" Drew asked with a smirk and a single raised brow.

"Diet." Brigid smirked back, playing his game.

Except, Drew suspected they were playing different games. He also had a feeling he would much rather be playing hers. And he definitely needed to win.

He wound through the canyon toward Second Dam. It was the best place to drive when you had no place to go. Brigid hadn't said much since they'd gotten their drinks, but she'd watched him closely. Drew let her. Whatever she was working through, whatever she was calculating, he'd just have to hold on to the hope that it'd come out in his favor.

Drew slowed into the small outcropping that led back to the bridge and overhang. Brigid unbuckled her seatbelt, and they both walked to the center of the bridge. Gravel and twigs crunched under their feet as they approached. Drew rested his forearms against the railing and looked out over the river. The only light was the moon, but his eyes adjusted quickly.

The water moved steadily down the mountain, reminding him of the river in Zion's Park, except that water had posed a threat while this seemed welcoming. Safe.

Trees surrounded the bridge and overhang on every side, hiding them from the view of the road, not that there were many other people nearby after dark.

It was still pretty cold in the canyon, but they had both dressed warm for the ride. His hoodie was enough for him, and Brigid looked almost too warm in her light pink coat. Drew glanced to see how she would be reacting to the chill, but found her again watching him.

"Do you want to tell me why you've been staring at me since I picked you up?" He let enough of a smile into his words that she would know he wasn't upset.

Brigid immediately turned her body to face the river, but they were close enough that her shoulder brushed Drew's.

"I've just been thinking a lot is all," she said.

Her hands clasped onto the wooden railing. He didn't dare look higher. He didn't know what he'd see in her face and wasn't ready to find out.

"About me?" Drew forced the words from his lips.

She nodded slowly.

"And what have you been thinking?" Drew pushed again. His chest tightened, and his breathing sped up. He took another deep breath to slow it back down and dared another glance at Brigid. She bit her lip as she thought out her answer. Drew immediately regretted his choice. He gripped the railing tighter and tried to erase the thought of how those lips would feel against his own.

"Honestly, I'm a little confused," Brigid said. "We've been friends for a long time, and I have seen you with a lot of girls." She swallowed and went on. "But this week . . . you've been different. Not different—more. Like I only saw the surface of you."

Drew let the question show in his face.

"I feel like I'm finally getting to know you. And the way you've been this week, the way you have always been toward your friends, that isn't someone who is disloyal." Her eyes were full of unspoken questions he was aching to answer. It was now or never. He wanted to tell her everything, but Drew could only give so much.

"I'm sorry I ever made you think I was like that. I have dated around a lot, but I've never used girls or taken advantage of them. I just couldn't ever commit to a relationship with anyone who wasn't . . .," Drew stopped. Her eyes held his in a firm lock as the crash of the river circled around them.

Brigid swallowed. "Who wasn't what?" Her voice was barely a whisper.

Drew's muscles tensed and his heart raced, but he pushed past it. She'd never want him if he couldn't do this.

"Brigid, I've wanted to be with you for a long time, but you were with him. So, I let him win. Until you broke up. And now," Drew dared move just a little closer, "I just want to make you happy."

He lifted his hand and pushed a strand of hair behind her ear, brushing her cheek with his thumb. His inked fingers created a stark contrast to her smooth pink skin. She leaned into his hand and blinked slowly.

Drew tried unsuccessfully to steady his breathing as he waited for Brigid to say something. It was all he could do to keep himself still as her eyes darted briefly to his lips. He let his hands move to clasp her hips, bringing her just slightly closer to him. She leaned the rest of the way until they were nearly touching and her hands rested on his biceps.

Brigid's breath hitched as she whispered, "I want to try. This. Us." Drew's entire body shuddered. It was more than he'd let himself hope for. "But can we take things slow?"

He could no longer repress the grin that took over his face. "As slow as you want."

Brigid's smile was paralyzing. Drew stood frozen in place admiring every piece of her.

Brigid rose onto her toes and brushed her lips against his cheek, barely making contact. But it was enough to completely wipe him out. Words were gone. Thoughts were only of her. She pressed herself against his body, burying her face in his neck, and Drew instinctively wrapped his arms around her shoulders and held her tight. He'd hold her all night if she'd let him.

Drew swallowed the lump in his throat. He didn't deserve her, but here she was. Even walking disasters get lucky sometimes.

***

Drew's back pushed against the cool metal of Brigid's locker early Monday morning, his hands in his pockets and iPod blasting through an earbud in one ear. Nate sat on the worn, gray carpet beside him, knees up and a phone in each hand.

Drew closed his eyes, his mind floating back to the night at the bridge. He and Brigid had stayed as long as they could, his arms wrapped around her waist, her back pressed against his chest. They'd stared out over the rushing water for hours, sometimes in silence, sometimes talking about anything at all, before she'd realized how late it was and asked him to take her home. He'd kissed her cheek when he dropped her off, a soft goodbye, barely more than a brush of lips. He hadn't pushed for more.

But damn if he didn't want more.

He was crazy about Brigid, but the last thing he wanted was to scare her away by coming on too strong. He'd meant it when he'd said they could go as slow as she wanted. He'd waited this long just to get to this point. He could wait for whatever she needed, as long as she needed.

Drew had realized the next day, though, that "going

150

slow" was the vaguest phrase ever. Go slow how? Physically? Sure. But should they go out? Were they a couple now or just friends with potential? He'd spent half the night worrying about how to act around her at school this morning.

He'd eventually decided to get to school early and let her take the lead.

Drew opened his eyes and spotted Brigid and Cam walking toward them down the hall. His knees buckled at the sight of her, and he nearly slid to the floor.

In all the best songs, there is a moment of intensity—a moment when the music builds and builds and builds until you think you are going to burst listening to it. Brigid was all those moments in one.

Drew rocked forward and pulled out the earbud as they approached. A knowing smile lit up Brigid's face, and his shoulders relaxed a bit.

She slid her arms around his neck and pulled herself against him. His breath caught, but he instantly reciprocated her hug, wrapping his own arms around her waist. Her breath tickled his ear, and he felt her cheeks heat before he stepped back. He was sure everyone within fifty feet could hear his heart racing.

"Morning." He offered half a smile.

"Morning." Brigid bit the corner of her lip, and Drew shoved his hands firmly into his pockets to keep from pushing her against the lockers and discovering just how soft those lips would feel against his.

Cam snorted from behind them.

"You're cheery this morning," Drew shot at her. Brigid

stepped away, and Drew crossed his arms, hiding the goosebumps that he told himself were from the cold.

"I'm just enjoying whatever is happening here." She moved a pointed finger between him and Brigid, eyes darting along.

Nate coughed from the ground, and Drew kicked his foot out from under him, which only resulted in Nate laughing at him. Drew would get an earful from Nate when he heard that Drew had spent hours alone holding Brigid and *hadn't* kissed her. Nate was not a slow-and-steady-wins-the-race kind of dater.

"See you at lunch?" Brigid asked, like they didn't eat together every day. Yes, things were definitely different now.

Drew's gaze didn't leave Brigid until Cam grabbed her hand and dragged her toward class and out of sight.

"What the hell was that?" Nate stood beside Drew, apparently unconcerned about being late to first period. He disconnected the cords from his phones, wrapped them into tights coils and shoved everything into his backpack.

"Something happened with me and Brigid Saturday." Drew spun the black dial on his locker until he heard a click and a pop and it swung open.

"I'm going to need more details than that."

"Too bad."

"You know I could beat it out of you. Just spill."

Drew rolled his eyes, a sure sign he'd been spending too much time with Cam. "There's nothing to tell. Brigid wanted to talk. So, we talked."

"Talked?" Nate grinned stupidly.

"Talked." Drew slung his backpack over his shoulder. The halls were beginning to clear out and only a handful of students remained. He lowered his voice. "She wants to take things slow."

Nate shrugged. "Slow is better than nothing."

"Agreed." Drew shoved the image of Brigid's hair blowing in the cool mountain breeze out of his mind. Nate would see right through him.

A shadow approached from behind, and Mike Allen slammed his shoulder into the locker next to Drew's.

Even if he hadn't dated Brigid, the cocky, narcissistic ass-hat that was Mike Allen still would have easily been one of Drew's least favorite people on earth. His too-tight jeans, perfectly destroyed t-shirt, and bleach-blonde pompadour haircut screamed "look-how-hard-I'm-not-trying."

Drew had no issue with people who had money—Cam's parents could run circles around Mike—but the flaunting got old, and Mike had no issue looking down on those without it.

"Things are looking pretty cozy between you and Brigid." Mike's eyebrows were raised, but there was no question in his voice. Avoiding Mike's extremely punchable face was generally the best plan of action, but it was too late for that. Instead, Drew clenched his jaw hard and closed his locker with significantly more force than necessary.

Mike was undeterred. "She's not your type, Cox," he clicked his tongue, "and she deserves better." He eyed Drew up and down before turning on his heel and strutting away.

"Forget about him. That asshole can go to hell," Nate

nudged Drew in the back.

Mike could go to hell. Drew would happily escort him there. But his words stung all the same. Mike was right. Brigid deserved much better than Drew.

Drew buried the thought with the rest of his unwelcome truths and headed to government.

CHAPTER 15

Not many seniors ate in the cafeteria—most went out to lunch—but there was one particular senior that was noticeably absent as Drew's eyes swept over the large expanse of circular, blue and white tables.

Florescent lights flashed along the high ceilings, their buzz drowned out by the noise of students yelling over each other. "School lunch smell" filled the air, a blend of prepackaged meals and preservatives. Drew tipped onto the back legs of his chair to get a better look around.

There was no sign of Ronny. Even in third period physics, the one class they all had together, his desk had sat empty.

Worry brewed in Drew's mind. Ronny didn't cut classes, so he was either so upset with Cam he was willing to miss, or his parents had killed him for knocking her up. Drew didn't care for either option.

As he glanced around the cafeteria, he noticed a few girls at the next table staring at them. The three girls were all in his government class, and he wanted nothing to do with them. Drew returned to the conversation Cam and Brigid were having about their homework for that night.

"Of course we can do it together. Preston's physics projects are easily a two-person job." Brigid ripped a piece off her sandwich and popped it in her mouth.

"How about three?" Drew asked. His throat tightened.

Brigid's eyebrows raised slightly. "You want to come?" Drew generally did not join the others for homework sessions.

Drew nodded once.

Brigid bit her lip faintly before responding. "Okay. Three." Drew nodded again but his eyes never left Brigid's face.

Cam looked away, and Drew felt like a dick. She was clearly happy for them, but it had to be painful to watch a new relationship right after hers had just ended.

"You coming too, Nate?" she asked.

"Nah. I think I'll stay in tonight." Nate held a potato chip between his fingers, the same chip he'd been holding the last fifteen minutes. As far as Drew could tell, he hadn't eaten anything.

"We'll be at Cam's if you change your mind." Brigid sipped her Diet Coke and Drew buried another smile. She hadn't forgotten about their deal.

"Where's tall, dark, and handsome today?" A nasally voice sounded behind them. The girls from his government class stood with their arms folded and their noses stuck in the air, Kaitlyn Howser at the helm.

Kaitlyn might have been really pretty if looks were all

that mattered. Her narrow face accentuated her full lips, and her bouncy, red ponytail trailed all the way down her back. Her narrow eyes were a similar color to Brigid's glittering ice blue but held none of her warmth or insight. Kaitlyn wore a pink V-neck and a skirt Drew would bet was much higher than two inches above the knee.

Cam turned to face the wolves head on.

"None of your damn business." Cam's voice was solid, but Drew noticed the shake to her fingers.

Kaitlyn put a manicured hand on her chest. "We were just worried about you, Cam. If Ronny finally realized what you are and dumped you, then it will only make this situation more difficult."

"What the hell are you talking about?" Drew cut in.

Kaitlyn sneered, face full of spite and condescension. Her predatory gaze roamed over Drew before she moved on. "Just that breakups are tough enough, even when a girl isn't in Cam's condition." Her sneered moved to a full grin. "Right, mommy?"

Cam's face fell, all color draining with it.

Nate shot out of his seat. "Get out of here, Kaitlyn," he growled.

She shrugged and walked away, her pack following close behind.

Cam didn't move.

Kaitlyn knew. She knew Cam was pregnant, which meant the entire school would know within a matter of minutes if they didn't already. Drew played through their options in his head.

None ended well for Cam.

"We need to get her out of here," Brigid said. Nate wrapped his arm around Cam and led her out of the cafeteria. She gulped for air and stumbled across the parking lot beside Nate. Drew and Brigid followed close behind. Nate rushed them to Drew's car, and the girls fell into the backseat. Drew pealed out of the parking lot.

"Did you tell someone?" Brigid demanded from Drew.

Drew found Brigid's eyes in the rearview mirror. "Not a word."

"I haven't talked to anyone outside this car since we got back." Nate was turned sideways in the passenger seat watching Cam, brows pulled together.

There was only one other person who knew.

"Why would he do this?" A tear streaked down Cam's cheek. It was an entirely new sensation for Drew. Cam was a rock. She always had the upper hand. Seeing her defeated, abandoned and betrayed in her time of need, snapped something inside him. Heat seared through his veins, and blood pounded in his ears.

Ronny was angry, furious even, with Cam—and Nate. But this was low. Cam was still coming to terms with everything, and Ronny was spreading the news across their school, starting with Kaitlyn Howser.

None of this made any sense. Even if he had been angry enough to screw Cam over like this, he was screwing himself too. Knocking up your ex-girlfriend wasn't exactly the kind of achievement Ronny-the-Golden-Boy was looking to add to his perfect record.

Unless Ronny genuinely believed he wasn't the father.

Drew swung into Cam's driveway, and the others climbed out of his car.

"You're not coming in?" Nate asked through the passenger window. Brigid was already halfway up the steps with Cam.

Drew shook his head. "I've got someone I need to see."

***

Drew was sitting against his hood outside Ronny's house when Ronny arrived. He was driving his mom's minivan. Drew usually drove him to school in the morning, but he didn't this morning due to the situation with Nate. It had seemed like a bad idea.

Ronny parked and walked to Drew's car. He leaned next to Drew on the hood, still warm from the drive over.

"What's up?"

Drew shrugged. "You tell me. No school today?" His voice was clipped.

"I was there. I just didn't make it to physics. I had a meeting with my counselor."

"Excellent timing."

"I'll be there next time."

They sat in silence for a moment. Drew fumbled aggressively with the pen in his pocket, waiting.

"You really aren't going to say anything?" The words burst from his lips.

Ronny lifted one eyebrow. "About what?"

"About announcing that Cam is pregnant to the whole

damn school."

"What?" His voice was louder, but a crack undercut any authority he may have had.

"Don't act all shocked about it. Kaitlyn knew Cam was pregnant."

"I didn't say a word to her. Why would I?"

"Well, someone did, and you are the only one that could have shared that information. No one else knows."

Ronny stood and paced a few feet from Drew, chest heaving but silent. His scrunched face contorted his freckles. He was playing confused, but Drew saw it for the lie it was.

Ronny had abandoned and destroyed Cam.

Drew stood from where he leaned against his car. His pulse raced. Ronny had him by a few inches, but at that moment, he seemed small.

"I get that you are pissed, but dumping Cam at her lowest was plenty to get back at her even if she had been cheating on you—which she wasn't. Pulling this kind of shit is low. It wasn't enough to leave her to raise this kid on her own? You had to make her as miserable as possible along the way?"

Drew crossed his arms and lowered his voice. "You've hurt her in every way possible. So, unless *she* wants you around, stay the hell away from her."

Drew climbed into his car and slammed on the gas leaving Ronny standing in the middle of the road, completely alone.

***

Fresh ink gleamed on his arms as Drew tuned his guitar. He'd spent the last hour pouring his anger into his pen, but even that hadn't been enough. He needed the music.

Blood pounded in his ears as he pulled his faded iPod from his pocket and hit "shuffle". It didn't matter what came on. He could play all of it.

He'd let his temper get the better of him. He shouldn't have gone after Ronny. It wasn't his battle to fight. He'd just gotten so used to taking care of other people, he sometimes forgot to let them take care of themselves.

He needed to apologize to Cam tonight.

Panama burst through the speakers, and Drew spun the volume knob on his amp. He needed the sound, the pulse of the music, loud enough to drown out any thoughts in his head and burn through the lingering anger in his veins.

Cam was going to have a baby, and Ronny wasn't going to be there for any of it. He hadn't even talked to Cam since that hotel room in Vegas, and if today was any indication, he didn't give a shit about her at all.

Or about the kid.

He wouldn't be there for the kid's birthdays, first day of school, or graduation. He'd choose to miss all of it. He was being a selfish asshole.

His dim bedroom did nothing to calm Drew's mind as his fingers raced through the motions on his guitar, matching the recording perfectly. He barely had to think to keep up with the riffs.

Cam would resent the kid eventually. Maybe not at first, but someday. She'd realize that the kid was what ruined everything. Life was fine until she got pregnant, then she lost everything she cared about.

That kid would grow up knowing he wasn't wanted. None of it would be his choice, but it would be his problem—his meaningless, insignificant life to live.

Drew sunk onto his bed, guitar forgotten beside him. He wiped the moisture from his eyes and cleared his throat.

There was nothing he could do about it. It was entirely up to Cam and Ronny.

The notification light gleamed on his phone. Two messages. Drew swiped open the first.

Mom: *Staying at Benny's tonight.*

No surprise there. She'd practically been living there for days.

He opened the second message.

Brigid: *You still coming to work on the physics project tonight?*

Physics was the last thing Drew wanted to do right now, but he would deal with it to see Brigid. And he really did need to apologize to Cam.

His fingers dragged over the screen.

Drew: *On my way.*

CHAPTER 16

Cam had recovered from the fiasco at lunch, and immediately forgave Drew when he'd confessed his blow up at Ronny. Apparently, she was too tired to yell at him herself, so Drew had saved her the trouble.

Cam's house was enormous compared to Drew's, compared to anyone's, really. Everything was clean and organized, like a home you'd see in a commercial. In the kitchen, pots and pans hung above the island stove in a casual, definitely on-purpose arrangement, and two white canisters labeled "Flour" and "Sugar" were the only belongings on any of the marble counters other than a candle warmer contraption that made the whole house smell like citrus.

The fridge was the only part of the kitchen with any personal touches. On the left, photographs of Cam's parents in different countries scattered the freezer door. Cam was in a few of them, but not many. However, the fridge side on the right was covered in pictures of Cam. Gold medal at a track meet. Swimming at a beach. Junior prom. She and Ronny had doubled with Brigid and Mike. Nate and Drew had stayed home watching stupid movies and eating their weight in microwave taquitos.

Drew, Brigid, and Cam had passed nearly three hours hunkered over physics textbooks around Cam's unnecessarily oversized kitchen table creating charts, graphs, and diagrams of different speeds, velocities, and about a thousand other vocabulary words that all meant basically the same thing. Drew's back ached from the metal chairs that were clearly more decorative than functional. He shifted in his seat, and Cam rolled her eyes at him.

"We're almost done."

"We should have done this on the couch." Drew motioned to the oversized grey sectional with electric reclining seats, built in cup holders, and phone chargers in the armrests sitting ten feet away.

"I would have fallen asleep on that." Cam's words were light, but an almost imperceptible headshake from Brigid told him to drop it.

He'd noticed Cam's dark, puffy eyes when he'd first arrived but had assumed it was due to the Ronny/Kaitlyn situation. Maybe it was more than that. He'd never known someone who was pregnant before. He needed to do some research on what Cam's life would be like the next nine months.

"If you want to head to bed, Drew and I can finish up this last part." Brigid nudged Cam's elbow.

Cam shook her head but couldn't hold back her poorly-timed yawn. Brigid stood and pulled Cam to her feet.

"Come on. Drew and I can manage a little coloring. You sleep."

"Thanks." Cam wrapped an arm around Brigid's shoulder, and the two headed down the hall toward Cam's bedroom. "Night, Drew! Behave yourself."

"Goodnight, Cam," Drew called after her. He pulled his phone from his pocket. Nate had been silent all evening. Drew had hoped he might change his mind and show up. Cam had even called to invite him again right after Drew arrived, but Nate hadn't answered.

Drew: You up?

Nate: yup

Drew: Why didn't you come tonight?

Nate: tired

Drew: Bullshit. Why didn't you come?

Nate went silent on the other end. Drew tucked away the nagging feeling in his gut as Brigid reappeared from Cam's hall.

"You get her all tucked in?" Drew wished Nate would have joined them, but he wouldn't waste this time with Brigid. They hadn't been alone since the night at the dam. Now it was time to make good on his promise to go slow.

"We just got talking for a sec. She warned me about your irresistible charm."

"Irresistible, huh?" Drew shot her a crooked grin as she slid back into her seat around the corner from his own. He didn't imagine her scooting it just a touch closer to him.

"According to Cam." Brigid winked at him, and Drew's stomach did a full backflip.

Go slow, he reminded himself. *Do not throw her onto this enormous table and make out with her until you both see stars.*

Drew cleared his throat and burned his eyes into the charts and graphs sprawled across the table.

"She's okay? After everything today?"

Brigid shrugged. "Mostly just tired. I think making a baby must be exhausting." Her eyes grew wide. "Not what I meant!"

Drew held back the words he knew would only embarrass her and removed the green and blue colored pencils from their box. He passed Brigid the blue one, and they both went to work.

"I don't get why these have to be colored." Drew shifted the paper and held it with his forearm as he colored the nearest graph.

"Even more insane is that it's ten percent of the grade." Brigid sharpened her pencil and went to work on her own paper.

They colored in comfortable silence for a while, switching papers and sharing pencils as they worked.

More than once, Drew found himself watching Brigid work. If he didn't feel bad making her do it all alone, he could have sat back and watched her all night—the way her brow furrowed when she focused really hard or that gleam in her eyes after each completed chart.

Slow. Go slow. But moving slow was still moving, right? Drew thought through his options. He couldn't hold her hand without interfering with their work. She'd moved her chair close enough to his she was easily within reach. Okay, so something small. Almost imperceptible.

Drew let his right knee fall toward Brigid, enough to rest against her left knee, but without pressure. Let her decide how to interpret and move forward.

A quick intake of breath was her only reaction. They continued in silence. She hadn't objected or pulled away. A win.

Drew switched papers again, and as he did, he felt a hint of pressure against his knee. His eyes slid slowly to the right to find Brigid watching him, purple pencil frozen in her fingers. Her brow was furrowed, questions and hope written all over her beautiful face. She swallowed.

She was trying. She was offering him a piece of herself, the most she could give at this point.

Drew's heart stopped beating completely, he was sure of it. That small bit of contact—an inch of knee, separated by denim, under their friend's kitchen table—had done more to his heart than anything any other girl had ever done. His fingers tingled, and his mouth went dry.

Drew returned the pressure, barely enough to register, but enough to answer her questions. Yes, it was welcome. And no, he wouldn't push her for more.

Brigid's brow smoothed, and a soft smile broke through the worry there.

"You know, if I had known it was just going to be the two of us tonight, I would have made some plans." Drew returned to his graph, but Brigid continued watching him.

"Plans?" Her voice was soft, nearly a whisper.

"I just hope you don't consider this our first date. I'd like to make a bit more of an impression than an evening of physics homework."

"Anything specific in mind?" She returned to the graph closest to her.

Drew shrugged like it hadn't been all he'd thought about for over a year. "I don't know. I thought we'd get something to eat. Maybe some Bluejay's custard."

"That's my favorite." Brigid was playing his game. Keep it light, non-committal. No pushing. Just a conversation between friends.

"And then I thought I'd take you to the Book Garden." Brigid's favorite bookstore, The Book Garden, was a small, used bookstore tucked away on the south end of town. A remodeled, Victorian-style home, the walls were covered in disorganized novels whose chaos was only rivaled by the piles of books scattered haphazardly through the rooms. A nightmare to many, but a treasure to the girl he adored. Brigid rarely went because it was far enough away that her parents didn't like to go, and she didn't have her own car to drive herself. But he'd seen the way her face lit up anytime she talked about it.

Brigid looked up again. "You'd take me to The Book Garden? On a date?"

Drew nodded.

"Why?"

"Because you love it there."

A grin lit her face. "You want to—"

In an instant, Brigid's face fell. She shook her head

fiercely once and clamped her eyes shut.

"Brij, is everything okay?" As quickly as Drew could process what was happening, Brigid escalated to full panic mode. Her hands shook, and her breathing accelerated. She was nearly hyperventilating in a matter of seconds. "Are you having an attack?"

Brigid nodded and slammed her hands flat against the table like it could ground her.

Drew had seen Brigid escalate before, but never this quickly and never without someone there—usually Cam— who knew how to help her. But Cam was fast asleep. He wouldn't leave Brigid alone, not even for the time it would take to get to her.

But if he didn't do something fast, she'd only get worse. He wasn't sure what a full attack looked like, but he wasn't going to let her get to that, not if he could stop it.

He'd never experienced this kind of anxiety, the kind that came from nowhere and nothing to completely paralyze you. He'd helped Nate work through some depression lows, but that was different. He never had to calm Nate from a faceless enemy, only lift.

Drew's heart raced, but he shoved away his own fear. He would not let this girl suffer because he couldn't keep his shit together.

Drew put his left hand over Brigid's, lying flat on the table. Her eyes were still closed tight, and he could hear her trying to count between breaths, each coming way too fast. She was trying to slow her breathing. He could help with that.

But he only knew one way.

He ripped the pen from his pocket, bit the cap off, and spit it to the ground.

"It's going to be okay, pretty girl. I'm here."

As gently as he could, he touched his pen to her wrist, just above where his other hand rested on hers. She continued counting as he dragged the pen across her arm, a river of ink in its wake. Her voice was barely more than ragged breaths, and she skipped numbers as she ran out of air. He arced the pen around her elbow and brought it back down, overlapping the line with itself. The tension in her arm shifted, but Drew adjusted immediately.

"I've never told anyone this, but I started drawing when I was just a kid. When I was only six or seven, I think. I had trouble focusing in school, and my hands would get fidgety whenever I tried. I'd play with stuff during class and get in trouble." Drew swirled the ink into a small flower near Brigid's wrist.

"My teacher, Mrs. Laker, realized what was going on and made me a deal that I could draw whenever I needed something to do with my hands. So I'd take a sketchbook and a pen with me to school every day. Then when things got . . . tense with my parents, I started doing it at home too."

Brigid continued to count her breaths, but Drew could sense them beginning to slow. Her arm relaxed enough that he could remove her palm from the table and cradle it in his own.

"As I got older, it got difficult to carry a sketchbook with me everywhere, so I switched to my arms. Now I just keep a pen on me. It gives me somewhere to focus when I need it and something to keep my hands busy."

"I thought . . . you were . . . hiding tattoos." Brigid's words were broken and barely audible, but her breathing continued to slow.

"Well, not there."

Brigid's face softened and a hint of a smile formed. They were almost out of this.

"I hear the rumors about the ink. None of them are true." Drew continued tracing lines across the fair skin on the inside of Brigid's arm with one hand as he dusted his other thumb softly across her wrist. Her pulse continued to race, but her breathing had slowed almost to normal. "The drawing has nothing to do with looking like a rebel or getting girls."

Brigid slowly opened her eyes and dragged them to meet Drew's. Her gaze traced his face as intimately as he'd just traced her arm before looking down at her hand, still resting in his palm, and finally her own arm, now inked to match his. The design had similar elements to his own, but with more feminine flourishes and finishes. He'd weaved flowers and sunshine through the twirls and twists.

When Brigid raised her face again to meet his, her bright eyes were gleaming, and a single tear trailed down her cheek. Drew brushed it away with his thumb and cradled her face in his hand. At some point during the attack, Drew had moved his chair beside Brigid's, leaving almost no space between them.

"What can I do, pretty girl?" Drew's own fears were finally breaking through his wall now that she was returning to him. How could anyone stand watching her go through that? But he knew instantly, he'd do it every day if he had to. If it meant she never had to go through that alone.

And she had. He was sure of it. The way she knew immediately to count breaths and ground herself told him she'd fought this battle alone more than once.

Brigid was braver than anyone he'd ever met.

"Just be here," she whispered, and another tear escaped.

Brigid sank into Drew's side and laid her head against his chest. Drew wrapped an arm around her shoulder, supporting her as best he could. He thought about carrying her to the couch, but she seemed content in these uncomfortable metal chairs, and that was good enough for him right now.

She breathed a shuttered breath, deep and slow.

"Do you want to talk about it?" This was all new territory for Drew, and even though they seemed to be through the worst of it, Brigid might still need to work through something. Drew would be here for whatever she needed.

Another slow, deep breath, like each was a deliberate struggle, before she answered.

"There's really not much to talk about. I get panic attacks sometimes. They are like my anxiety attacks, but they come on fast and hard instead of a slow build like the anxiety ones."

"No warning?"

"No warning."

"So..." Drew cleared his throat, "I didn't do something?"

Brigid squeezed his hand, still holding hers. With their

fingers weaved, it was hard to tell where her ink stopped and his began.

"No, Drew. You didn't cause it. Sometimes they just happen."

Relief flooded Drew's body. It was bad enough she had to go through these. If he'd been the cause, he'd never forgive himself.

"How long do they last?"

"If we can't stop them? Depends. Some are only a few minutes. I've had some last up to half an hour."

Half an hour of complete hell. Drew squeezed Brigid close.

"Do you need anything?"

She didn't respond for a moment and then sat up and faced Drew. Her eyes were tired but clear, and most of the color had returned to her cheeks.

"I need you to not treat me differently. Everyone tiptoes around me once they've seen an attack, like I'm breakable. Even Cam is more careful about what she says or does. She watches how I react to things. She's trying to protect me, but I don't need shelter from the storm. I need someone to sit with me under the umbrella."

"I won't treat you differently. I promise."

Brigid smiled at him, a true smile, and his heart squeezed so tight he thought it'd burst. There wasn't a thing in the world she could ask of him that he wouldn't do for her.

Brigid inspected her arm again. She was nearly back to her normal self, despite being in full panic only minutes before.

"Is this you claiming your property?" She quirked an

eyebrow at him.

"Never," he pretended to inspect his work, "but you have to admit it looks pretty great on you."

Brigid leaned closer and lowered her voice to a whisper. "I think I could get used to it." She trailed a finger down Drew's arm.

Drew's blood heated, and his arms ached under Brigid's touch. His earlier thought about the many uses of this table resurfaced, and he pushed it out again. He slid his free hand to her waist, wrapping her firmly in his arm. She was almost completely on his lap, her sweet scent wrapping around him. He stroked his thumb slowly over her hand, still entwined with his own.

"Brij, we don't have to—"

"I know." She traced her finger back up his arm and a shiver tore through his body. Her gaze flashed to his mouth, and a low growl escaped Drew's throat as she bit her lip. His pulse raced as the little space between their bodies closed. He wasn't sure who was leaning in anymore. Brigid's face tilted up to his. "I—"

Brigid's phone erupted from its place on the table, and Brigid jumped enough Drew was grateful he had an arm around her to keep her from falling off his lap. She snatched her phone and swiped open the call.

"Hello? Yeah, I'm still at Cam's." She slid into her own chair again and ran a hand through her hair.

Drew was going to need a cold shower later. He took a steadying breath but his heart raced on. Cam's house had somehow become a sauna.

"I'll be home soon. A ride?" Brigid looked to Drew for confirmation. He nodded, unable to form words yet. "No, I can get a ride home. K. Bye." Brigid clicked off the call and shoved her phone into her back pocket. "I need to get home. It's a school night."

She bit her bottom lip again, and Drew swore Brigid's phone was going to end up at the bottom of Second Dam one of these days if it kept him from those lips again.

They gathered the mostly finished physics project, and Brigid slid it carefully into her backpack.

They were quiet on the drive to Brigid's. Her house was just down the street from Cam's, but her parents didn't like her walking home in the dark, something Drew wholeheartedly supported. He pulled into her driveway and shifted to park.

"Thanks again for tonight." Brigid unbuckled the seatbelt she'd worn for half a block.

"I'm just glad you weren't alone." Drew kept both hands tight on the wheel. He was not going to make any moves in a car in her parents' driveway. Somehow that was way worse than at their sleeping friend's kitchen table.

"And thank you for telling me all that stuff about your drawing. I know that's not the easiest thing for you—opening up like that."

Words caught in Drew's throat, but he forced them. "But I want to. To you."

Brigid opened her door. "Goodnight, Drew."

Drew watched Brigid slip into her house before pulling out his phone to check the time. Almost ten. There was still time.

Drew clocked in.

CHAPTER 17

"You've got two weeks until the AP exam. I expect that each of you is studying rigorously in preparation. Don't blow it off. You'll regret it come test time."

Mr. Hibbert was in fine form today. A collection of low scores on the day's practice exam had resulted in one of his more exuberant lectures. His glasses bounced on the bridge of his nose as he passionately pleaded with each of them to take the test more seriously.

No mention of how their scores might reflect his teaching.

The bell interrupted the closing of his big speech and the room exploded in a mass of scooting chairs, closing laptops, and swinging backpacks. Drew stood but hesitated, letting Ronny get well on his way before following him out the door.

"Drew." Mr. Hibbert leaned against his desk, arms folded across his body. "A word."

Drew approached the man. He smelled of strong

coffee and disappointment.

"I'm concerned about your score on the practice exam today."

How did Hibbert expect him to respond to that? Apologize? Me too? Drew was well aware that his score was less than acceptable. He opted for silence.

"Do you need a study partner? You and Ronny are friends, right?"

"I just started studying with Brigid Foster. She'll help me catch up."

"Brigid Foster? In my honors English?"

Drew nodded.

"Well, okay. But if you need more help, don't hesitate to ask."

Before he could get roped into after school tutoring sessions, Drew bolted from the classroom. Brigid was waiting for him outside the door.

"Everything okay?" She twisted the elastic on her wrist.

"Of course. Another lesson this weekend? " Drew asked, all smiles for her.

"How about my house this time? Saturday night? My parents are getting pizza, and I thought we could eat before our lesson."

Drew stumbled slightly, but recovered without Brigid noticing. She wanted him to eat dinner with her family. His mouth went dry. He'd never had a girl want him to meet her parents before. He was the guy girls hid from their parents. Drew had snuck out of more than one bedroom window to avoid just that.

He shouldn't have been so surprised. His relationship with Brigid wasn't like the ones he'd had in the past. It was a normal thing for a girl to want her parents to get to know the guy she was dating.

Even though they had never technically been on a date.

He shouldn't really be nervous either. He'd met the Fosters before, many times. But even he knew this was not the same thing.

Brigid had stopped walking and was staring at him strangely. He hadn't answered her.

"Sounds great." He plastered a smile on his face. A genuine one crossed hers.

"No pressure."

Yeah, right.

They met up with Cam as quickly as possible, flanking her in the hallway. High school had taken on a whole new level of painful in the last twenty-four hours. Drew had been right that word would spread quickly. By the time they'd arrived that morning, it seemed like every person in the school knew about the pregnancy. Cam was going strong despite having to rush from class to class to avoid the taunts and jabs that followed her through the halls.

Students who were feeling kind kept to stares and whispers. Assholes like Kaitlyn were more vocal as calls of "whore" and "tramp" followed them everywhere they went. Teachers remained silent, but their pitying looks were nearly as bad as anything they might have said. Drew and Brigid did what they could to shield Cam from the judgmental world that was high school.

"Have either of you talked to Nate today?" Drew scowled at a cluster of students gawking in their direction. Nate had sent him a super vague text this morning, something about not "making it to school" today. Drew had noticed Nate skipping a class here and there before spring break, but he didn't usually peace out for entire days.

Cam shook her head. "He's barely said a word to me since Vegas."

"Not really. A few texts," Brigid said.

They turned the last corner before the hall opened into the large common area that connected to the main doors of the school. They merged into the crowd winding around the school's eagle mascot statue in the center of the space. The gift from the first Skyline graduating class had always seemed unnecessarily large, but it somehow looked smaller now. Unrideable.

"I'm going to pass on lunch today." Drew hung back as the girls rushed to Cam's car through the chilled air. Drew was unclear on the details of how the new car had come to be. Cam told her parents about the pregnancy, and two days later she had a car.

Cam and Brigid waved a goodbye and took off. Drew headed the other direction in his own car.

Five minutes later, he knocked on the Lankford's front door. When no one answered, he felt for the spare key he knew they kept tucked behind an old dog statue on their porch. He let himself in and replaced the key.

The house was dark, no lights or sound from any room. Drew snuck down the stairs and into Nate's bedroom, where there was no sight of Nate, but a very quiet snore coming from the bed.

"Get up. It's noon." Drew kicked the bedframe, and Nate emerged from the mound of pillows and blankets he'd been buried beneath. His eyes were foggy, and the corners of his mouth pulled down when he realized who'd woken him.

"I'm tired."

"You've been tired for a week."

Nate rubbed his face with both hands. "Must be the time change. I haven't adjusted back from Nevada time."

"That whole hour difference?"

"It's known to be a real killer." Nate smirked and disappeared into the bathroom. He returned looking more awake. He'd combed his hair at least.

"Why are you here, Drew? I'm not going to class."

"Fine. Let's go to the gym." Nate loved the gym. He tried to go every day but usually missed one or two a week. Drew guessed he'd only gone once or twice since they'd gotten home. He picked up a pair of basketball shorts off the ground and threw them at Nate.

"Fine, but you're coming with me. You're in terrible shape."

Nate's gym was tucked in a strip mall between a nail salon and a frozen yogurt shop. It was the kind of place only serious exercise nuts worked out, people who could practically bench Drew and all referred to the owner by name.

Drew did not belong here.

181

But he'd stay as long as he needed if it meant getting Nate out of bed and away from his house.

Black mats blanketed the floor. The walls were covered in floor to ceiling mirrors that reflected the florescent lights. Along the wall to the right were racks of weights—dumbbells and kettle bells ranging from two pounds to fifty pounds. In the back were two doors, one marked "Women" and the other "Men," each leading to lockers and showers. On the left and down the center were rows of machines. Drew didn't know what most of them did, but he figured Nate would.

He followed Nate to an open area near the back, and they began their warmup.

Drew followed Nate through his sets, keeping up as best he could. He was in better shape than Nate gave him credit for, but he didn't have Nate's strength. Nate was a gym rat and had the muscle to prove it. Drew's build was leaner.

Sweat dripped down his face and his heart pounded in his chest, but Drew pushed forward. Adrenaline pulsed through his veins, and by the time they completed Nate's workout, Drew was ready to pass out.

Nate handed him a water, and he downed it in one go.

"Careful. You'll hurl it back up." Nate sipped from his own bottle.

Drew took a few deep breaths before he could respond. "You suck. I can't believe you do this almost every day."

Nate chuckled to himself. He pressed the ball of his foot against the wall and straightened his leg, stretching his hamstrings. "I like it. I always feel better after."

Despite the exhaustion settling through his entire body and the sore muscles he knew would greet him tomorrow, the strain and struggle had been somewhat therapeutic. For the first time, Drew wondered if Nate exercised for the release, not the results. His own pen and ink.

"I'm having dinner at Brigid's on Saturday."

Nate's eyebrows shot up in mockery of Drew's discomfort. "That's fast. Do you need help picking out a ring?"

Drew flipped him off. Nate laughed a deep, comfortable laugh. It was hard to believe this was the same guy who'd ditched school to stay home and sleep only an hour ago.

"Seriously, though," Nate continued as he stretched his other leg, "Meeting the parents is big for you. You ready?"

"It's not really meeting them. We've all met the Fosters before."

"Okay, so, re-meeting them. As the potential boyfriend."

Drew shrugged. His shoulders already felt tight. He followed Nate's lead and reached his arm across his body, stretching his shoulders and back before they seized up. "You know I don't care what parents think of me, but her parents approval means so much to Brigid. If I screw up, that's it."

Nate switched arms. "First off, they are going to love you. You practically worship their daughter, and you are a hundred times better than that ass hat she was dating last year.

"And second, Brigid isn't going to give up on you based on her parents' opinion. I've watched both of you drool over each other for months. It's disgusting, but kinda sweet. She wants this, too. Don't sell yourself short."

Drew rubbed his already aching thighs. Had Brigid really been into him for that long? It hadn't seemed like it, but he also hadn't done anything to encourage her, or even show her he might feel the same.

Nate could always tell, though. He could read people like that, like they had something they needed to say but couldn't find the words to say it. So he'd say it for them without them ever having to ask. Time to return the favor.

"Why are you avoiding Cam?"

Nate interlocked his fingers and pushed his arms straight out. "Wow, just going right for it, huh? No foreplay?"

"Answer the question." Drew mimicked Nate's stretch.

"I'm not avoiding Cam."

"You haven't spoken to her. You weren't at school today. You wouldn't come over last night. It's a pattern."

Nate dropped his arms and sank onto the mat, back against the mirror. He did look different. Maybe he really was just tired, but Drew didn't believe it. He looked like his usual self, but somehow dimmer—like only half of him could get through.

"Is it something else?" Drew hated asking. He knew this conversation, as badly as it needed to happen, would sting.

Nate's eyes darkened and his shoulders sagged. "I can't . . . do a lot right now."

"Like school?"

"Or facing Cam." Nate took another sip of water and

ran his hand through his hair, the blonde darkened with sweat. "It was bad enough that Ronny left her, but seeing her at lunch yesterday? I've never seen Cam broken like that."

"I was with her an hour ago. She's doing alright."

"Maybe."

They sat in silence and watched as a girl in a blue polo wiped down machines and stacked weights.

Mental illness was not something Drew understood. It didn't make sense that a brain could have all the same parts and work the same way as his but result in the hurt he saw in his friends. Brigid's fear and anxiety were real. Nate's depression and guilt were real. But how was Drew supposed to help them fight an enemy he couldn't see?

"It's not your fault." Drew could say the words, but Nate may never hear them.

He pulled Nate to his feet, and Nate nodded toward the door. "Let's get out of here. We could both use a shower. You smell terrible."

The Foster's home was loud.

Generally, Drew's time in Brigid's house was long after the youngest kids were in bed for a movie night, or right after school when they were still on the bus ride home. But when all eight Fosters were home, it was all volume.

There were kids everywhere. The Foster's had six children, each with their mom's blonde hair and ice blue eyes. Ashley, the sister a few years younger than Brigid, was nowhere to be seen, but Drew assumed the music blasting down the hallway was from her room. The next in line, a girl of about twelve was using the kitchen island to work on her homework. Mrs. Foster would pause loading the dishwasher every so often to lean over her shoulder and correct an error or explain a math problem. The youngest Foster stood a few feet away openly staring at Drew and ignoring the Disney movie playing on the tv. Something purple was smeared across her cheeks.

Drew sat stiffly on an oversized blue velvet couch in

the living room. Brigid relaxed in the spot next to him, and her two brothers, Finley and Peter (Drew had no idea which was which), lounged on the carpet on the other side of the coffee table. Scrabble letters cluttered the space between, and it was hard to tell which letters belonged to which words.

"That's not a word," the younger brother pointed at the letters the older had just placed on the board.

"Sure it is. It's the past tense of think: thunk." The older brother smiled proudly at his ridiculous word.

"It's isn't! Brigid, is thunk a word?"

"Hmm," Brigid faked a look of deep thought, "I don't think it is. Sorry, Peter."

Peter frowned deeply. "Fine. How about thud?" He replaced the offending letters.

"That's a word." Finley nodded, and, like any six-year-old with glasses, had the appearance of an adult trapped in a little kid's body. His neatly combed hair and buttoned polo didn't help either.

"Hannah, stop staring at Drew. Go find Mommy." Brigid shooed the little girl, but Hannah ignored her and continued watching Drew with wide eyes.

"Come here, Nana!" Mrs. Foster's bright voice rang from the kitchen. Hannah immediately disappeared toward the island, tiny feet pounding against the tile.

Brigid's dad burst through the garage door, a stack of at least five pizza boxes towering in his arms. His tie hung loose around his neck, and his sandy, brown hair was mussed from the wind.

"Look who's home!" He sent Drew what appeared to

be a genuine smile and a nod and headed to the enormous kitchen island to deposit the boxes.

"Pizza!" Both boys immediately forgot their game and scrambled over each other to get off the floor. Brigid's mom kissed her husband lightly and retrieved a stack of napkins to add to the table. Brigid took Drew by the hand and pulled him into the kitchen behind her.

Drew and his mom never ate at their kitchen table, but they did have one. It was a round, wooden table with a chair on each side. They had three chairs when he was a kid, but one had broken a few years ago, and they hadn't ever had a reason to replace it. One of the table legs was damaged, causing the whole thing to wobble if you leaned on it too much. Nothing like the Foster's table.

A giant rectangle of gray wood stretched the entire width of the kitchen. A bench spanned the length of each side and matching chairs filled the spaces at the ends. Drew had expected Mr. Foster to take the place at the head of the table, but it was Mrs. Foster who sat in that spot, with Mr. Foster perched on the bench to her right. The kids filtered into the rest of the seats. Little Hannah took the available place next to her mother, and Brigid landed on her other side. Drew climbed across the bench next to Brigid.

The group destroyed the pizza. Within seconds, plates were filled with slices of pie and dripping cheese. Drew took the slice of Hawaiian Brigid offered and ate in silence.

"Drew, Brigid says you are teaching her to play the guitar. That's very exciting." Mrs. Foster looked expectantly at Drew from across the table. Eight sets of eyes turned his direction.

Drew swallowed the scalding cheese. "She's a fast learner."

"That's no surprise," Mr. Foster's deep voice filled the room, "Brigid is good at everything she does." He beamed with pride for his daughter.

Brigid stared at her pizza, a deep blush creeping up her neck.

"Oh, don't be embarrassed, Pancakes. It's just the truth."

Brigid slunk lower into her seat, and her blush deepened. Drew tucked away his amusement and let Brigid escape.

"I agree, sir." Drew said.

"Where did you learn to play, Drew?" Mrs. Foster asked.

Drew's chest tightened. If it wasn't Brigid's parents, he would be tempted to lie, make up some story about years of lessons or summer camp. But Brigid knew the truth, and even if she didn't, he wouldn't want her believing the lie. He needed to be better than that.

But there was no way in hell they were about to have a conversation about his dad. This dinner was his chance to prove to the Fosters he could be good enough for their daughter. Bringing up his past was definitely not the way to do that.

"I've played since I was a little kid." Not a direct answer, but not a lie.

"And you want to study music in college?" Mr. Foster's

question was genuine. Most adults tried to talk Drew out of a career in music. Drew's chest warmed slightly at the lack in skepticism.

But Drew had no intentions of going to college.

He snuck a glance at Brigid. She knew he'd decided against getting a music degree, but maybe she wasn't ready for him to share that with her parents.

Brigid avoided his eyes and sipped from her water.

"I'm still figuring out what's next." A coward's answer.

"Nothing wrong with that. You're young. Think it through. It took me years to decide I wanted to dive into the wild world of accounting." Mr. Foster smiled at his wife. She swatted his arm gently in return.

"Did you know a music major's salary is 37% lower than the national average?" Finley asked from his spot at Drews left. He set down his knife and fork. "I looked it up earlier."

"I'll keep that in mind."

Finley nodded once, and his eyes locked on Drew's arms. Drew immediately regretted not wearing a hoodie.

"Why are there drawings all over your arms?"

"Finley, we don't pry, honey." Mrs. Foster scolded her youngest son.

Finley continued to stare, wide eyes magnified by his glasses. "Did you draw on Brigid's arms? I saw them. My teacher says that you shouldn't write on your arms because the ink will sink into your skin and get in your blood, and you'll get lead poisoning and die."

Peter burst out laughing from his spot across the table

and nearly spewed chewed pizza everywhere. Brigid rolled her eyes and threw napkins at him.

"Drew isn't going to die, honey." Mrs. Foster smiled sweetly and took a bite of her pizza.

"Finley worries about people," Mr. Foster said. He wiped his hands on a napkin, laced his fingers, and rested his wrists on the edge of the table.

Mr. Foster was the perfect blend of likeable and intimidating. His wide, square face and salt-and-pepper stubble were all business, but he had a friendly smile that softened his image. "We're sure glad you could join us for dinner. Your mom didn't mind letting us borrow you for the night?"

"Um, no, she didn't mind." Drew instinctively felt for the pen in his pocket. "She's got plans this evening."

"Well then, I'm sure glad you came here so you wouldn't have to eat dinner alone." Mrs. Foster said as she wiped sauce off Hannah's cheeks.

Drew nodded, unsure of how to respond to that. What would these people think if they knew he ate dinner alone basically every night, if he ate dinner at all?

"May we be excused?" Ashley asked, eyeing him indiscreetly.

"Yes. You may be excused," Mr. Foster waved his hand, and as quickly as they'd gathered, the family dispersed. Brigid stood slowly.

"We better get started on our lesson if we are going to have time to study before curfew."

"Oh, of course. It was nice to see you again, Drew," Mrs. Foster smiled warmly at him.

"You too," he replied, "Thank you for dinner."

Brigid laced her fingers through Drew's and pulled him toward the stairs he knew led up to her room. It hadn't been a disaster, but he couldn't imagine he'd impressed Mr. and Mrs. Foster either.

"Keep the door open!" Mr. Foster called after them.

Drew and Brigid slipped into her room, and Drew noticed she left the door open about an inch.

Drew hadn't ever been in Brigid's room before, but it was exactly what he'd thought it would be. White walls were covered in pictures of her friends and posters of her favorite books. A *Count of Monte Cristo* print caught Drew's eye, and he bit back a smile.

Everything was where it belonged. Nothing looked out of place. Her bookshelf overflowed with books, organized by color to create a rainbow effect. Her bed was made with a fluffy, white comforter and pillows piled high at one end. A plush blanket plastered in flowers was balled up at the other.

Brigid removed a bag of cinnamon bears from her desk drawer and popped one in her mouth before offering them to Drew.

"I'm so sorry." Brigid sat on the edge of her bed.

"It's fine." Drew took the bag from her hands and bit into one of the candies. Heat flooded his mouth.

Brigid looked at him incredulously.

"Really." He sat next to her. "Actually, it's kind of nice."

"The chaos and probing questions are nice?" she asked.

"No, Pancakes." Brigid covered her face with her

hands, and Drew gently pulled them away. "It's nice that your family cares that much about you. That they have dinner together every night and want to meet the people in your life." He squeezed her hand. "Do they know we're…?"

He didn't know how to finish that sentence. What were they?

"They know."

Drew nodded but didn't push. He rubbed his thumb along the back of her hand and over her wrist. Her ink was long gone by now.

"My siblings might not," she continued "They don't catch on to things as quick. Except Ashley, but I think she's pissed. She's always had a crush on you."

That explained a lot. Ashley was a freshman, and he'd see her around school every now and then. Her eyes would always go buggy, and she'd dip into a hall or classroom out of his path.

"I think I'm a little old for her."

"Is that your only objection?" Brigid quirked an eyebrow. He'd never get tired of her challenging him. Drew leaned close and brushed his cheek against Brigid's.

"And I want *you*." Apparently, he was being bold tonight.

He eased back, and Brigid studied his face in silence. Whatever she was searching for, she either found it or gave up before she stood and pulled Drew's guitar from under her bed. His hand was instantly colder without hers in it.

"I have something to show you." She removed the guitar from its case and sat in a pink desk chair a few feet from him. Drew waited patiently as she tuned her instrument and positioned it just right in her lap.

"Okay, I'm ready. But be prepared. It's not very good." She bit her lip and shifted in her chair.

"I can't wait to hear it." Drew braced an arm on either side. Brigid's blankets were soft against his calloused hands. He tried not to think too hard about the fact that he was sitting on Brigid's bed and put all his focus on the girl across from him, nervous as he'd ever seen her.

Brigid carefully placed her fingers into position over the frets and began to strum. He'd expected her to show him the chords they'd worked on last time, but as Brigid continued playing, goosebumps covered Drew's arms.

She'd learned a song.

Drew listened closely as Brigid moved through the chords. The tune took shape, and sparks shot through Drew's entire body as he realized what it was.

She was playing Foo Fighters.

It was a simplified, acoustic version of *Learn to Fly*, hesitant and full of pauses, but it was the most magnificent thing Drew had ever heard. Sorry, Dave Grohl.

Drew's chest burned, and he clutched the plush fabric of Brigid's blanket in his fists begging it to ground him as he watched Brigid lay herself bare. He knew Brigid. He knew her reservations and anxieties. They were a lot alike in that way. They'd both been hurt, each seen the dark side of love in different ways. But they were learning to trust again. This was as close to confessing her feelings as Drew could ever hope for.

But he still needed to hear the words from her. He

could never assume she was ready for anything more, or even wanted it.

Brigid's face was scrunched in concentration. Her guitar, because it was definitely hers now whether she knew it or not, trembled on her lap, but her fingers were sure. When she finished, she placed the guitar gently to the side, leaning it against her bookcase.

"I only know the first bit. Could you tell what it was?" She spun the elastic around her wrist.

Drew swallowed the lump in his throat and nodded. "How did you…?"

"YouTube. I've been practicing all week." She rose from her chair and reclaimed her place beside him on the bed. Her movements were slow. Careful.

"Foo Fighters?"

Her hand slid closer to his, and her finger traced circles on the back of his own, still clasping the blanket. Her touch left a wake of fire along his skin.

Burn away, pretty girl.

"I looked it up that night I saw the poster in your room." She swallowed.

Drew grasped for an ounce of the boldness he'd felt earlier.

"Why?" His voice was low and gravelly. They could power half the city with the electricity filling the inches between them.

She licked her lips, but her eyes held his. Drew's chest rose and fell with each breath, fighting to barricade his crumbling walls.

"Because I want *you*."

All the heat coursing through his body streamlined directly for his chest. He dropped his head and pressed his eyes closed, unwilling to let her see the effect her words had on him. They were an arrow, a cannon aimed for that last bit of wall he was holding up with nothing but sure will. And it was a direct hit. He couldn't let her see it fall, even as he knew it was nothing but rubble now. His face would betray all of him.

Delicate fingers pressed against his chin, gently lifting his face. He kept his eyes closed and inhaled a deep, raspy breath. Brigid's lips brushed his and sent a shiver through him.

Drew matched her touch, caressing her lips with his own. They were every bit as soft as he'd thought they'd be. He moved cautiously, allowing Brigid to lead. Her hands traced up his arms and locked behind his neck. She ran her fingers through his hair. He clasped her hips firmly in his hands and deepened the kiss. She returned his intensity.

She tasted like cinnamon bears, sweet and spicy. His entire body craved her, but he kept his hands at her waist, still earning that trust he so desperately needed.

She wanted him. Not to support her or save her, but just him. No girl had ever wanted him just for who he was. He'd never let them know him well enough. Brigid did, though. He didn't deserve her, and he wasn't dumb enough to believe he ever would. But for just this moment, she wanted him.

Brigid smiled against his mouth and he gently kissed the corner of her lip where he'd jealously watched her bite it for months. He traced his nose along her jaw and planted a light kiss on her neck. He pulled back, but only a breath's distance. Her arms stayed locked behind his neck.

"Looks like Cam was right. You are irresistible," she whispered.

Drew returned her smile with his own—full and unrestrained, a smile she'd likely never seen before—and met her lips with his own once more.

★★★

It was nearly two hours later when Brigid packed up the guitar, replaced it under her bed, and walked Drew to his car. He would have enjoyed spending all that time kissing Brigid, but they'd spent most of it practicing chords and reviewing for his exam. He hadn't kiss her again once they'd switched to lessons.

Kissing her at all had been more than he'd hoped for. He didn't want to push it. They had all the time in the world.

"Thanks for the lesson," Brigid leaned against the driver's door, blocking him from getting in.

Fine by him.

Drew neared her, stopping only a foot away. She studied his face, eyes darting to his lips, but Drew stood firm. He couldn't kiss her again. Not yet.

Dating Brigid wasn't about rushing the relationship and pushing boundaries. He still had way too much to prove. If he went too fast too soon, he'd scare her and she'd be gone.

Drew wrapped his arms around Brigid and pulled her against him. Her hair smelled like pineapple, and Drew had to once again restrain himself.

"I better get inside." Brigid stepped away but didn't let

197

go completely. Her hands linked behind his neck and she twisted his hair in her fingers.

Holy hell.

"We have an audience," Brigid whispered. His heart rate rocketed again as her breath tickled his ear, and it took him a moment to process her words.

But sure enough, when Drew looked up to the window above the garage, at least four sets of eyes were peeking through the blinds. They disappeared when they noticed Drew's gaze.

He squeezed Brigid's hand once more before she walked back to her front door and disappeared inside.

As he drove home, Drew's chest burned with longing for more than just the girl he'd spent the evening with. He had forgotten what it was like to have a real family, a group of people who wanted to know where you were and who you were with, who spied on you through the blinds, or even worried that you might be getting lead poisoning.

Drew tried to remember having that. Elliott had never been that kind of father, even before he left. Mom was that way when Drew was really young, but that had faded and disappeared over the years.

Drew killed his engine in his driveway, but remained behind the wheel. He couldn't bring himself to go in. The house was dark and quiet. Empty. Void of life. The opposite of the home he'd just left.

Instead, he pulled his phone from his pocket and clocked in for a late-night shift. Someone had to pay for that empty house.

CHAPTER 19

Sunday was clutch for takeout. Drew made more money on Sundays than all the weeknights combined. In a college town, he spent most of the day running back and forth from campus with a few stops in the surrounding neighborhoods in between.

It was late into the night before he'd been ready to go back to his own home after dinner with the Fosters, but he had to make Sunday count. He'd given up hours of pay this week to spend time with his friends, and now he was paying for it. So, with a only few hours of sleep, he clocked in for a long Sunday shift.

Drew shuffled his iPod and hooked it into his car stereo as his phone rang.

"We're having a movie day at my house," Cam announced through the speaker. "You're in charge of drinks because I never know what you want."

"Literally any diet soda," Drew said. "But I can't make this one."

"Why not? It's Sunday. And I know you aren't with Brigid or Nathan because they're both coming."

Nate was going to be there. Drew squeezed the wheel and dropped his shoulders. He'd barely seen Nate all week. Since their gym visit, Nate had declined any invitations to hang out, missed more classes than he'd attended, and even his texts were hit and miss. But Drew had been blowing off shifts all over the place lately to spend time with Brigid, not to mention their five-day disaster of a spring break. He couldn't miss out on a Sunday afternoon's profits. Rent was due in a week.

"I've just got some stuff going on today."

Cam whined into the phone, "What stuff? Come on, Drew. You're going to say no to your pregnant friend?"

"Mean. I'll catch the next one. Promise."

He hung up before should could say anything more and immediately regretted it. She'd make him pay for that later.

By eleven, the orders were coming in faster than Drew could deliver them. He had six orders of Chinese from the same restaurant dropped of to the same dorms. Couldn't these people coordinate?

His phone dinged: another order for Chinese. He stopped by Dragon Hill, picked up the order, and plugged the address into his GPS: 2753 Oakland Way. He recognized the street. It was Brigid and Cam's street. Easy delivery and sure to be good tips.

He tapped the brakes as he turned onto the street, searching house numbers for the correct drop off. 2733. 2745.

Shit. In the year he'd been working delivery, he'd

managed to avoid this.

Drew pulled over in front Cam's house, the vinyl 2753 mocking him from the side of the West's mailbox. He breathed out and leaned his forehead against his steering wheel.

Maybe he could drop the food and leave. But if they answered before he pulled away, he'd look ridiculous. Plus the West's were super rich. There was no way they didn't have one of those video doorbells. They'd know it was him from the footage.

He could skip the delivery. Trash it somewhere or drop it off to the wrong house. But Cam would just order more.

There was no way around it. Drew grabbed the bag of Chinese from his passenger seat and headed for the door.

Cam answered almost immediately.

"Drew! You came! Guys, Drew's here!" She yelled over her shoulder. She turned back to him and poked him in the chest. "You hung up on me."

Brigid appeared next to Cam, and Drew could see Nate waving from his spot on the giant sectional inside.

"Why do you have the food?" Brigid asked. Her brow's pulled together as she tried to make sense of what she was seeing.

"Actually, I'm just delivering. I can't stay." Drew handed the bag awkwardly to Cam.

"Why are you delivering it?" Cam asked. "Are you a delivery driver?"

"I just do it every now and then to pick up a little extra

cash. No big deal." Understatement of the year, but not a total lie. Drew inched his way backward, wanting more than anything to make a break for his car.

"That's why you couldn't come over today? You have a job?"

Drew nodded.

"You could have just said that." Cam looked hurt. Drew refused to look at Brigid. Guilt swam through his stomach, and his throat tightened.

"I really should get back to work." He shoved his hands into his pockets and backed away another inch.

"Okay, but we're gonna be here all day. You should come over when you're done." Cam gave him a half smile and waved.

"Maybe I will." Drew stepped off the porch step, and glanced at Brigid as the door closed between them. Her eyes were cold, and her arms wrapped tightly around her.

Drew rubbed his hand down his face. He'd screwed up.

He should have trashed the food. Or paid a stranger on the street to deliver it for him. Or pretty much anything other than showing up at Cam's door with damning evidence of his inadequacy.

Brigid's family wasn't nearly as wealthy as Ronny's or Cam's, but they did alright. She would never have to have a job to keep her family from ending up on the street. Drew didn't know if the pity or the judgement would be worse. Either way, even a glimpse into this part of his life would change things and likely ruin everything they had. He had to control the damage before it sank in.

His fingers hovered over the CLOCK OUT option on his phone. His body was heavy in his seat, and a headache was growing behind his eyes. He could do it. Clock out, walk back up to Cam's door, and save his relationship—or at least slap a Band-Aid on it and hope for the best.

And then what?

He still had bills to pay. As far as he knew, his mom hadn't heard back on that job yet, and until she started bringing in a paycheck, it was his problem. Besides, damage control now would likely be just as futile as it would be in a few hours. His stomach churned at the thought.

At least they only knew a piece of truth. The whole truth would sink him for good.

Orders continued to pour in, but he wasn't nearly as quick as he'd been before. He checked his phone every two minutes to see if Brigid had texted yet.

Drew pushed through the guilt of clocking out an hour early, and headed to Cam's after the dinner rush. The sky was dark, but Cam had said they'd be there all night.

A case of soda in each hand, Drew rang Cam's doorbell for the second time that day. Nate answered this time.

"We didn't think you were coming. It's been . . ." he checked his phone, "ten hours since you were here. Have you been working this whole time?"

"Long shift." Drew followed Nate into the house and dropped the soda on the kitchen counter among a mess of nearly empty Chinese containers, pizza boxes, and soda cans. Behind them, Cam and Brigid were curled up in blankets on the sectional watching *The Princess Bride.*

"It's classic movies day," Nate explained.

"I'm a little surprised you're here." Drew raised an eyebrow at Nate, and popped the top on a can of Diet Dew.

"Cam threatened to kidnap me if I didn't come." Nate grabbed a blanket from the edge of the sofa and curled up next to the girls who only then registered that Drew had arrived.

"You made it!" Cam's eyes peaked over the back of the couch. "Come sit with us!"

Drew walked toward the couch but hesitated before sitting. His gut twisted and his mouth went dry. Watching movies on a couch was a minefield even when you knew where you stood with a girl.

Dating was the worst. If you could skip all the dumb games and societal rules built into relationships, it would be much more enjoyable for everyone involved.

"Brigid, could I talk to you for a minute?" Drew shoved his hands into his pockets.

Brigid looked at him for the first time since he'd arrived. She eyed him and then nodded. He followed her down a hall and into Cam's room. Photos covered every square inch of her walls. She'd gotten a Polaroid camera for Christmas last year and had taken thousands of pictures before she'd accidentally left it outside in a rainstorm.

Brigid folded her arms and waited.

"I just want to explain. I took the job last summer to help my mom, but things have been a little tight so I kept it. I get it if you don't want to be with someone with those kinds of problems." He'd been planning what he would say for nearly ten hours now. Enough truth to not be a lie, but no new information. And an easy out if she wanted it.

Brigid's eyes widened. "I don't care that you have a job, Drew."

"You don't?" His chest loosened.

"I care that you lied to me about it. Why didn't you tell me?"

Drew squeezed his eyes shut. She wasn't disgusted. She was angry. He'd spent weeks convincing her she could trust him only to keep something so important from her. He'd undone all that work in one moment.

He should have told her.

"I'm sorry, Brij. I screwed up."

"I just don't get why you didn't tell me." She rubbed her arms.

"I thought that if you knew the truth, you'd leave."

Her face softened.

"Not everyone is looking for a reason to leave you, Drew." She pressed her palm to his cheek. "I don't care that you have a job or help your mom. But if you and I are going to work, you can't keep stuff from me." Her eyes warmed, and Drew placed his hand over hers.

"You and I?" He moved her hand to his lips and placed a kiss in her palm.

She bit her lip. "I mean, if you and I are . . whatever we are."

"We are." Drew squeezed her hand gently. "Would you like to go out Friday night? With me?" he asked. The words came out fast and urgent.

Brigid smiled. "Yes. I would. Very much."

Drew restrained a sigh of relief. He'd been building up his courage all day to ask Brigid out for the second time. She'd given him signs all week long that she was interested and would say yes, but he could still see her face when he'd asked that night by the yurt, the fire dancing in her eyes as she rejected him. If she'd said no again, he would've stopped trying, let her walk away. As badly as he wanted to be with her, he would not become the guy that wouldn't stop.

"It's a date, pretty girl."

Brigid slipped her fingers through Drew's and led him back to the couch with her.

"All good?" Cam asked. Her eyes darted between them, somehow even larger than normal.

"All good." Brigid pulled him on to the couch beside her. They took the spot in the corner of the sectional, and she curled up against him, leaning into his side and resting her head on his chest. The scent of pineapple tickled his senses and made his vision go blurry.

They watched the movie, or at least tried to through Cam's constant line-quoting and tossing popcorn at the screen whenever the villain appeared. Drew had been so focused on Brigid cuddling against him, his fingers trailing up and down her arm, he hadn't noticed Nate nearly asleep a few feet away.

He slipped his phone out of his pocket, careful not to disturb Brigid.

Drew: I'm glad you're here.

Nate: I could say the same about you. All those nights you were busy and we thought you were with girls?

Drew: Shifts. Or at least, a lot of them.

He didn't really want to talk, or even think, about other girls with Brigid in his arms.

Drew: You and Cam okay now?

Nate: I'm here.

Nate clicked his screen off and tucked his phone into his pocket. Apparently, their conversation was over.

Drew's phone buzzed once more.

Mom: *I'm going to be home Friday afternoon. Will you be there?*

Drew tried to remember the last time his mom had asked him when he'd be home. Maybe never. His mouth went dry, but a heat radiated in his chest as he responded.

Drew: *I'll be home.*

She responded almost immediately, like she'd been waiting to hear back.

Mom: *See you then.*

Drew nearly dropped his phone. His mom had initiated communication, and made plans to see him. He pushed the hope that threatened to bloom in his chest back down. This didn't mean anything.

Or it could mean she was finally coming around.

Drew had grown accustomed to the idea that he would spend most of his life taking care of things that weren't his to take care of. He wouldn't get to have the things he'd dreamed of. It wasn't in the cards.

But as Drew glanced around the room at the people he cared about most in his life, a smile spread slowly across his face.

Cam had been beaten down hard the last few weeks, but still she found the strength to laugh at stupid movies and shovel fistfuls of popcorn into her face, not giving a shit what anyone else thought of her.

Ronny would come around sooner or later.

Nate stared blankly at the screen and sipped from a can of soda. He wasn't better, but he was here. And for Nate, that was huge.

Drew's eyes stopped on the girl snuggled comfortably in his arms. He squeezed her gently. She looked up at him, smiled, and brushed a soft kiss against his jaw before returning to the movie.

His mom's text still lit up his phone, and for the first time in what could have been years, Drew let hope in.

***

Drew offered to help Cam clean up since Brigid needed to get home for curfew and Nate had taken off after the movie, claiming to be tired.

Cam sat on the floor picking up kernels of popcorn that had missed her mouth and throwing them into the giant blue bowl that had once been overflowing but now sat almost empty on the edge of the couch.

"Seems like things are going good between you and Brigid," Cam said without looking at him. It was more of a question than an observation.

"Did Brigid tell you to ask me?" Drew threw empty Chinese takeout containers and soda cans into the black trash bag he held in his hand as he made his way around the spacious kitchen.

Cam's house was one of those open concept designs where the living room, dining room, and kitchen were all one giant space. And in the matter of one day, they'd managed to completely destroy all of it.

"No," Cam responded, "I'm just nosy and want to hear about it." Zero apology in her voice.

Drew smiled anyway. "We're going out on Friday."

"Woo-hoo!" Cam hollered from her spot on the floor. "I love that you two are happening. She deserves someone amazing after that catastrophe with Mike."

Drew didn't respond, hoping Cam would go on. She did.

"Did she ever tell you what happened between them?" Drew shook his head.

"Last December, he took her on a date. Normal deal. But when they got back to his house, no one was home. He tried to make a move. She shut him down, told him she wasn't ready for sex. Mike didn't care. He told her she owed him after months of dating, and that it was part of being a girlfriend."

Red spots flickered in Drew's vision. If he'd known this before, Mike would be dead—which is probably why Brigid had never told him or Nate or Ronny.

"Did he hurt her?" Drew ground out the words.

"Not physically, but when she still refused, he dumped her on the spot. She found out later that he'd been sleeping with other girls for months while they were together. Douchebag."

His stomach turned. Brigid, his smart, caring Brigid,

had been treated like a piece of ass and made to feel like it was her fault. No wonder she'd needed some reassurance before she'd been willing to give Drew a chance. He was lucky she'd been willing to even consider it.

"She's okay, you know." Cam was staring at him from her spot on the floor. She was no longer cleaning but eating the popcorn she'd piled in the bowl. Drew nodded. Of course she was. She was with him, and he'd never hurt her.

He needed a change in subject. Talking about Mike was making his ears ring.

"What about you?"

"I'm fine. I'm always tired, and I'm always hungry. But at least I'm not throwing up all the time." She leaned against the couch and continued eating.

"Your parents took the news well?"

"They took it like champs." Cam smiled at something Drew couldn't see. "It helps that my mom has literally been in my position. Well, almost." Her smile disappeared.

"Have you talked to him?" They hadn't discussed Ronny since Drew had blown up at him outside his own house.

"He came over yesterday."

Drew nearly dropped the now-full bag of trash he was holding.

"He came here?"

"It's okay, Drew. He apologized for everything: accusing me of cheating, ending things in Vegas, not being more supportive with all this." She pointed to her stomach with a flick of her wrist. "He asked to get back together."

Drew slunk onto a bar stool. "What did you say?"

Cam stood from her spot and made her way to the stool next to Drew's before answering.

"I said no. I forgive him for what happened, and I hope we can get to a place where he can be involved in the baby's life, maybe even as a couple. But for now, that place isn't a possibility. Me forgiving him doesn't change what he did, and I can't be with someone who would think those things about me. I love him, and I miss him, but I need more than that." Cam's eyes were filled with tears, but she held them back.

"What about the kid?" Drew asked.

"I'll raise it."

"You sure? How can you love a kid you don't want?"

Cam leaned against the counter and blinked a few times before answering.

"Unexpected isn't the same as unwanted."

Drew pressed his back into the stool and rubbed his hand down his face. This was all coming out wrong.

Cam grabbed his hand and walked him back to the couch, snatching a bag of barbeque chips off the counter on her way. She pulled a blanket over her lap and motioned for Drew to sit. He took a seat a few cushions down.

"I was unexpected," Cam started as she reached her hand into the bag for a chip. "My parents were seniors when they found out they were pregnant." She raised her eyebrows meaningfully. "You know all of this."

Drew nodded. Her family was very open about their history.

"Regardless of how my story started, I've never felt

unwanted. My parents travel a lot, but they take me whenever they can. Especially when I was little. They took me everywhere with them. And now, when I can't go, they call. Or they send pictures.

"Sometimes life makes choices for us. But just because we didn't make the choice doesn't mean we have to be unhappy with the outcome. This isn't what I planned, but I already love this kid more than anything. We always have a choice, Drew Cox. And I choose him."

CHAPTER 20

Drew pushed aside his panic and knocked on the door at the Lankford home after school on Thursday. It was the third day in a row without a word from Nate.

Nate's dad answered, still in his work clothes. Without a word, he ushered Drew inside, and pointed to the stairs that led to Nate's basement bedroom.

Drew and Mitch Lankford didn't have a very solid relationship. Drew didn't appreciate how Mitch treated his son and the choices he made for him, and Mitch didn't see Drew as a very good influence on Nate. But they put up with each other for Nate, or at least that was why Drew didn't let Mitch have it every time he was in the man's presence.

Drew proceeded down the stairs and into the basement. Nate's door, just off the main room, was closed. Drew knocked once. "Nate, it's me."

A muffled reply sounded through the door, "Come in."

Drew opened the door and stepped in. He could barely see the room around him. Nate's lights were off and the blinds had been pulled closed. Drew crossed to the window and opened them.

Sunlight flooded the room, and Drew cursed under his breath. Dirty clothes draped across nearly every surface. Empty cans littered the floor, nightstand, and desk. Tangled cords were piled over the workshop, and a stack of phones and tablets leaned against the trash can.

Nate was laying in his bed, a pillow over his face to block out the light.

Drew kicked some clothes off the beanbag in the corner, plopped down onto it, and waited.

It took Nate nearly fifteen minutes to pull the pillow off his head and sit up.

"What's up?" His voice was muted and groggy. He reached for a can of something from his nightstand and took a long drink. The label flashed as he set it back down. Still soda.

"You weren't at school again. I've barely heard from you in days."

Nate shrugged. "Just wasn't feelin' it today. I'll be there tomorrow." Drew watched Nate as he padded to his dresser. He ripped his T-shirt off over his head, dropped it to the floor, and pulled on a fresh one.

Drew pushed a little harder. He needed answers, but if he pushed too hard, Nate would break. "You struggling?"

Nate stilled. He took his time before he answered, "Maybe. A lot going on right now."

Drew nodded. They returned to silence.

He'd seen this a few years ago when Nate's depression had taken over and he'd gotten really sick. Nate became unresponsive and disinterested. He'd pull away and shut everyone out. This was the worst Drew had seen him since then, but last time it had been triggered by his mom's death so Drew hadn't recognized it as anything besides grief. He wouldn't make that mistake again.

Drew waited a few more minutes before he got up to leave. Nate had gone back to sitting on his bed, a blanket pulled around his shoulders. Drew paused in the door way.

"Tomorrow?" he asked.

Nate didn't respond. Drew wasn't even sure he'd heard him.

"Nate." He let a little bit of bite into his voice. Nate finally looked up at that. "Tomorrow. School. You'll be there?"

"Tomorrow," Nate whispered, but it was hollow. Lifeless. The echo of a promise.

Drew turned and headed back upstairs. He found Mr. Lankford reclining in his chair in the front room.

"He's not okay," Drew said. Drew wouldn't let Nate go down this road again. Not alone.

Mitch studied Drew for a moment before responding, "He'll be fine. Needs to get his lazy butt out of bed and do some work is all."

Drew planted his feet and crossed his arms. "He needs help."

Mitch closed his recliner, stood, and matched Drew's stance. He was taller and stronger than Drew, but Drew couldn't be intimidated that easily. He had learned long ago not to let shitty fathers get to him.

"Don't you have enough of your own problems

without causing any here?" Mitch's face was steel, but his neck flamed red.

Drew contemplated turning around and heading right back downstairs. But as empty as Nate's voice had sounded, it was still there. The promise that he'd be here tomorrow. Drew walked out the door instead.

***

Nate made good on his promise. He was at Drew's car when Drew stepped onto his driveway Friday morning. He didn't say anything, just nodded in acknowledgement, but at least he was there.

School crawled by. Drew had taken the whole evening off work for his date with Brigid. He'd thought about squeezing in a few orders before picking her up, but the last thing he wanted was to smell like pizza and French fry grease.

Sunday's movie night had left Drew feeling pretty confident about his relationship with Brigid. She'd instigated the cuddling on the couch, and they'd been texting nearly nonstop since. He hadn't opened up further about his job and his family situation, but he still wasn't really sure she needed to know more than she did.

They sat around their usual booth at Joey's, and Drew snuck a glance at Brigid as she sipped her Diet Coke. She'd been sneaking glances at him for the last hour with no stealth whatsoever, and it was adorable. They'd decided that although they weren't a secret, they weren't going to flaunt their relationship either. Cam was still dealing with a more than difficult situation in her own love life. No need to rub it in.

But the tension was unreal. They hadn't kissed since their first nearly a week ago, but it wasn't because he hadn't wanted to. He'd craved her touch every day since. He'd nearly kissed her at Cam's movie night, but it hadn't felt right after he'd lied to her.

Drew grazed the back of his hand against Brigid's and felt her leg press into his under the table. His stomach fluttered as her finger traced circles on his knee. He laced his fingers and squeezed his drink between his palms. Busy hands. Busy hands would keep him from doing anything rash.

But it wouldn't stop the heat radiating through his body from her touch.

"Drew?" Cam quirked an eyebrow. "Are you with us?"

Drew cleared his throat. "Yeah, sorry. What did you ask?"

Cam gave him a knowing smile. "I asked if you were ready for your AP test on Tuesday."

"Should be." It was an optimistic answer but not a lie. He was in a much better place than he'd been before he'd started tutoring with Brigid. And he didn't need a five. A three was passing and therefore a passing grade in English. He didn't care about the college credit for obvious reasons.

It was past time to head back to class, but Cam was still eating, and none of them had any inkling whatsoever to hurry her along. In fact, Drew was pretty sure he'd seen Nate sneaking some of the food from his own untouched plate onto Cam's. And he was more than content playing this game with Brigid.

"Are you all waiting for me?" Cam glanced between

them, suddenly realizing they'd all been done for a while.

"You're fine, Cam." Brigid's finger trailed up his thigh and hooked into his pocket. It shouldn't have affected him the way it did—a single finger pressed against the outside of his thigh with a layer of denim between them—but it was enough to blur his vision and spike his heart rate, each beat pounding in his ears.

Cam shoved one more fry into her mouth and wiped her hands on a napkin. "I'm done. Let's get out of here before Drew can no longer walk."

If Brigid hadn't completely stolen his ability to speak, he'd have told her off, but as it was, he simply nodded and headed for the car.

The ride back to school was no different: Brigid beside him, stealing glances and discreetly tracing the ink along his right arm from her place in the passenger seat. Her teasing was somehow both excruciating agony and complete ecstasy.

I'm ready when you are, pretty girl.

Drew never wanted to push Brigid for anything more than what she was offering, but as he shifted to park, her gaze dropped to his mouth, she bit her lip, and it was pretty clear what she was offering.

They climbed out of his car. The wind blew her hair gently around her shoulders, and her eyes sparkled at him. Cam and Nate headed toward the school, and Drew let himself give in, just a little.

He grasped her hand firmly, spun his body to place her between him and his car, and captured her lips with his. He cupped her face in his hands, and his fingers tangled in her hair.

She responded instantly. Both hands grabbed his jacket and crushed his body against hers. Her urgency and demand surprised him, and the tension they'd both been fighting erupted. His hands slid over her shoulders and down her back, somehow pulling her even closer. He clutched her hips and lifted her onto the trunk of his car.

He moved between her knees. Brigid's fire matched his, and she wound her hands securely around his neck. Heat radiated through him as Brigid opened her mouth further. A low growl escaped him and he took advantage of the invitation. He nipped gently at that bottom lip that drove him crazy before brushing his tongue across hers.

A car honked a few rows over, and Drew broke their connection.

Which was probably a good thing. Drew was having a hard time remembering they were in public, even if the parking lot was mostly empty. His chest heaved as he tried to regain his breath. Brigid's rose as fell as quickly as his own. She didn't say anything but smiled shyly when he helped her off the back of his car.

Drew waited by Brigid's locker after school, but she never showed. Drew shrugged off the worry. She'd ridden to school with Cam. Maybe Cam had needed to hurry out.

Nate was also missing, and that worry burrowed down deep. He should have been here. Drew had been . . . *busy* with Brigid when they got back from lunch and hadn't seen if Nate had gone to class or somewhere else entirely.

Drew sprinted to his car. Someone was leaning against the trunk, but as he got closer, he realized it wasn't Nate as he'd hoped. Instead, he found Mike Allen playing on his phone and clearly waiting for Drew. Drew's throat burned, and worry shifted to anger. He stopped a few feet away and crossed his arms, keeping his distance. The last thing he needed was to get caught fighting Brigid's ex in a parking lot.

"What do you want?" Drew's voice was edged.

Mike took his time putting his phone away. His designer jeans were too tight to fit the phone properly. The guy had some balls to act like Drew wasn't worth his time when he was the one hanging out at Drew's car.

"Just needed to pass along a message," Mike smiled a cocky sideways grin, "from Brigid."

"Why are you delivering messages from Brigid?" Drew asked. His fists clenched at the sound of her name on Mike's lips.

"Because she and I are trying to work things out. I helped her through a panic attack last period, and we really connected. *Someone* pushed her too far after lunch. Good news is I was there to help, and she realized how badly she missed me. I told her I would let you know so she doesn't have to." Mike produced a serpentine smile. "She doesn't want you, Cox."

"Get the hell away from my car," Drew spat. Mike shrugged and walked past him and into the parking lot without looking back.

Drew fell into the driver's seat and slammed his door closed. Nausea overtook him, and he nearly lost his lunch in the passenger seat. He had to call Brigid. His phone was in his hand, and he was about to hit send but stopped. If there was even the slightest chance that what Mike had said was true and he really had sent her into a panic attack, he wouldn't chance calling and upsetting her further.

He never should have kissed her. It was a mistake. Now she probably thought he was after the same thing Mike had been. He should have waited for her to decide she was ready for that kind of relationship.

But if that was really the truth, why get back together with the asshole who'd hurt her the first time?

Drew thought back to that night at Cam's. Brigid's breathing rising to unsafe levels. The fear in her eyes had been unbearable.

He'd helped her then. And now he was the cause.

Cam would know what happened. They had last period together, and Drew would bet all the money he had stashed that she'd been there for the attack.

Drew dialed Cam's number. He ripped the pen from his pocket and clicked the lid as he waited for the pickup. It took six rings.

"Hey, Drew. I really can't talk. Brigid had an attack after lunch, and we can't get it under control," Cam spouted.

"Mike?" Drew demanded. He couldn't even form the whole question.

"Yes, Mike. I'm sorry, Drew, but we'll have to talk later. Brigid's parents just got home."

Click.

Drew's pen snapped in half and ink bled onto his fingers.

She was getting back with that creep.

Numbness overtook his limbs and his head spun.

Drew had pushed her. She'd said weeks ago that she didn't want to date him, but he'd pushed. He'd kept asking and flirting and finding reasons to be around her. So she agreed to go slow. And he'd pushed again. She'd kissed him back, but he'd instigated making out in the damn school parking lot. He should have known she didn't want that. He thought she had but he'd misread everything. From the very beginning. She hadn't wanted him, she simply hadn't wanted to hurt him.

But he'd hurt her.

CHAPTER 21

Drew spotted Benny's blue pickup parked in front of his house and groaned. He'd completely forgotten about his mom being home after school today. He'd been looking forward to possibly seeing her all week, but now he just wanted to be alone.

Maybe they'd be in the kitchen, and he could sneak to his room without his mom and her boyfriend even noticing.

He had no such luck.

His mom and Benny sat on the worn couch in the living room. Drew nodded briefly to the man his mom was seeing. His mom jumped up and met him just inside the door.

"Drew! I'm so glad you are home. We have big news!" Her eyes were wide, but clear. She clapped her hands together.

Drew raised his brows, urging her to explain. He couldn't quite manage forming words yet.

"I got the job! They called a few days ago, but I wanted to tell you in person and this week has just been a whirlwind. I start next week." She smiled brightly. Benny stood from the couch and wrapped an arm around her shoulders. He was beaming.

"That's great, mom. Congratulations," Drew mumbled weakly. He tried to muster up some excitement. This really was good news, the news he'd been hoping for, waiting for for over a year.

"And that's not all." She tucked both lips in and looked excitedly at Benny before going on. "Benny and I are moving in together! We've spent the whole week finalizing the details, and we're moving in tomorrow." She smiled from ear to ear and gripped Benny's arm.

"You're moving out?" Drew must have understood that wrong. He couldn't live with his mom's boyfriend. That was way too weird. He barely knew the man.

"Tomorrow! Benny and I found this cute little townhouse a few miles from here, and with my new job, we could finally afford it." She skipped into the kitchen, Benny on her heals.

"What about this house?" Drew asked, following her through the doorway.

"Oh, I already talked to the landlord, and he said he could have new tenants by next weekend. He sounded a little relieved to be honest. Rentals are going quick right now, and we both know you've been late with the rent a few times." She climbed onto the counter and rifled through the cabinet over the fridge before emerging with a bottle. "I knew a had some champagne up here somewhere. This is a celebration!" She popped the cork and bubbles and booze spilled out the top of the bottle and onto the floor.

"We're getting a townhouse?" Drew couldn't keep up. His heart was still shattered on the asphalt of a high school parking lot, and now visions of him and Benny sharing a bathroom clouded his mind.

"Not we—you and us. We—me and Benny. Just the two of us. Remember? I told you this was my chance for a new beginning." She poured three glasses of champagne and handed one to him and one to Benny.

Drew's stomach dropped. Cold settled through him, and his hands began to shake. He set the champagne flute on the counter.

He wasn't being forced to move in with a stranger.

He was being kicked out.

"Where am I supposed to go?" He hated the weakness and desperation in his voice.

"Honey," she lowered her glass and her face turned serious for the first time in the conversation, "you are eighteen. I know I am your mother, but I can't baby you forever. You've got to get out on your own. Make something of yourself. Chase that music dream of yours if you want." She patted him on the cheek lightly.

Drew nearly argued back, but he didn't have it in him.

He'd been supporting his mother for over a year, but she was somehow cutting him off. And she'd never looked happier. Maybe Benny really was good for her. He certainly seemed to love her. Smile lines creased the skin by his eyes, and he leaned across the counter to kiss her cheek.

"I guess this is congratulations then," Drew lifted his glass to them, but set it down on the counter without drinking any. He wandered to his room, or what was his room for the remainder of the week.

The floor shifted beneath his feet, and he landed on his bed.

One week. He had one week to find a place to live.

Drew couldn't afford a place on his own. He couldn't even afford this house, and it was rent controlled.

Drew rifled through his drawers until he found a fresh pen and went to work on his arms. Long strokes crossed over each other, black lines dragging behind and blending into the pools of ink staining his hands.

Ronny's parents might have a spare room, but Drew still wasn't speaking to Ronny, and even if he was, Ronny would be moving to California in a couple months. He couldn't live with a friend's parents if the friend wasn't even living there.

Cam had room and would say yes if he asked to stay with her, but she had a baby on the way. She had more than enough on her plate already. The last thing she needed was a bum friend to worry about as well.

Drew watched as the ink spread across his skin, swirling across veins and dipping between his fingers.

Drew's eyes swept over the band posters on his wall. Brigid had liked those.

His gut twisted at the thought of Brigid—of her and Mike together.

He threw his pen against the wall. He'd been so stupid to think life was finally lining up for him. It had been so close. For just a moment he'd almost believed he'd had a mom who gave a shit and a girl who'd wanted him regardless of his mess of a life. It was more than he ever should have let himself hope for.

He had to figure out where to live first though. Maybe Nate would let him crash there for a while, at least until Drew figured out a better plan. Mitch hated him, but maybe not enough to throw him out on the street.

Not like his own mother had.

He'd ask Nate about it.

Shit. Nate.

He'd been so distracted by Brigid and Mike and his mother, he'd forgotten his best friend had gone missing halfway through the day.

He bolted out of his room and raced to Nate's house.

***

Drew threw his car in park but left it running and ran to the door. He shoved it open without knocking. Mitch was nowhere to be seen.

Drew bolted down the stairs and into Nate's room.

Nate was curled up under a ratted blanket.

Not moving.

Drew shook him roughly, ignoring the racing in his chest and tightness in his throat.

"Nate!" Drew's voice was raspy and strained. Nate startled awake and sat up abruptly. Drew pushed his shaking hands against his eyes and stumbled back a step.

"What the hell, man? I was asleep." Nate chucked a pillow at Drew and returned to his previous position.

227

"Do you realize how terrified I was when you disappeared today? You scared the shit out of me." Drew's breathing was ragged.

"Why?" Nate remained in his bed, eyes closed.

"Because you promised me you'd be there today."

"I don't answer to you, Drew."

"I was just worried about you." Drew braced a hand on the doorframe. Nate was here. He was fine.

"Well don't be. I don't need you taking care of me."

"Someone has to." It was out before Drew could stop it. Nate stood from the bed, and Drew finally got a good look at him. His gut twisted.

Nate looked like shit. Physically, he'd seemed mostly normal at school, maybe a little worn, but this was a completely different Nate, like those hours in public had drained the life from him like a battery. His skin was sallow, and his hair lay limp around his face, much longer than he normally wore it. Anger darkened his dull eyes.

"What does that mean?" Nate spat. And something in Drew finally snapped.

"You've clearly been spiraling for weeks. I tried to talk to Mitch about it, but he's too much of an asshole to do anything. So, it falls to me to keep you in one piece until you can do it yourself. One more problem for me to deal with. I try not to push you, but you've lost control anyways."

Nate flinched and took a step toward Drew. His voice was low and threatening, nothing like anything Drew had ever heard from him. "I haven't lost control. And if I'm such a burden, then why the hell are you here? You think you can help everyone, but you can barely help yourself. Get your own life together before you try to run mine."

And there it was. The truth Drew had been burying deep down every time it reared its ugly head. He'd been trying to take care of his friends—Cam, Nate, Brigid, and even Ronny—but how could he help anyone when his own life was a disaster?

You can't fix other people if you are broken. And Drew was broken.

He'd fractured that day his dad had walked away. He'd cracked a little more every time his mom had chosen her life over his. Every unanswered call. Every dirty look and veiled comment about his father. He'd finally shattered the moment she'd told him he had to leave.

She was going to live her own life, and she didn't want him in it.

Just like Brigid didn't want him in hers.

Nate didn't even want him.

Nate was right. Drew thought he'd been helping, but he'd done nothing but been a burden and a bother to each of them. He'd hurt them all.

Drew retreated from Nate's room without another word. He climbed into his car, but idled in Nate's driveway. He had nowhere to go.

He had no one. He was completely alone.

Almost.

There was one more person, someone who needed him. It wasn't the best, but it was all he had now.

Drew pulled out his phone and dialed before he could

think twice. He answered on the first ring.

"Hello?"

"Hi, dad."

CHAPTER 22

If Elliott Cox had been surprised by his son's call, he'd hid it well. Within 24 hours, Drew was in Los Angeles in a ritzy high-rise apartment. His father had done well for himself.

The apartment had two bedrooms and a huge kitchen. A small laundry room was off the hallway bathroom, and the living area was big enough to boast a 70-inch flatscreen. This was practically a mansion in L.A.

Regardless of the high-end finishes and expensive furniture, the apartment was anything but homey. It reminded Drew of the room he'd stayed in at the Cosmopolitan. Everything was modern and sleek. There were no colors, just an array of blacks, whites, and grays. Art was displayed throughout the rooms, but nothing personal. A giant canvas painting of Los Angeles from above at night hung on the wall by the couch. Geometric shapes were a prominent theme. No people. No photos.

Elliott had offered the spare bedroom to Drew, and with nowhere else to go, he'd accepted. He'd brought almost nothing with him. A backpack of clothes and his guitar, just the one since he'd left his other with Brigid.

As he walked into the bedroom—his bedroom—he let his backpack fall to the floor and placed his guitar gently across the bed. Elliott's living room was equipped with all the latest music accessories including multiple top-of-the-line amps and pedal boards with more pedals than Drew had ever used. He'd have to mess around on those later.

His dad had filled him in on the job on the elevator ride up. Small band. 80s sound. Needed a new guitarist after their last guy decided to get married and move to Vermont. Apparently, they weren't all that famous, but Elliott swore they were the next big thing.

Drew slipped his phone from his pocket and stared at the screen. No notifications. He hadn't expected any. The only people who knew where he was were his mom and Cam.

His mom hadn't reacted as poorly as he'd expected. Although, as she was the one who'd made him homeless and told him to make something of himself, she couldn't have justified being all that upset.

He'd texted Cam from a gas station just south of Vegas.

Drew: *Leaving town for a while. Check in on Nate.*

It had been as much as he'd been willing to share. Opening himself to his friends hadn't turned out to be a good idea, but he also couldn't leave Nate alone in his condition. Someone had to know.

She'd responded immediately.

Cam: *Where are you going? What's wrong with Nate?*

Drew: *LA. Just keep an eye on him.*

This response took longer. He was halfway through the California desert when her text came through.

Cam: *What about Brigid?*

What about Brigid? He'd given her everything he'd had. He'd let her see as much of him and his messy life as he could. She'd taken it all in her own flawless way—until he'd pushed her too far and destroyed everything they'd built in a matter of moments.

Drew: *Tell her I'm sorry.*

He tossed his phone on the bed next to his guitars and walked back out to the overstuffed couch that screamed "wealthy bachelor." Elliott was on the phone again.

Drew used it as a chance to study his father. He'd been a broken child the last time he'd seen this man.

Not much had changed.

Elliott looked older though. His once dark hair, similar to Drew's own, now had a sprinkle of grey through it, more distinguished than old man-ish. Wrinkles creased the skin by his eyes, but overall, his face was the same, sharp jaw and dark eyes.

Drew didn't realize how much he'd grown to look like his father. No wonder his mom hated him.

Elliott hung up and called across the kitchen to Drew, "You hungry? I'm thinking Chinese."

Drew nodded, and Elliott made another call. He plopped into a chair across from Drew. After a moment, he set his phone face up on the coffee table between them. "So . . . you're eighteen, right?"

Drew nodded.

"Graduated?"

"Basically." Drew had enough credits to graduate. He'd make the call next week and get approval to make up his failed English online. Somehow the AP test that had seemed like such a big deal only two days ago no longer mattered.

"That's good. Graduation is an important step in a man's life. Closes one door so more can open." He sauntered to the fridge and emerged with a beer bottle. He offered one to Drew, but Drew shook his head. Elliott brought him a Coke instead.

"I noticed you brought a guitar with you. What do you got?"

Drew relaxed into the leather against his back. Music was a safe topic.

"Gibson Les Paul."

Elliott whistled. "That's an alright guitar for a kid your age. How'd you find yourself with one of those?" He took a swig from his bottle.

"Saved up."

"Well, that was a good call. Nothing better than a guitar worth playing."

The doorbell rang and Elliott swaggered to the front door, reappearing a moment later with more Chinese food than the two of them could eat in a week.

Drew reached for his wallet. He'd brought all the cash he'd had left with him, but at this rate it'd be gone in a matter of days.

Elliott waved a hand at him. "Don't worry about that.

This one is on me."

Drew paused. "You're going to pay for my meals?"

Elliott shrugged and took a large bite of an egg roll. "At least this one. I am your dad, right? Isn't that part of the job?"

So was not abandoning your family. Apparently, they were going to just pretend that hadn't happened.

Fine by Drew.

"You got a girlfriend?" Elliott asked between bites of chow mein.

Drew forked a piece of cashew chicken and ignored the question. He wasn't going to answer that. Elliott couldn't make a few calls, bring him to California, and suddenly expect Drew to be his son. That door had closed a long time ago. Drew didn't need a dad, just a manager.

And if Drew was being honest, he wasn't ready to face the answer to that question. Things had been great with Brigid. They'd only been together a couple weeks, but he'd been in love with her since he met her. She clearly didn't feel the same.

So, he'd left. He had no reason to stay. He needed a job and a place to live. Elliott had offered him both.

Elliott took Drew's silence as a no. "Well, that's probably good news anyway. You'll have girls all over you by the end of your first gig next week. You can take your pick of them. I always do." A slimy smile slithered through his words.

Drew would not have this conversation with Elliott. Appetite gone, he stood and walked to his room. Without turning back, he replied, "I'm not you." Elliott didn't respond before he closed his door.

***

"Fellas, meet your new lead guitarist. This is Drew." Elliott motioned to Drew with far too much exaggeration.

Drew's new band mates did not respond. Elliott took that as a signal that he should take over the introductions.

"This is Keith. Keith is lead vocals and guitar. He knows everything there is to know about music, and he's the best songwriter this side of Nashville." Keith nodded a hello, causing his curly brown hair to fall across his face. He was draped across the couch, one gangly leg hanging over the arm rest. Elliott had told him Keith was a few years older than Drew, but his curly hair and pointy chin made him look younger.

"Next to him is Calvin. Bass." Calvin looked like a Calvin. He sat up too straight on the couch by Keith, and his glasses slid slightly when he smiled. He stood briefly, long enough to shake Drew's hand at which point Drew caught a flash of a skull tattoo on his forearm. It seemed Calvin wasn't all he appeared to be.

"And, of course, your drummer, Fallon." Fallon sat on the opposite end of the room on a bar stool. Her long, black hair shimmered in the light as she sipped from a can of soda. She had a lot of olive skin showing in shorts and a sports bra, but Drew wondered if that was partially functional. He knew a lot of male drummers who played shirtless. Fallon raised one eyebrow like she knew what Drew was thinking. Drew looked away quickly.

"Drew's the best guitarist out there." Elliott beamed as

236

though he was somehow entitled to a piece of Drew's props. Whatever. Drew was never one for words of praise. He'd much rather prove himself.

"I got word that we are definitely opening at The Garage next Saturday. You all have a week to get Drew up to speed and ready to go. He's got the skill, just needs to play with you to get a feel for the style." Elliott flashed one last manager-smile and walked out the door, leaving Drew alone in a room of musical strangers.

"Let's get to work," Calvin said. He grabbed a case from behind the couch and removed a beautiful bass from inside.

"Everything you need to hook up is over there," Keith told Drew as he plugged his own guitar into an amp. Keith's guitar was one of those that was well-played but well-cared for. An American Fender if Drew was seeing correctly.

They were in a large warehouse that seemed to be half music studio and half apartment. The couch Keith and Calvin had been on was adjacent to a bar with stools and a fridge. On the other side of the space was all the equipment Keith had motioned to. A decent set-up. High quality, but nothing overly pricey. They were just starting out after all. Fallon eyed him as he tuned, and she took a seat behind her kit.

"You know a lot of classic rock?"

"Most of it."

"Then let's see what you got." A mischievous smile crept along her lips, and for the first time since Drew had arrived in Los Angeles, nerves fluttered through his stomach.

He'd wanted to play music so badly, and he'd had

nowhere else to go. He'd never considered this long enough to wonder if he was good enough.

Heat radiated from his neck as he slung his guitar strap around it and pulled a pick from his pocket.

Fallon counted off, and Drew immediately recognized the opening riff of Guns N' Roses "Sweet Child O' Mine" floating from Keith's guitar.

Drew listened for a few lines before joining. He needed to get a feel for their sound. Elliott had been right. They were good. Really good. Keith's voice had a raw edge and grit to it that was unusual but captivating. Calvin sang backup but could have held his own on lead. The bass and guitar blended perfectly, neither taking over the other.

And Fallon was a damn rockstar. Her drumsticks flew between her drums like fire, never stopping long enough to cool. Drew had been right about her lack of clothing being functional. She'd be in a full sweat by the end of the song.

All they needed was a kick-ass guitarist.

Drew let the sound fill him, breathing in the notes and the rhythm until it was a part of him and he could blend seamlessly with the sound.

They finished the song and immediately started another. Song after song, strung together with barely enough time to gulp down water and set for the next.

They played for nearly an hour before Keith let his guitar rest against his thigh. He gave Drew a once over before he spoke to the whole band.

"This is gonna work. I'll have a set list by tomorrow." He faced Drew, "I've got some ideas for altered chord progressions for you."

Drew spent every hour he could in the rehearsal space with Keith. If they weren't rehearsing with Calvin and Fallon, they were going over chord progressions and riffs.

Elliott hadn't lied about Keith's music abilities. He knew his stuff and had some incredible instincts. Drew liked him. He was chill but also didn't bullshit. He'd bluntly admit that something he'd try sounded like trash, or praise his own ideas if they panned out.

He reminded Drew of Nate.

Drew's thoughts drifted regularly to the phone in his pocket. He hadn't heard from his mom since he'd moved out. He'd considered calling her but decided against it. She'd made it very clear he was no longer a child and needed to do this on his own. He wasn't sure that a call from him only a few days later would be welcome.

He'd call after the gig on Saturday.

None of Drew's friends had called either. That was the greater surprise. He hadn't expected to hear from Brigid or Ronny. Or Nate after the way they'd left things. But he'd thought he'd at least get a text or call from Cam. Back home, she was constantly calling to tell him about the new releases on Netflix or to ask him what she should have for dinner. Sometimes he wondered if Cam was really that social or if, deep down, she was as lonely as he was.

Her parents were always traveling and she didn't have any siblings. She'd been in a relationship with Ronny and close friends with Nate and Brigid, but it seemed like if she wasn't with one of them, she was on the phone with Drew.

Which was why it was so strange he hadn't heard from her. Maybe she hated him too.

She could get in line.

"You okay, man?" Keith stared at him, brows drawn together.

He lifted his guitar back into his hands. "I'm fine. Let's run it again."

***

By Friday night, Drew had fresh callouses across his fingers. He'd played until they stung, but he was ready for the gig. Keith had signed off on the final set list and declared them ready to go for the following night. He said no practice Saturday morning. According to Keith, it was bad luck to practice the day of a show.

It was long after dark before Drew returned to Elliott's apartment. He dropped his keys on the counter and headed for the fridge to find leftovers. His eye caught movement out on the patio.

He found Elliott relaxing in a patio chair, amber drink in one hand. A large plate of sushi, easily enough for six people, sat on the table next to him as he peered out over the city.

Elliott's condo was near the top floor of a very tall high rise. The result was an incredible view. Rows of lights crossed over each other, some moving and others still. They chased each other until it looked like they dropped off the horizon, meeting a dark sky, empty of both clouds and stars.

"Drew! Come. Sit. Eat." Elliott motioned toward the chair across the small sushi-wielding table. Drew sat slowly

240

and took a California roll from the enormous platter.

Despite living with Elliott for nearly a week, they'd barely had more than passing conversations. Drew had spent every spare moment at the warehouse, and Elliott was generally gone late into the night.

"You guys ready for tomorrow night?" Elliott asked.

"Yup."

"I'm sure." Elliott uncrossed his leg and leaned forward, resting both elbows on his knees and pegging Drew with a contemplative look. "You know, I'm really glad you decided to take my offer. I'd hoped you would, but I was beginning to wonder before you called."

"I almost didn't." Drew took another roll from the tray.

"What was stopping you?"

"I had responsibilities back home."

"And now you don't?"

Drew shrugged. "Things change."

Elliott nodded slowly. "I'm glad you see that now."

"See what?" Drew asked.

Elliott leaned back into his seat. Drew had been living with Elliott for almost week now, but it had taken only hours to see how similar he was to his father. A stranger on the street could point them out as father and son. Drew looked like a younger version of Elliott. When Elliott wasn't in "manager mode" and plastering on a fake smile and charming persona, when he was the real Elliott, they had the same shadowed eyes, wicked grin, and dark chuckle. But it was more than that. It was the movement. The shrug. The crossed arms.

"Life changes. One day, you are on a path. You have responsibilities and certain priorities, and then that path changes. Suddenly you no longer want the responsibility of being a father and a husband. You realize you had the wrong life. And then you find a new life."

"That's why you left?"

"I was never meant to be a father. It wasn't what I wanted. But your mom wanted a kid, so. . ." He shrugged. "I stayed for years knowing it wasn't right. Eventually I knew I couldn't stay any longer. I needed to make my own choices and find the life I'd always wanted. The right life."

"The one we weren't in."

"It was never personal, Drew. I liked you, even as a kid. I always knew we'd be part of each other's lives again." Elliott took another drink and shoved a sushi roll into his mouth.

Drew watched Elliott. He'd always thought his father had left them because he didn't want them, but it was more than that. He hadn't wanted to be a father. He'd been given responsibilities he'd not signed up for, consequences for choices he didn't make. Something Drew knew too much about. Because of this man.

Consequences weren't stop and go. You couldn't just end a consequence. It was like the law of conservation they'd learned about in physics. Energy didn't ever die, it just changed. Consequences worked the same way.

Elliott hadn't outrun his consequences. He hadn't escaped. He'd just passed them on to the next man in line.

So, who the hell was now stuck with Drew's?

The Garage was a relatively small venue in downtown L.A., too small for the big names, but a great place for up and comers and some of the less well-known bands. The stage was large enough they'd be able to spread out without too much empty space. The crowd was mostly standing, but there was a bar along the back wall and a balcony with tables where people could sit, drink, and enjoy the music. The whole place was 21 and older, but even as they headed to the backroom, Drew passed plenty of people who were obviously still in high school.

The greenroom had a faded yellow couch, a white fridge, and a table with stools around it. The lights were dim enough to hide the filth but light enough to tune successfully. They'd each perched themselves on surfaces throughout the room, readying their instruments for the show. The band before them had been playing for nearly half an hour and should be off any minute. Drew itched to get onstage, but the others seemed calm.

Calvin was unrecognizable. He'd traded his polo and khakis for shredded jeans and a Metallica T-shirt. His hair, usually neatly combed, was rumpled and messy. He'd ditched his glasses, and Drew was pretty sure he was wearing eyeliner.

Fallon, on the other hand, looked exactly how she did at every practice. A black sports bra was all she wore on top, her smooth hair reaching most of the way down her back. The only differences were her black leggings and a significant increase in makeup. Her skin was shiny, and her eyes were shadowed in blues and purples. She twirled her drumsticks casually around her fingers.

Elliott burst through the door. "How's my favorite band?" The smile plastered on his face was large enough Drew could see nearly all his teeth. Drew held back a huff of air. Elliott's favorite band was U2, and it always would be. Drew remembered sitting in his dad's Mustang listening to Bono wail out "Sunday Bloody Sunday." But apparently, he'd spout whatever bullshit he needed to keep his paychecks happy.

"Who are these rookies? They're terrible," Keith answered without looking up from his strings.

Elliott shrugged. "They are learning. But they are nothing compared to you guys. This is their closer. The venue is ready for you to head back."

Drew wrapped his guitar strap over his shoulder and followed Fallon out the door. Elliott clapped him on the back as he walked past.

They wound through the dark halls before arriving in the wings. Black curtains hung around the space, dimming the area further. The air smelled like booze and sweat but pulsed with an energy he couldn't identify.

This was all he'd ever wanted.

But all he could think about was a fancy, new townhouse, a boy lying in bed unable to stand, and a girl with the most beautiful blue eyes he would ever see.

CHAPTER 23

The screams continued long after the final note faded and the band had disappeared from view.

Keith immediately packed up his guitar and weaved his way into the crowd. There'd be a gathering of girls somewhere in the sea of people, and he was determined to find them.

Calvin headed home.

Drew took a seat at the bar and sipped from a water bottle. Sweat soaked through his black T-shirt, and he considered following in Calvin's steps, if only to get to a shower, but he couldn't bring himself to go back to Elliott's apartment just yet.

Playing on that stage had been everything Drew had thought it would be. He'd played small gigs back home: coffee shops, background music and such. But he'd never played like this. This was the real deal. And the crowd had loved them.

They'd already been booked to come back the next weekend—headlining.

Elliott had been thrilled when he'd delivered the news.

He was waiting in the wings when they left the stage, eyes ablaze and smile plastered. Then he'd disappeared into the crowd with his arm around a girl who was much closer to Drew's age than his own.

Drew hadn't seen him since. Another reason he didn't really want to go back.

Fallon slunk onto the stool to Drew's right. The bartender immediately brought her a drink. Drew huffed a laugh. He'd waited ten minutes to get his water. Apparently, the bartender was a little more interested in a hot, drummer chick than in him.

Fallon scrutinized Drew without shame as she sipped her drink. He wasn't sure if he should watch her back or not. That seemed a little predatory, but he couldn't just ignore her either.

She saved him the choice by finally saying something. "Why are you sitting here? This how you celebrate?" She nodded at his water and raised her eyebrows.

"I could ask you the same."

"Ah, but mine is a little stronger than yours. Celebratory alcohol." She lifted the glass of clear liquid. Drew wasn't sure she was even old enough to drink legally, but it wasn't his job to police the bar. "To you, Drew Cox."

Drew raised an eyebrow. "Elliott told you I'm his . . ."

"He didn't have to," Fallon smiled her wicked smile, "I'm not an idiot. But you clearly aren't like him or you'd already have a girl in your lap."

"I guess not then."

"So why don't you?"

"Why don't I what?"

"Have a girl in your lap. That's what Keith always does after a show. And Elliott. And Brian before he left the band. There're probably fifty girls in here that would love to go home with you. You're hot, and you crushed it up there. Girls love a guy who plays the guitar." Fallon continued to sip her drink. She spun on her stool and leaned her back into the edge of the bar, eyes scanning the crowd before her. Goosebumps covered her shoulders and arms. Apparently is wasn't nearly as warm in here once you were out of the lights. "What about her? She's already undressing you with her eyes."

She motioned to a group of girls at the other side of the bar. The one on the end had been staring at Drew for a few minutes, but Drew had been adamantly avoiding her gaze. She was cute, with freckles speckling her pert nose and purple glasses that made her eyes look especially large, but Drew wasn't interested in anyone in this room. Or state.

"I think I'll pass tonight."

Fallon returned to staring at him. She was much too perceptive. Her eyes thinned as she studied him, like she could read his thoughts as easily as she could read the drink menu.

"You have a girlfriend?" she asked.

"Nope." Drew spun the water bottle lid back and forth. He should have grabbed a pen before he'd left.

"Oh, I see." Fallon's smooth grin slowly reappeared. "You're getting over someone."

Drew sipped his water but said nothing. He didn't want to have this conversation. Maybe he should order something a little stronger.

"Mmm," Fallon hummed, "then you are going about it all wrong, lover-boy. The best way to get over someone is to find someone new, even if it's just for a night. New lips. Different skin. Fresh sheets." She set her drink on the bar.

"Thanks for the advice, but I don't need some stranger in my bed to feel better." In fact, the idea alone made him queasy. How had he ever been with anyone else the first time Brigid was with Mike? The idea seemed ludicrous now.

"Then pick someone who isn't a stranger." Fallon's dark eyes burned straight through him. She leaned in and her long, slim fingers slid through his hair. "It doesn't have to mean anything."

Drew closed his eyes, hating every inch of himself for how good it felt to be touched. He slowly brought a hand to her waist. Her skin was cool and his hands immediately craved more.

Now he remembered. This is why he'd been with all those other girls. Fallon could help him forget everything.

Her lips brushed against his jaw, and Drew stepped off his stool and against her, still sitting higher up on her own. Her eyes met his for just a moment before their lips crashed against each other, desperate for distraction. They were all heat, lips, and teeth. Nothing soft or tender between them.

She tightened her grip and pushed against his chest. He ran his hands down her back, his callouses brushing her bare skin.

But it was all wrong. Her lips, her skin, her taste. None of it was what Drew really craved, it was just that: a distraction. Just like Matias had used on that stage in Vegas.

Fleeting enjoyment that would keep his mind occupied followed by regret and emptiness when he realized it meant nothing. Just like those girls Drew had dated while he waited for Brigid the last year.

He pulled back as quickly as he'd fallen in. Fallon's eyes shot open. Her chest rose and fell in heavy breaths that matched Drew's. He shook his head.

"I can't, Fallon. It's not you." He swallowed. "It's her."

Fallon smiled knowingly. "Then why the hell are you here?"

***

The condo lights were on when Drew entered at nearly three in the morning. He dropped his keys on the counter and noticed a woman's purse sitting at the other end.

Lovely.

Drew carried his guitar into his room and pulled his phone from the pocket of the case. He never checked his phone during shows, but he knew he wouldn't have missed anything. His phone hadn't buzzed all week.

He nearly dropped his guitar as he unlocked his phone to find six missed calls and at least ten texts.

Cam.

Something must have happened. His heart dropped as he listened to voicemail after voicemail.

Nathan. Missing. Dam. Ambulance. Hospital. Still alive.

Cam hadn't been descriptive, but Drew could put the pieces together.

249

Drew dropped into a chair, head spinning. He'd done this. He'd left when he'd known. He'd known Nate was sick. That he needed help. He'd tried to make himself feel better by warning Cam, but she didn't know. No one knew what had happened all those years ago when Nate had spiraled. What he'd tried to do one night. That until he found help, he'd been a suicide risk. Worse. And that he still was.

Drew had to leave, to get to Nate. If he left right now, he could drive straight through the night and be there by evening. It might not be too late.

Drew grabbed his backpack from where it was slung over the back of his chair. Guitar in the other hand, he headed for the door.

Elliott and his guest, the girl from the venue, had made their way to the balcony, each trying not to spill a glass of wine as they shoved their tongues down each other's throats.

Drew pocketed his keys and opened the fridge. He loaded a few water bottles, energy drinks, and protein bars in his backpack and zipped it closed.

"I'm going back," he called to Elliott, who was still making out on the balcony behind him.

Elliott broke away from his girl. He was wrapped in a navy blue, silk robe and still held a glass of wine.

"What do you mean you're going back?" Elliott asked.

"They need me at home."

Elliott staggered into the condo and toward Drew before remembering they had an audience. "Babe," he called out to the woman behind him, still looking at Drew, "Why don't you take that drink back to the bedroom? I'll meet you there in a minute." The girl shrugged and left them alone.

"She old enough for that drink?" Drew planted his feet, ready for whatever Elliott would throw at him to keep him here.

"She's 23, alright? It's all legal," Elliott responded, "Now what do you mean they need you in Idaho?"

"Something's happened. I have to go."

Elliott's anger contorted his normally handsome features. "I thought we talked about this, Drew. You get to choose. You get to decide what and who you want in your life."

Drew turned to leave but froze as Elliott's next words hit him in the back as hard as if he'd thrown an actual knife.

"I'm your father, and the only family you have left."

Years of anger, fear, and pain crashed down around Drew. Suddenly he was twelve and trying to explain to his mother that dad had left. Watching her sit on the floor crying while he could do nothing to bring back the man who had hurt them both. Years of emotional damage and financial struggle because the man who had promised to take care of them both had decided he had a better life to live. They hadn't been what he wanted.

Until Drew could serve a purpose. Until he needed Drew to be there for him, to help his career.

Words flew through Drew's head. All the things he'd wanted to say to his father over the years. The "how could you's" and "why would you's" that had built up. Explaining just how terrible life had been since Elliott had left.

But it hadn't all been terrible. He'd had Nate. And Cam

and Ronny. And Brigid. They'd been there. They'd stood by him through all of it. Even when his mom left, he'd known they would have taken him in. Any one of them. They'd been all the family he'd ever needed.

And he'd left them. Abandoned them in their time of need.

Drew looked his father over. And he let it all go. He didn't need this man in his life to feel like he belonged to someone.

"I choose them." Drew picked up his bag and guitar and left.

His family needed him.

***

Drew listened to Cam's messages again once he was in the car and on the road. It was hard to string together what had happened based on her broken thoughts and scattered retelling, but Drew caught pieces between sobs.

Nate was missing.

Cops were looking.

He was found.

He's in the hospital.

It's bad but he's still alive.

Drew laid into the gas pedal. There were no cars in sight in the middle of the California desert, and every minute mattered.

Drew slammed his hand against the steering wheel and wiped the moisture from his eyes.

He'd done this. There was no one to blame but him.

He'd been the one who knew what was happening, who could find Nate the help he needed. Mitch hadn't believed him. Cam didn't know that part of Nate's life. It was up to Drew.

And he'd left. He'd torn Nate apart about it and then left him. For what? Elliott?

Elliott wasn't the same man who'd driven away six years ago, but he was no better. He still saw family as a burden, people who held you back and pulled you down. In some cases that may be true, but not the family Drew had left behind: Nate, Brigid, Cam, and Ronny. The family he'd chosen for himself.

Drew's stomach swirled as he pictured Nate dying a hospital bed somewhere, and he pulled over just in time to lose the contents of his stomach on the side of the road.

Nate was going to be okay. He would get through this.

Drew drove straight through the night, only stopping for gas, and arrived at the hospital an hour earlier than he'd expected. He parked in visitor parking and burst through the main doors. Inside was a large, steel and glass reception desk. People raced around him, each on their way to find their own loved ones. Drew approached the man sitting behind the desk. A brief conversation ended with Drew headed to a waiting room on the third floor.

The elevator ding announced his arrival, and the doors opened to reveal a white tile path leading in both directions. To the left, the path curved around a corner to some unknown location, but to the right it led down a hall to a set of large glass doors with signs that read "Authorized Personnel Only." Across from the door was an open seating area with three rows of blue chairs that stretched from wall to wall and a smaller version of the glass and steel desk from downstairs.

Drew hesitated before stepping out. He'd been so focused on Nate, he hadn't thought about the other faces that would meet him here.

Cam looked up from her phone as he walked in. Her eyes were puffy, and dark smudges revealed her lack of sleep. Brigid laid across a few chairs, her head in Cam's lap, hair draped across her face. Drew's chest tightened painfully.

Mr. Lankford sat a few seats down the same row, staring blankly at the wall ahead of him. His face was pale and void of any emotion.

Ronny was on the other side of the waiting room, sleeping with his head against a wall. Had they all been up all night too? From the looks of it, everyone was exhausted.

"You came," Cam said. It was somehow both a question and a statement.

"You didn't think I would?"

She shrugged. "I wasn't sure."

"You called." He took a seat on her empty side.

"I thought you'd want to know."

"Any news?" Drew asked. He swallowed hard, terrified of the answer. "How is he?"

"Not sure yet. He's been back there for hours, but they haven't made any promises yet."

Brigid shifted, and Drew waited to make sure she was still asleep before speaking again, quieter than before. "What happened?"

Cam's voice was barely a whisper. "I went to see him

yesterday morning. Oh, God. I can't believe that was only yesterday. He hadn't been at school all week, and he didn't return any of my texts or calls Friday, so I thought I'd check in. When I got to his house, there were cops there, and Mr. Lankford was freaking out. Nathan had been missing when Mr. Lankford got up that morning. No note or text. Just gone.

"We waited for a bit, but couldn't stand just sitting around, so we started looking too. It was almost dark before Nathan was found. He'd gone to the dam." Fresh tears filled her eyes. "He was nearly dead when the ambulance arrived. They brought him here, and we've been waiting since."

"He'll make it." Drew squeezed Cam's hand. Cam blinked and gazed at the glass doors across from them. "Who found him? Mitch?"

"Ronny."

Drew's eyes flew to the boy sitting alone in the corner of the waiting room. Ronny's clothes were covered in dirt. He was technically an adult, but at this moment he looked like a little kid. A kid who'd saved the life of Drew's best friend.

"He'd heard about the search and had just known Nathan would go to the dam. He went straight there and found him unconscious by the water. Ronny carried him all the way back to the road to meet the ambulance." She wiped a tear away and leaned her head on Drew's shoulder.

"Get some sleep," Drew whispered into her hair, "I'll wake you up if we learn anything." Cam nodded sleepily and closed her eyes.

"You came," she breathed, already drifting off.

***

255

Nurses walked in and out of the waiting room, never with any updates, but Drew's heart raced every time.

Mitch sat silently a few seats from Drew. Cam, Brigid, and Ronny were all still asleep. Drew had gotten another energy drink from his backpack, careful not to wake Cam in the process. He was going on thirty-two hours without sleep and had no intention of sleeping until they got word that Nate was going to be okay.

Beeping came and went from somewhere behind the glass doors. A new receptionist started her shift. People came and went. Still nothing.

Drew was about ready to go find Nate himself. He had to be back there somewhere, and Drew was done waiting.

A doctor in dark purple scrubs and a white coat emerged from the glass doors.

"Mr. Lankford?" she called.

Mitch started at the sound then rushed to her side, and the two disappeared behind the doors.

"You have got to be kidding me." Cam sat up from his shoulder, and Brigid stirred on her lap. "They aren't going to tell us?"

"I don't think they can, technically. They tell the family, and then the family tells who they want," Brigid yawned.

Drew avoided looking at her. They could deal with that mess later. His focus was all on Nate right now.

Drew heard steps from behind and found Ronny pacing back and forth in front of his row. He rubbed at his neck, but stopped when he caught Drew watching him and slunk back into his seat.

Minutes dragged on until Mitch reemerged from the doors, face still blank.

Drew shot to his feet. Cam rushed at Mitch so quickly she nearly knocked him over.

"Is he okay?" she blurted.

Mitch met her eyes, all pain. Drew braced for the worst.

Mitch nodded. "He's still unconscious, but he's going to make it." He locked eyes with Drew for a moment before disappearing behind the doors.

Cam sunk to the floor as sobs wracked her whole body. Brigid kneeled next to her and rubbed her back, wiping her own tears from her cheeks.

Ronny slunk back into his chair for the second time and let his head fall into his hands.

Drew stood frozen in place watching his friends, his family, fall to pieces.

Nate was going to live.

Numbness flooded Drew's body, and he fell back into his chair. His chest ached and his shoulders tightened as he held back his own grief-choked sobs.

Nate was going to live.

CHAPTER 24

Cam and Brigid went in search of food after Cam mumbled something about throwing up from hunger. Pregnancy sounded terrible.

They disappeared around the corner on the other side of the elevator, leaving Drew alone with Ronny in the waiting room. He hadn't seen Ronny, aside from brief passings at school, since he'd torn into him about Cam. It had weighed on him since then, but he hadn't expected to get the chance to apologize face to face.

Drew drug himself over to Ronny's row of chairs and sat, leaving an empty space between him and Ronny.

"Hey." He wasn't sure Ronny would even talk to him, but he'd talk either way. Ronny only had to listen.

"Hey." Ronny's voice was strained, tired from lack of sleep and raspy from sitting in silence for the last twenty something hours.

"I'm sorry about what happened. I had no right to lay into you about announcing the pregnancy. It's between you and Cam, and honestly, I was letting some other stuff get to me and took it out on you."

Ronny blinked at him. "You're apologizing to me?"

"I was a dick."

"You were a dick. But I'm still surprised. I'm the one that owes you an apology. I was an ass back in Vegas and didn't handle things the way I should have."

"Sounds like you should be making that apology to someone else."

Ronny focused on the glass doors leading to Nate, his eyes full of pain, shoulders curled in. "I almost didn't get the chance to."

"You will."

"I will." Ronny sat back up and eyed Drew from the side. "I figured it out, by the way." Drew raised an eyebrow in question. "I didn't tell Kaitlyn about Cam, but I figured out how she knew."

"Who told her?"

"Technically me, but it was an accident. Remember how I had that meeting with my counselor at school that day?"

Drew nodded.

"Well, the meeting was to discuss scholarship options for people with families. Options that might cover things like off-campus housing or help with living expenses. I realized a few days later that Kaitlyn is a TA in the counseling center during the time I had my meeting. She must have overheard it."

It made sense. Drew had thought at the time it was out of character for Ronny to hurt Cam that way, and Kaitlyn is just the kind of person who would love snooping on people's private moments to get a bite of the most recent gossip.

Now he felt even worse about biting Ronny's head off. It really had been an accident. And to try to get help with being a father.

"Wait. What do you mean by "a family"? Are you and Cam . . . ?" Cam hadn't said anything about being engaged, but Drew also hadn't spoken to her in over a week.

"No, she still wants nothing to do with me. I spoke to her a few weeks ago, and she said she forgave me for how I acted, but that she couldn't be with someone who didn't trust her. I don't know how to show her I do. I just reacted poorly to shocking news."

"But you want to marry her?"

Ronny nodded. "We're young to be married, but we're also young to be parents, and we're going to figure that out." He looked at his hands, clasped in front of him. "I love her. I want to spend the rest of my life with her. And our kid."

Drew scrutinized Ronny. His brows drawn together created a deep wrinkle between them, and he frowned at the floor.

"That's really what you want? Because if someday you decide you no longer want that life, the wife and kid, you can't just walk away without leaving the shattered remnants of that family behind you."

"I know, Drew." Ronny clapped him on the shoulder.

Ronny was a better man at eighteen than Elliott had ever been.

Mitch emerged from the glass doors, looking better

than he had since Drew had arrived at the hospital. Color was starting to come back to his face, and his eyes were actually focusing.

"He's awake. Tired, but awake. He's asking for Drew."

***

Drew followed Mitch down a long hall with rows of doors on both sides. Cleaner fumes filled the air, and the lights were too bright. They slowed as they rounded a corner, and Mitch motioned to the second door on their right.

"I'm going to go find some food while the two of you talk. Let him know I'm still here, would ya?"

Drew nodded, and Mitch headed back the way they'd come.

He was suddenly very nervous. What do you say to your best friend who you'd abandoned when they needed you most?

Drew slowly edged into the room. As he took it in, he was glad he hadn't eaten anything. He likely would have thrown it right back up on the floor of that room.

Nate lay in the bed, hooked to half a dozen monitors. Wires and tubes lined the bed, and an IV dripped fluid into his arm. Nate's eyes were closed, and his head rested against the mound of pillows propping him up. Dark smudges lined his eyes and made him look like a different person. And he was pale. So, so pale.

Drew dropped into a chair at the foot of the bed. He'd done this. He'd caused Nate to look like this. Even knowing the truth, it hadn't sunk in the way it did as he surveyed Nate in this room.

He'd almost died.

Nate opened his eyes. The rest of him stayed still. Drew just stared at him. He couldn't form words, but he couldn't look away either.

Nate didn't seem to expect anything. They just sat there. But Nate found his voice first.

"I'm sorry." He whispered. His voice was raspy and weak.

"Why the hell are you sorry? I did this. It's my fault." Drew dropped his head into his hands.

"Drew, look at me." He made himself meet Nate's eyes. "You did not do this. I did this."

"But I drove you to it. I said all that screwed up stuff and then left. I knew you were hurting, and I deserted you." Drew's gut twisted, and he again thought he might throw up.

It took a minute for Nate to respond.

"I've been struggling for a long time. Things have been getting worse the last few months. I should have gotten help, but I told myself it wasn't happening. I didn't want to go down that road again."

Drew shook his head. "You should rest. We don't have to do this now."

"I do." Nate took a sip of water before continuing. "It finally got so bad that I finally gave up. I didn't think I could take it for another day. I felt trapped. I decided things would be better for everyone if I was gone. I didn't see the truth of things until I was dying in that canyon. By then, I couldn't stop it. I'd gone too far. The doctor said that if Ronny had found me even a few minutes later, I'd be dead."

A tear slid down his cheek, and Drew realized that his own were wet as well. He clasped Nate's hand in both of his.

"But I'm ready now. I'm ready to live. I'm ready to be the real me." A small smile lit up Nate's face.

"You're going to come out?" Drew asked. He'd never said the words out loud before. Nate had never wanted him to, not since the day Nate came out to Drew two years ago. He'd been confused and more than a little scared. He'd told Drew he was terrified that admitting he was gay would change their friendship. It never had.

Cam was the only other person who knew. Nate came out to her not long after Drew. He'd given her permission to tell Ronny when he started noticing how jealous Ronny was of their relationship, but Cam refused. She said it was a piss-poor reason for him to come out and that she'd rather lose Ronny than force that on Nate.

And she had.

"Soon. Not yet, but soon." Nate closed his eyes and another tear slid down his cheek. "I miss my mom."

"I know." There was nothing more for Drew to say.

They sat quietly for a few minutes before Nate opened his eyes again.

"You were in California." Nate stated it like he just now was remembering a fact buried deep down.

"Yes, I was."

"But you are here now." Nate glanced around the room as though looking for answers that he might have left sitting on a shelf somewhere. His brows drew close together.

"You came back."

"Of course, I came back. What is it with everyone?" Drew reached for the pen in his pocket and clicked the lid. "I came as soon as I heard."

"But what about California?" Nate asked.

"Overrated."

Drew told Nate all about Los Angeles. He talked about the band and the gig and even Elliott. Nate laughed when Drew told him about walking out on his father.

"It was about time that bastard got shut down," Nate smirked.

A small knock on the doorframe announced a timid nurse.

"I'm sorry gentlemen, but I really couldn't hold her off much longer."

They heard her before they saw her.

"Which door? This one? I get to see him. I have been waiting forever."

Cam stormed in and put both hands on her hips. She shot Drew a look with those giant eyes. "You have been in here for an eternity. It is *my* turn."

Cam didn't wait for a response before climbing into bed next to Nate and burying her face in his shoulder. Drew chuckled when Nate's eyebrows shot up in surprise. But he wrapped his arms around her and held her close to him.

Drew waited until they both drifted off to sleep before leaving. They would be fine that he didn't say goodbye.

Not goodbye. See you soon.

***

The vending machine ate his first dollar, but Drew was so tired he tried a second one without even thinking and it worked. He was sipping another energy drink a few moments later when Brigid arrived at the machine, her hand full of quarters.

Drew stood back to let her get to the machine, and a few buttons later, she was twisting the top off a Diet Coke.

"Diet, huh?" Drew asked.

A half-smile fought its way through Brigid's restraint. "You got me hooked. Normal soda is too syrupy now."

"Told you." Drew let his own smile in just a little.

They nodded awkwardly. What do you say in this situation?

Hey, how's that asshole you chose over me?

Brigid spoke first. "How is California?"

"It was fine. Nothing too exciting."

"When do you head back?" Her icy eyes bore into him, and the pain was unreal. Drew swallowed hard.

"I'm not going back. I'm home for good."

"Oh," Brigid drew back, "I guess I didn't realize it was just a short-term deal. Cam made it sound like a more permanent move. And you didn't say anything . . ." She drifted off, not stating the obvious. She bit her lip.

They watched each other, unable to say anything but unwilling to move on. It had only been a week, but she somehow looked different. Guarded.

Thanks to him.

Someone cleared their throat behind him, and he took a step away from Brigid.

Cam and Ronny stood at the edge of the waiting room.

Cam's eyebrows were raised and her arms folded. Ronny had a deep look of confusion.

He didn't know. Why would he? He'd been MIA since before anything had happened with Brigid.

"Visiting hours are over. They said we can come back in the morning," Cam said. Her judgmental stare said much more.

As they wandered to the elevator, a hand clasped Drew's shoulder. Mitch motioned for Drew to follow him, and they stepped out of hearing of the others.

Mitch clasped his hands together nervously.

"I'm glad I caught you before you took off. I heard your mom moved out last week. You got a place to stay tonight?"

Drew hid the shame barreling through him. Of course, word had spread through the neighborhood that she'd moved. Luckily, none of his friends seemed to know.

"I'm staying here tonight," Mitch shifted on his feet. "If you need a place to stay for a bit, you're welcome to stay with us." He locked eyes with Drew for a moment—an apology and an understanding.

Despite his issues with Mitch, Drew appreciated the offer. And he'd probably take him up on it. He had nowhere else to go.

Drew nodded and followed his friends into the elevator. They wound their way through the rows of cars until they approached Cam's.

Cam folded her arms and leaned against her car door. "I need to talk to Drew."

She scowled at him, and Drew sighed heavily. Apparently, he wasn't done with unpleasant conversations for the day.

Ronny eyed them both before gesturing a few spots down.

"I can take you home, Brigid." She nodded, and Drew watched them climb into Ronny's parents' minivan. He couldn't help noticing Cam's eyes follow Ronny's movements.

Drew leaned against the car beside Cam as the van disappeared into traffic.

"I'm mad at you." She kicked a rock on the pavement.

"I'm sorry I left you without saying goodbye," Drew muttered. He'd never been very good with apologies.

"You should be." Cam rubbed her arms. It wasn't a cold night, but she was probably still recovering from shock. Drew shrugged off his hoodie and handed it to her. She slid her arms through the sleeves. "But that's not why I'm pissed at you."

"It's not?" Drew leaned his head back against Cam's car and thought through all the stupid things he'd done in the last week. There was a lot.

"You hurt Brigid." Cam looked at him expectantly.

"Brigid?" Drew crossed his arms and straightened his back. "I shouldn't have made out with her."

Cam scoffed. "Of course, you should have. But you also should have said goodbye when you took off."

"I mean, I guess, but I didn't really think I owed her one."

"You didn't think you owed her a goodbye? After all

that had happened with you two?"

"Sure, but she definitely didn't feel the need to say goodbye to me. She sent Mike to do it."

Cam's brows pulled together. "What are you talking about?"

Drew rubbed his temples. This conversation was doing nothing for his sleep-deprived brain. "The day I left. She sent him to tell me. He met me after school to fill me in on how they'd gotten back together. The panic attack, all of it. Then I called you. You confirmed it. How do you not remember any of this?" Cam was no longer leaning against her car. Her face dropped and her hands slid into her hair.

"I confirmed that Mike had *caused* her panic attack that day. He was waiting for her outside her classroom and tried to make a move. Apparently, he'd seen you two making out in the parking lot and decided that meant he was owed something similar. He was a dick. We left. That's it."

Drew froze in place. Red blurred his vision and blood pounded in his ears.

Mike had gone after Brigid only minutes after they'd been together. Drew was going to kill him.

But if that's really what happened, then—

"Then they aren't together?" he asked, not caring about the desperation in his voice.

"No," Cam shook her head, hair falling out of the knot she'd tied. "They never got back together."

"So, she thinks that I just—" Drew couldn't even finish the thought.

"Yes, she thinks you took off without a word and left

her behind," Cam all but shouted.

He'd ruined everything. He'd promised her he wouldn't hurt her. He'd promised. And then he'd been so stupid to believe that asshole. He'd left without even talking to her.

He had to fix it. Now.

"Go." Cam smiled at him. "Get her back. She deserves that."

He nodded once and rushed to his car. The sun was setting, but it was still early enough for a stop.

CHAPTER 25

He reached Brigid's house just as the sun sank behind the mountains and cast a shadow over the valley.

Drew rushed to the door and pushed the bell before he had a chance to think through what he was going to say. She'd never forgive him, and he probably didn't deserve it. But he had to explain. He had to tell her what happened.

Footsteps sounded from inside the door, and Drew's entire body stiffened. Mr. Foster appeared. As he realized who was at his door, his jaw tightened and he somehow grew at least 6 inches.

"Why are you here, Drew?" Mr. Foster pulled the door closed as much as possible without completely shutting it.

"I just need to talk to her." Drew was ready to beg if he had to. He'd swallow every last bit of his pride if he could even slightly ease the pain he'd caused Brigid.

"Why?" Those warm eyes and friendly smile were nowhere to be seen.

"I made a huge mistake. I just need to tell her I'm

sorry." Drew didn't break eye contact. He let Mr. Foster see him for what he was. No mask. Just a kid who'd do anything to see the girl he loved.

Mr. Foster said nothing. He looked Drew up and down, taking in all he saw. Drew knew he looked terrible. He'd driven all night and spent the day in the hospital. A few short naps in the waiting room was all the sleep he'd had in two days.

Mr. Foster closed the door without a word. So that was it. Maybe Drew could catch her at school next week or something. But Drew wouldn't be at school. He'd called and switched to online school a few days ago.

Drew slunk onto the top step and let his head fall into his hands. He'd junked everything up. She'd said yes. They were going on a date. He was sure she'd been into him. And he'd let all of it burn because he'd been so sure that no one could ever want him.

"Drew?"

Drew shot up from the step, losing his balance and catching himself against the railing. There she was. Even a week without her had been torture. But that was nothing compared to the pain that tore through him as he saw her now, knowing he had pushed her away.

"My dad said you needed to talk to me." Lines creased her brows and her eyes widened. Beautiful ice blue eyes. She pulled a hair band off her wrist and twisted it between her fingers.

Drew nodded slowly. He wasn't sure where to start. The beginning.

"I need to tell you a story." He motioned toward the step. They sat together, and Drew told her everything. He told her about his father leaving. About supporting his mom for the last year. He told her about the calls from his dad. His mom kicking him out.

He told her about meeting her the first time and his devastation at finding out she was dating someone. He told her about what he'd thought had happened that day at school with Mike. How he'd left town to chase a dream because he'd thought the dream that had been here was over. He told her about the band and the gig. About Elliott.

She listened to every word. She never spoke, but Drew knew she was listening.

When he'd finished his story, they sat in silence. His emotional exhaustion had overtaken any physical weariness he'd been fighting earlier. He slid his hands over his face and sighed deeply. Brigid still hadn't said a word. Maybe she wanted him to leave. Drew stood and walked down the steps. He turned back when he got to the bottom.

"Brigid, I never meant to hurt you. I left because I thought you had found someone else who made you happy, and I couldn't bear to watch. I thought I'd lost every reason to stay. But I was miserable in California. I missed Nate, and Cam, and Ronny. I missed *you*. I'm not here to ask you out again. I just wanted to say I'm so sorry I hurt you."

Brigid stood slowly and edged her way down the steps, stopping on the one just above the one Drew stood on. She was just slightly taller than him with the added step. She folded her arms awkwardly behind her back.

"You thought I was happy without you?" She gazed at him through her long lashes, reading him as openly as one of her books.

Drew nodded once.

"So, you left." The sting of those words cut through Drew. But he had to finish this. Had to let her see all of him. No walls.

"I will never forgive myself for giving you up. I should have stayed. I should have trusted you."

Before Drew could register, Brigid pushed her lips against his. It took him less than a second to respond. He wrapped his arms around her waist and pulled her against him. She moved her hands up his chest and grabbed his shirt in her fists, pulling him in as well.

Drew couldn't think straight.

This girl.

He couldn't get enough of her.

He couldn't breathe, but he didn't care. He let his hands move up her back and into her hair. He deepened their kiss, and Brigid met him with passion of her own—an urgency he hadn't expected, like the last week had been hell for her too.

The porch lights flickered, and Drew pulled away, immediately cold and empty. Brigid glanced back toward the house and held up a finger to say she'd be in in a minute.

"I guess Dad wants me to go in."

Drew only nodded, still processing what had just happened.

"See you tomorrow." She took a step toward the door and paused. "Thank you, Drew, for telling me." She slipped into the house.

Drew walked back to his car, head in a daze and hands hanging loosely by his sides.

***

Walking into Nate's bedroom was eerie. Just over a week ago, Drew had been in this room and seen the messy piles and discarded trash.

Now it was spotless. Empty. Deserted. Like a hotel room after the tenant has checked out.

Seeing Nate's room so sterile and detached made Drew realize just how close he'd come to losing him. A lump formed in his throat, and his fingers went numb. He wasn't sure he'd ever move past feeling responsible for what happened.

Drew wandered around the room, looking but scared to touch, like he'd somehow crack the life that was already so fragile.

Nate's chargers were wrapped in tight spirals, hanging in their place above the workshop. The stack of tablets, phones, and laptops were organized neatly in their bin. The dirty clothes and empty cans were gone.

Sitting on Nate's desk, the only things out of place in the room, were two photos. Drew picked up the first and recognized it immediately. It was one of Cam's Polaroids, taken the previous summer.

All five of them were at the lookout at Second Dam. Nate held the camera, arm extended to get everyone in the shot. Ronny stood behind Cam, arms wrapped around her waist. Brigid and Drew were on either side. They were happy. No one had any idea the mess that was headed their way.

Drew caught a glimpse of something scrawled on the back in Nate's sloppy handwriting.

The whole fam

Nate may have a long road ahead of him, but he had some things figured out way before Drew.

Drew set the picture back on the desk and picked up the other.

He recognized the woman smiling at the camera. She was much younger than Drew remembered her, but the little boy version of Nate sitting on her lap identified it as being taken years before the cancer took Mrs. Lankford.

Nate looked much more like his mom than his dad. They had the same straight smile, blonde hair, and even from the picture you could see she had the same charm that Nate always exuded.

She'd been a good mother.

Drew slowly set the photo down by the first. He fought off a yawn and eyed the bed longingly, but turned and climbed back up the stairs and out the door.

He had one more person he needed to see.

***

Drew knocked quickly and took a step back, gluing his feet to the porch. He'd nearly turned around twice on the way over. He hadn't been invited, but he didn't need an invitation to visit his mom, right?

Benny answered the door and greeted Drew with a

warm smile and an invite into the townhome.

It was even nicer than Drew had expected. His mom's job must be paying pretty well. And Benny was probably bringing in more than an eighteen-year-old delivering food on nights and weekends.

"Good to see you. Your mom said you'd gone to California. Didn't think you'd be back any time soon." He motioned to the faded leather couch for Drew to sit and called up the stairs, "Steph! Drew's here!"

"Drew?" His mom was at the top of the stairs a second later. Drew's mouth fell open at the sight of her.

She looked great. Her hair was pulled up and clean. Her clothes looked fresh, maybe even new. Her skin glowed, and her eyes were clear and bright.

She shuffled down the stairs, and she and Benny each took a seat in a set of matching armchairs across from Drew.

"What are you doing here? California didn't pan out?" Her words sounded less spiteful now than they had last time he'd returned early from a trip. She sounded . . . disappointed.

"I decided I wanted to be here." Drew clicked the pen in his pocket.

His mom's throat bobbed, and she looked at her hands. "How is he?"

Drew wasn't sure how to answer. Was there something he could say that would be less painful?

Benny's eyes remained on Drew, but he reached a hand across the small table that separated the chairs and gently placed his hand on top of his mom's clasped ones and rubbed the back of her hand with his thumb.

Drew faltered. He'd never seen anyone treat his mom like this. Even before Elliott left, he was never a touchy, feely kind of husband. Drew's parents never held hands or cuddled on the couch.

"He's living his life the way he thinks he should." It was the truth. Elliott was who he was.

"He always did." His mom glanced around the room like she wasn't sure where to look. Drew followed her gaze and took in the home around him.

The living area they sat in opened to the small kitchen where two stools were tucked under a peninsula counter. A few moving boxes were scattered across laminate floors, but it was homey. Like a family lived here.

No booze anywhere in sight. Even if it was tucked in a cupboard, that was still improvement. Maybe she was getting help.

"Did you need something? It's been a long day." She was starting to sound more like her normal self.

Drew shook his head and stood. "No, I just wanted to let you know I'm back if you need anything. I'm staying at the Lankford's."

"You don't have to take care of me." She stood and followed Drew to the door.

"I know, Mom."

He closed the door behind him.

***

"Shut up. You did not," Cam shouted across the bed between laughs.

"We did!" Ronny confirmed. "The three of us. Thanksgiving break."

"You went skinny dipping?"

Drew held back his own laughter. Nate was smiling as well, and it both soothed and hurt Drew's heart to see. Nate had been quiet for most of the afternoon. He was still tired and weak, and he still had a long road ahead. But he was there.

"Why didn't you invite us?" Cam's eyes thinned, but she couldn't dim her smile.

"Oh, come on." Ronny wiped at his eyes. "You two would have hated it. It was excessively cold." The three boys burst out laughing again at the memory, the cool water coating their skin in the chilled autumn air.

Cam folded her arms in defiance, but her dimples gave her away. "Well, you still should have asked."

The four of them had spent the last few hours rehashing old jokes and poking fun at their past selves around Nate's hospital bed. It was time well spent.

Mitch had brought Nate a change of clothes this morning while the rest of them still slept. He looked much more like himself in a light blue V-neck and basketball shorts. His hair was slicked back and clean. Even his color looked better today.

Cam was lounging in the bed beside him, legs hiding from the AC under the white sheets. The other three had pulled in chairs from the waiting room.

Something had changed among them, more than just a few patched relationships. Even Cam and Ronny were on friendly terms. They hadn't made up as far as Drew knew, but the tension between them had dissipated, leaving a connection of respect Drew hoped they'd be able to build on as time went on.

"Next time." Nate wrapped an arm around Cam's shoulders and squeezed.

"I'm holding you to that."

"Speak for yourself. I think I'll stick with a suit." Brigid's smile sent a shiver down Drew's spine. Even across a hospital room she had full control over him. They hadn't talked about all that had happened the night before. No kissing or hand holding, but that was okay. It had never been about the physical anyway. Just being near her was enough.

The nurse arrived to inform them that Nate needed to rest, and Cam, Brigid, and Ronny each said their goodbyes to Nate and shuffled to the door. Drew hung back.

"How long do you have to stay?"

Nate shrugged. "It's a process."

Drew stepped toward the door, but Nate continued.

"My dad said you need a place to live."

He faced Nate and returned the shrug. "I'll figure something out."

Nate sent him a crooked grin, and it was the greatest sight in the world. "I've got an idea—but you better not suck to live with."

Drew chuckled. "We can talk about it later."

Nate lifted his chin. "Tomorrow?"

"Tomorrow."

4 MONTHS LATER

"Are we almost there?" Cam leaned across Ronny's lap to peek out the car window. Despite being well into her second trimester, she only had the slightest bump to maneuver around.

"Navigation says we're less than half a mile away," Brigid shook with anticipation in the passenger seat.

"I can see it! Why can't we just park here?" Cam asked.

"Because we are in the middle of a busy street." Drew smiled at the girl in his backseat.

"Turn here," Brigid pointed to a small turnoff into a tiered parking lot.

The sun landed on the horizon as Drew inched carefully into a parking spot, shifted into park, and paused his iPod.

Salty air filled his car, and Drew breathed in deep. Even when he'd spent that week with Elliott in Los Angeles, he'd never been able to smell the ocean.

It smelled incredible.

No one moved or spoke. Cam giggled from the back seat, and Ronny kissed her cheek. The two of them had moved into their new housing three days earlier. They'd found a small apartment just off campus where Ronny could still walk to class, but Cam and the baby could live with him. Despite being only a short drive from the beach, they had sworn they'd wait until Drew, Brigid, and Nate arrived to go. Drew had driven straight to their apartment without even stopping to check in at the hotel.

They were only going to be in California for a few days. Brigid needed to get back to Boise before the beginning of the semester. Her first psychology class started early Monday morning, and she'd been talking about nothing else for weeks.

After Nate had been released from the hospital, Brigid had taken it upon herself to help him explore different treatments for his depression. They'd fought their battles together, him against depression and her against panic attacks. Day by day, she'd fallen in love with the fight, the hope that there was light and healing to be found.

Brigid would be majoring in psychology so she could someday work full-time helping teens with mental illnesses.

Drew ran his finger along the back of Brigid's hand. He couldn't be prouder of his girlfriend.

"You ready, pretty girl?"

Brigid shot him a wicked smile and burst from the car, sprinting straight for the water. That was all the invitation Drew needed. He flew from his seat and raced after her, followed closely by Cam, Ronny, and Nate holding hands and running as fast as Cam could go.

Brigid stopped dead in the sand at the shoreline, and they each slowed as they reached her.

Drew gazed across the rolling waves as the sun set off the edge of the world, shooting color over the ocean before them. Cool water crashed against his ankles, and he thought back to the canvas he'd bought in Vegas, the one that now hung on the wall in their apartment—his and Nate's.

A few weeks after the incident, Nate came out to his father. Mitch responded better than expected, but their relationship had somehow grown even more strained. Nate and Drew moved into a small apartment together not long after, and neither of them had regretted it for a second.

The painting was no match for the real thing.

Cam laughed wildly and bounded into the water. Brigid and Ronny followed after her, and Drew watched as his friends were instantly taken down by a wave, only to reemerge soaked through and grinning from ear to ear.

"How are we friends with them?" Nate chuckled and crossed his arms. "They could have at least worn swimming suits."

Brigid and Cam threw themselves into another wave, riding it as best they could without a board. Ronny trudged his way through the water and back to Drew and Nate. He rubbed his arms for warmth, and his teeth chattered behind his smile. His freckles glowed in the fading light.

"You two coming?"

About the Author

Born and raised in northern Utah, Annie has spent her whole life surrounded by books. She began writing her first novel in third grade and eventually earned a Masters in English. Now she teaches high school English and loves it.

Annie is obsessed with musical theatre, snowy days, her hubby and kiddos, and diet soda.

You can find Annie online:
www.anniejakes.com
Instagram: AnnieJakesAuthor

Acknowledgements

First off, I thank my wonderful husband for his support and patience as I leaned into my extreme tunnel vision throughout this process. I love you.

A big thank you to Lindy for being my sounding board, cheerleader, proofreader, and voice of reason.

And to my many friends and family, without whom this story never would have made it to the page, I thank you all.